Geza Gardonyi

Love and Loss:
Tales from Hungary

©Translated by Peter Nanasi, 2010
ISBN 1453886419

Contents

Where are you, Eve?

One Christmas Eve thirteen bachelors got together to celebrate. Kelemen, the youngest member of the group, got up to tell his reason for not getting married.

I was so young when my story started, that I don't even remember the beginning. My first recollection is from the time when an old maid was hitting my head with the palm of her hand and finally kicked me. I ended up falling down onto the dusty street.

"I will have you thrown out of the castle!" she screamed. "Naughty child! I will have you thrown out! You will not play with Martha any more."

She grabbed Martha's hand and started to drag her toward the castle. My sin was that I had walked out of the park with her. We had heard music from the village, where there was a celebration. People were dancing in the pub at the end of the village. There were children dancing next to the pub. Martha started to move and turn to the rhythm. We heard the music. Martha grabbed my hand.

"Dance with me!"

What could I have done? I danced with her. I was just a little, barefooted kid back then. I only had one little pair of pants and a shirt. I lived in the castle too. It is true that I lived among the servants, but I lived there. I was Martha's playmate.

My father worked for the manor. I was not yet five years old when he died. That happened right about the time Martha came to the castle. She was even more of an orphan than I was. The lord of the manor became her guardian.

She cried a lot during those times. She was given dolls and books with pictures, but she just kept calling for her mother.

"Where is mom? Take me to my mom!"

My mother was visiting the castle for some reason and I happened to be with her. Little Martha was staring at me. She hid behind my mother's skirt and was peaking toward me. I was trying to hide on the other side. Martha laughed. My mother had to leave me there that day. The next day her stepparents sent for me.

This is how I ended up in the castle. And this was how Martha and I became friends. And when my mother died, I was kept in the castle. But I don't remember these things. I just heard them when I got older. I only remember the day clearly, when Ms. Ilona beat me and threatened to have me thrown out of the castle. I was able to deal with the beating, but being thrown out of the castle would have been too much. Where would I go if they threw me out? Who would feed me? I was living on cake, but I wouldn't even be able to get bread. Where would I sleep? Would I be separated from Martha forever?

I was following them with a tight chest, from a safe distance of course. Little Martha was crying, as she ran next to the woman. I must have been pale.

We entered through the big, fancy, iron gate and crossed the sunny front yard. They entered the castle through a door by the porch. I stayed outside. I was whimpering as I tried to listen if Martha was getting a beating.

Her stepparents usually did not beat her. But because Ms. Ilona was screaming so much, I felt we had done something terrible. Martha was in my care and I was always watching over her. I treated her like a little angel dressed in human clothes. But now that I had made a mistake they would throw me out. I will never be able to set foot again in the beautiful castle with its towers, beautiful, clean, glass hallways, and some other child will play with Martha. Another child! But who will she be? That I could not figure out, but I hated whoever she was going to be.

I was crying for a long time near the porch. All of a sudden I saw Lord Akos, the Lord of the castle, as he was coming with his huge head and robust steps. He was coming from the castle toward me. He was wearing gloves. His black hair looked as if it was made out of cast iron. He was serious, as always, and as I said, he had a huge head. He was mainly made up of his head, like a tadpole. Even then, I was thinking about that, as he was approaching me. Lord Akos had such a big head, that he looked like he has exchanged heads with someone bigger than him. It may have been too heavy for him, because his head was always leaning forward. And everything was big on his tan head, the forehead, the chin, the mouth, the nose, the skull. Only his eyes were tiny; they were calm and cold.

Everyone was afraid of him. Even the horses seemed to pull the plough harder when he was going toward the fields. The trees seemed to huddle humbly together where he was walking by. Perhaps the sparrows were too afraid to chirp as well.

I was frozen as I waited for him to grab me and throw me out, or at least to stand in front of me and send me out of the garden with harsh words. But he barely looked toward me. He kept going toward the horse stables. He was constantly walking through the manor.

My heart started beating again. But his wife was still left, the lady of the castle... What would she say?

I anxiously searched the windows. I was wondering which one belonged to her. The maid had probably complained to her already and they were just waiting for me, so they could beat me and throw me out.

I started crying bitterly. All of a sudden a butterfly with black borders on its wings landed on a carnation in front of me. I stopped crying. I carefully grabbed my hat and swooped down. A stake which was holding the flower pierced my hat and the butterfly flew away. I was staring at my hat and had tragic feelings, which made me cry again.

I saw through my tears that Ms. Ilona was coming to get me; her skirt was flying. The upset turkey is coming. She is going to take me to the other upset turkey. What a day!

4

We went through a lot of rooms. (They will throw me out through a lot of doors!) There were pictures on the wall depicting lords in helmets and uniforms, and they all seemed to be looking at me with disapproval from their gold frames. Finally, there was a room with pictures of saints and of Mary. The second upset turkey was sitting there, the lady of the house, in black clothes. She was sitting among her tiny pictures and cactuses, by the window. Her thin body was stooped in her chair.

There was a parrot with green wings behind her, a smart little bird. When people walked by, she said:

"Good morning! Good morning!"

Even the bird was silent as she stared at me in disbelief with her smart, black eyes.

Martha was also there, next to the chair. She was pale and anxiously awaited what was going to happen next.

"You good for nothing!" began the lady.

Other times her sharp voice was full of gentleness and goodness. She was usually sad and apathetic. Her legs were disabled. She seldom moved out of her room.

"Put the good for nothing into jail!" she said harshly. "He will never play with Martha again!"

The jail was not exactly Venetian. It was only an empty room for the cook, next to the kitchen. They did not keep a cook back then, other than a deaf woman, who did their cooking. Ms. Ilona was a sort of maid for them. There was only one other person serving the family, the old butler, Mr. Lukacs.

I was crying. Martha started to cry as well. But there was no mercy! Ms. Ilona grabbed me like an eagle grabs a lamb, and she was taking me to prison.

Well, this scene was repeated many times! When the park's back gate was left open, we sneaked down to the Danube to bathe. A steamship went by. There were strong waves. A body of a woman with a puffy face surfaced the water. Her hat and the feathers on it were soaked. Her gray hair was floating in the water. We didn't know she was dead. Occasionally, bodies floating downstream got stuck by the curve in the river. We got scared and ran back to the castle without putting all of our clothes back on.

One time we sneaked into the forest and got lost. Another time we used the silver tea pot to hold the insects we were gathering. I don't even want to think about the time when the parrot scratched Martha. I held the bird and Martha got the scissors. We cut down the bird's claws.

We were especially scolded for getting lost in the forest. We were prompted to go there by a fairy tale. Ms. Ilona told us a story about an orphaned prince and princess. It was interesting for us to hear how their stepmother pursued them into the forest and how they found food. A good hermit provided them with shelter in a cave.

There was a forest over the village and we were interested in the hermit. But the hermit did not show himself anywhere. And we were not too unhappy about it, because we found some wild strawberries. We were eating happily. We got our hands and feet dirty. Finally we were found in the evening by the forester, instead of the hermit, and he took us back to the castle.

"These children are impossible!" said the lady of the house. "We have to find a girl to play with Martha."

Her calm voice was more terrifying to me, than Ms. Ilona's hair raising screams.

I was crying and bawling in the prison. All of a sudden I heard the doorknob turning. I looked at the door. Martha was peaking in through the opening.

"Kelen," she said anxiously, "where are you going?"

She wasn't able to say my name right. To her, my name was simply Kelen, instead of Kelemen.

"I don't know," I whispered, "I don't know where I am going."

"Don't go very far."

"Where should I go?"

"Only to the end of the garden, where the cactuses are kept."

"They won't give me any food."

"I'll bring you food, Kelen. I'll bring it to you every day."

"They'll beat you for it."

"If they beat me, we'll leave. And if the forester is going that way again, we'll hide in the bushes."

I stopped crying. We were deep in thought and looked at each other silently.

Martha was a chubby-faced little girl back then. She was wearing an indigo colored shirt with sailor collar and knee-length skirt. She had a boyish haircut. And I only remember her eyes; they were big back then and clear light blue. She had a cheerful personality. She was always smiling, always jumping, always happy.

There was only one other conversation I remember from back then.

There was a thick marble obelisk in the park with moss on it. It was about ten feet high. It was surrounded by old bushes and chestnut trees, which almost hid it. There was always some shade in that area, even in hot weather.

Martha had a doll, a little doll with red skirt and curly hair. The doll's name was Margit. A fly landed on Margit. Martha drove it away. The fly landed on the doll again.

"Let's take Margit into the shade," she said, "the flies won't bother her there."

We got to the shaded area. I saw a shiny, green insect land on the top of the pillar. We were looking at it.

"I will climb up for it," I said.

I tried to climb. Martha was helping me by pushing from behind. A gardener passed in front of us with a rake. He warned us.

"If the lord sees you, he will be upset. Don't you know that this is a grave stone?"

I sheepishly got back on the ground. Martha picked up her doll. And when we were left alone, we looked at each other wondering.

"There is a dead person here," I said to Martha.

The girl looked at the gravestone with amazement.

"Why do some people die?"

"Because they get old."

"Are we going to get old?"

"Perhaps. We'll grow up and then we'll grow old."

"And are you going to become a man?"

"Perhaps. And you will be a woman."

Martha appeared to be deep in thought, as she looked at me.

"If I become a grown woman, you will be my husband."

The sun was shining into her eyes through the bushes. She closed them. She lifted her palm to her forehead. What she said surprised me so much, that I was unable to answer her for a few minutes.

"But," I said, as I was shaking my head, "they won't give you to me."

"Why?"

"Because."

"Yes, they will."

"No, you are the rich kind, and I am not the rich kind."

She was thinking. Then she shook her head.

"I will not become anyone else's wife."

"You'll have to."

"No."

"Yes, you'll have to."

"I will tell them no, and then you'll be my husband, okay?"

"Okay. But still, they won't give you to me."

Martha threw her doll onto the ground.

"Then we'll cry, and they will agree in the end."

And her eyes were full of tears already.

This conversation always remained in my memory. I was looking at her from time to time wondering, would it be possible what she said? Sometimes I thought with pleasure that it was possible. Other times I thought with sadness that it was impossible.

After our adventure in the forest, a girl did appear in the castle. She was a peasant girl, the field guard's daughter. The servants washed her and put new clothes on her. She was hired to play with Martha all day long.

I was placed with the field guard. He was probably paid to watch over me. I cried and screamed. I escaped and waited in front of the park's gate all day long. A field laborer dragged me back to the field guard. But I escaped again. This painful time lasted for maybe four days, until Ms. Ilona came for me and took me into the castle.

"Martha is sick!" she said with tears in her eyes. "She may even die."

The little girl was really in bed. The lady of the house and the girl they hired were next to her. But Martha was asking only for me.

I don't remember what was wrong with her. She had been seen by a doctor. The only thing I remember is that they brought her medication from the pharmacy, but Martha did not want to take it. She held her jaws tight when they tried to force her and tossed, turned, and kicked. They were unable to restrain her. Finally, they persuaded her to take the medicine by promising her that she could play with me again. When she heard this, she took the medication.

When I was seven, Ms. Ilona took me to the school in the village and gave me to the teacher.

"Don't cry," she said. "You can come home at noon. But if you keep crying, you can't come home..."

Martha was observing with interest, as I was writing my first letters on a board in Ms. Ilona's room. She wanted to do the same and asked for a board. She was writing too. Everyone was amazed in the castle.

"This is a good boy," said the lady. "We are not going to hire a governess for her yet."

Little Martha really did learn from me to read, write, count, about the Bible, and all the knowledge a village school teaches to humanity.

I also want to mention that she did have an odd habit. She liked to kiss people. If she was able to reach someone's face, she kissed that person. And since I was always the closest to her face, I was kissed the most often. Sometimes she hugged me and kissed me ten, twenty or even a hundred times.

At first she was laughed at for this habit, and later nobody paid attention to it. But one day it became disastrous for both of us.

It made me feel good when she kissed me, because after my mother died, nobody ever kissed me any more. And I also kissed that little, dear, white lamb back and she was always happy when I did.

Once, when I was ten years old we were playing on a bench in the park. All of a sudden she hugged my neck and kissed me. I also hugged her and kissed her back. And she did it again. Then I saw Lord Akos standing in front of us. He was staring at us, as he was standing there, like a serious rhinoceros. We were frightened and stared at him anxiously. But he did not say a thing. He turned around and walked away. An hour later my teacher showed up at the castle.

"Where do I find the lord?" he asked. "He sent for me."

He put his long pipe down by the porch window. He coughed and went inside. He returned fifteen minutes later, lit his pipe, and came to me.

"My son, Kelemen," he said, "come with me."

I went with him and I even had to sleep at his house.

The next day he took me into the city. He bought me new clothes, shoes, and hat. They put them on me in the store. Then he took me to a locksmith who had a room to rent out and negotiated with him for a long time. From there, we went to a school. He enrolled me. The whole thing seems like a series of dreams to me now.

Around Christmas time my schoolmates were counting the days with joy, until the Christmas holiday. They all thought about going home. And I thought about going home as well. Where was my home back then? Was it the village? No. Was it Ms. Ilona's room? No. Was it the castle? No.

But still, I was anxiously waiting to find out if I was going to be able to go home. To me, being with Martha meant being home.

But the last class passed, and my mates cheerfully rushed out of the school gate, and I was the only one sadly lagging behind.

The locksmith asked me when I got home:

"Aren't you going home?"

"I don't know," I answered.

And I waited for someone to come and get me. But nobody came for me.

Still, I did receive a packet, the day before the holiday. I was reading with amazement that Ms. Ilona sent it. I was trembling as I opened it. In it I found a cake with walnut and poppy seed filling, quince jelly and a letter.

A silver twenty krajcar coin fell out of the letter first. I quickly put it in my pocket. Then I read the scribble written with a thick pen:

My dear son, Kelemen, you can't come to the cake so the cake comes to you and Martha was crying for a long time after you left, but she has a governess now. I am sending you my kisses.

Yours, Ms. Ilona

I read it a hundred times. The words, *my dear son*, surprised me every time, and the words, *Martha was crying after you for a long time*, filled me with sadness.

I ate the contents of the package. I also spent the twenty krajcars on candy, but my Christmas was still sad.

I kept pulling out the letter over and over. I only read the middle of it, where it said, *Martha was crying for a long time.* I felt as if the furniture and the walls were also whispering: *Martha was crying for a long time.*

I was thinking I should go home. Which way was my village? I didn't know. But the train passed by it and I would need to go toward the east. If I still had my twenty krajcars... And it is likely that Ms. Ilona would beat me, but perhaps not. After all, she did send me cake. And in the end, I could even play for a whole week with Martha.

One thought led to another. I could ask the locksmith for money. My teacher did say, if I needed to buy something, I should ask the locksmith for the money. He told me to write down my expenses on paper and to send it to him every quarter.

I looked out the window and saw that it was snowing outside. They wouldn't even notice if I went to the train station. I stopped debating. I asked for forty krajcars to buy books. I didn't dare to ask for more.

I sneaked out to the train station.

"Please give me a ticket for forty krajcars."

"Where would you like to go, kid?"

"Home."

"But where?"

I didn't like this question. Should I tell him? What if he were involved in my banishment, and wouldn't give me a ticket if I told him.

I didn't have enough courage to ask for a ticket again. I thought I would travel on foot, next to the rail tracks.

I was walking in the snow and later in the fog. My ears were cold, my hands were cold, my feet were cold, my whole body felt cold already, but I kept on walking. Some of the track watchmen shouted at me. At those times I just got off the tracks and kept treading through the knee-deep snow. I had shoes on, so my legs were wet. But I just kept walking. I also got off the tracks when a train came from either side.

Then the evening got dark, but I kept going. I was hungry, thirsty, and frozen to my bones. Still, I kept going. The road seemed endless, and I thought my feet had turned into lead. It felt like my feet were no longer carrying me; instead I had to keep dragging them. But I just kept going in the night, silently, in the snowy endlessness. I had been walking for a hundred years already, as if time became infinite, like the road...

By that time I even cried some. I must have gotten lost. I am sure I got lost. I would have arrived home a long time ago, if I was on the right road. Then I felt I was trudging slower and slower. But I just kept on going. My knees started to buckle. As time went on, I felt like the ground was being dragged left and right beneath me. I collapsed.

The only thing I could still hear was the furious bark of a little dog. He was barking by my head. I didn't care any more, even if he ate me. Somebody shouted and the dog quieted down. A lamp was shining into my eyes. It was a track watchman.

How long was I lying at his place? I don't know. He made me drink some brandy. He was interrogating me: Who was I? Where was I going?

I wasn't far from my village by then, perhaps ten, fifteen miles away.

The next day a horse drawn cart was sent for me by our lord. The cart was full of straw. I was placed in it. The cart took me to my teacher. I was laid in bed there too.

My first visitor was Ms. Ilona. She scolded me and almost slapped my face. I was fearfully peaking from under my cover and tried to see when she would lift her hand to strike me. I noticed with surprise that her eyes were full of tears.

My teacher made me drink some kind of a hot liquid. I thought it might have been tea with hot paprika in it. That tea made me feel so good that by the afternoon the teacher said to me,

"Would you be able to get up now?"

"Yes."

Just as I got out of the bed, the door opened and Martha flew in.

"Kelen!" she shouted. "Kelen! Kelen!"

And she hugged my neck. She was jumping with joy, as she was kissing me.

The teacher was amazed. He put down his pipe and went outside.

We were happy to be with each other.

How beautiful she had become! How much she had grown! Her hair had grown too. She had beautiful, blond hair, just like the color of corn hair. A blue headband was holding it together.

The teacher returned. He picked up his pipe and continued to smoke it.

"Well, how did you come here, Miss?"

Martha seemed embarrassed.

"I just came..."

"By yourself?"

"I heard Kelen arrived..."

"And you slipped out."

Martha cast down her eyes and smiled bashfully.

"You will be in trouble," the teacher said.

Martha became serious and fearfully looked in front of her. But then, she turned to me again.

"Are we going to play? What should we play? Where have you been for so long? You will move back to the castle now, won't you? I'll show you the beautiful picture book, the doll, and the full kitchen set which were given to me. The kitchen set even has a copper grinder in it. We'll cook something together."

Then Ms. Ilona and an older woman wearing pince-nez came to get her.

"Outrageous! Outrageous!" said the woman in a hoarse voice. "You will pay for this!"

"She'll be put into prison!" added Ms. Ilona.

She had a little fur-coat and a fur hat in her hand. They put them on her. Martha cried. They took her away.

My teacher took me back to the city the next day. He took it upon himself to educate me while smoking his pipe the whole way.

"Think about the fact that you are an orphan. You will be disgraced, if you make the lord unhappy. You should study as hard as you can, until he pays for it."

Well, I did study hard. I was not among the best students, but I was not among the worst either. The only thing I did not understand was why I was not allowed back into the castle.

My teacher came to get me at the end of the school year. He looked at my report card and shook his head.

"It could be better."

He paid what I owed the locksmith. He lit his pipe and was taking me home.

I was thinking about one question the whole way, but it took me hours, before I was able to utter it.

"My dear master, please tell me, are you taking me to the castle?"

"No, my son," he calmly answered. "You will stay with me. But we will go to the castle too. You will show the lord your report card. You'll thank him for sponsoring your education. And you will ask him to continue to extend his goodness toward you."

We arrived in the evening. We went to the castle the next morning. He put his pipe by the porch window. He made me stand in front of Lord Akos. The lord seriously looked through my report card. He kept nodding.

"Good. You did not fail. That is the main thing. I will continue sponsoring your education, as long as you don't become negligent."

The lady also welcomed me. She liked that I got an A' in religion. She didn't care about the rest.

"Well, good," she said, "you can visit Martha while we discuss some things with your teacher. She is down in the park, at the back, where the cactuses are."

I may have mentioned already, that there was a greenhouse at the back of the park and next to it there was a stand with three steps. It was full of cactuses. Some of them had thorns, some didn't. Some of them were round; others were flat or even angular. They had cactuses from all around the world. They kept them to please the lady. When a cactus bloomed, it was taken up into her room and placed next to the parrot's birdcage.

So, she was by the cactuses!

Well, I was running as fast as I could.

"Martha! Martha!" I shouted, even when I was still far from her.

Little Martha's body quivered. She left the lady, who was wearing pince-nez, and flew in front of me. We hugged and kissed each other.

"Martha! Martha!" the governess was outraged. "How inappropriate!"

"But he is Kelen. He is our Kelen!" Martha was explaining.

"Is he a relative? He is not!"

"No, but he is Kelen, Kelen, Kelen."

The next day I wanted to visit Martha again, but my teacher did not let me.

"You are not allowed to go there. The Lord said, you are not allowed."

I couldn't understand why. I thought through all my mistakes. I examined everything, from cutting off the parrot's claws to wandering in the forest. But they have forgiven me for everything.

I slipped out one afternoon. I went to see Ms. Ilona. I knew lord Akos usually took a nap after lunch. I sneaked into the castle. I didn't dare to go straight into the park. I felt the governess wearing pince-nez was my enemy. But I thought I could trust Ms. Ilona to some extent. She would scold me. She might even beat me. But in the end she would get Martha.

I opened her door. There she was, the turkey wearing a skirt, sitting on her couch. She lifted her head with alarm.

"Oh, you naughty boy! You scared me! How did you dare to come here? You rascal! Weren't you told you are not allowed to come here?"

I started crying.

"Is it true that I am not allowed?"

The woman continued scolding me.

"Well, what do you want? Are you hungry? Here is a piece of cake. But now get lost! Don't let the lord see you."

"Martha…" I whimpered. "Where is Martha?"

"That is none of your business! Martha is a lady and you are just a servant! You are a rag! You are nothing!"

She went to the window. She looked outside into the garden, and then returned.

"Don't cry," she tried to calm me in a softer tone. "Hide yourself here. The Miss may also be sleeping."

She left. A few minutes later I heard Martha running down the hallway. She hugged my neck and kissed me.

I was surprised that Ms. Ilona was not lifting her hand to hit me. She sat down next to us and started to mend some stockings.

But the door was left open. All of a sudden we heard a door opened upstairs. Ms. Ilona jumped up and looked out the door. We heard a carriage just arriving outside.

"A guest," said Ms. Ilona. "Martha, we need to get a dress on you quickly. And you, run away from here, as soon as we are all upstairs. And don't come here any more! If you do, I will beat you with a stick."

I knew the guest was a widow from the nearby village. She was our lady's childhood girlfriend. She visited her every week during the summer and usually brought her son with her. He was a sly teenager, much older than us. The ladies usually talked with each other, while the teenager looked through some picture albums and kept yawning. Martha was usually near the ladies and she was also bored.

I did not dare to set foot in Ms. Ilona's room again. But I kept going by the park from then on. The stone wall was very high! But the wild walnut trees around the corner were even taller. I could climb on them. I could see into the park from them!

I climbed up one of the trees. I kept peeking into the park from different spots. Martha noticed me. She signaled that I should hide myself. And when she was able to get away from her governess, even just for a minute, she ran to me. I rested my elbow on the stone wall and Martha climbed up on the three step cactus stand. The highest step was less than three feet from the top of the stone wall. Martha hugged my neck and rubbed her soft, little face against mine.

"Kelen! Kelen!"

We were joyfully exchanging a few words and questions, under the protection of the leaves. At times, we even talked for a long time. She told me the things that happened to her since I had not seen her. I also told her the things that had happened to me. We were talking, just as if we were siblings, until her governess started shouting for her.

"Martha! Where are you? What are you doing there for so long?"

Then Martha kissed all over my face and ran back.

The next fall I received a letter from her sent from Budapest.

I am writing to you in secret, Kelen. I am attending a school run by nuns. It is not as good being here as it was at home. They only put one dumpling into the soup. I am learning French and I got A's twice already. You cannot write to me, because it is not allowed, but think of me every evening. I will also think of you. I am sending you my kisses, sweet, sweet Kelen!   Martha

I am not going to tell you the story of my whole youth. I was tossed around, like a sparrow chick, which fell out of his nest and got thrown around, until his wings grew out or fell victim to some kind of danger.

There was only one sentence which gave me some strength. It was lord Akos telling me that he would sponsor my education as long as I didn't fail. It is true that he also threatened to make me a locksmith apprentice, if I didn't study.

Well, I studied and became one of the best students. If I became a locksmith, I would have to stay in the city. But if I studied, I could always take my report card into the castle at the end of the year, and I would hear those wonderful words from the lady.

"You can visit Martha until we talk with your teacher."

And those American walnut trees were growing leaves for me. But by the end of the second year, I did not run to Martha shouting her name, like I did the year before. It is true that she was not in the park that day. She was in the glass hallway. She had a different governess. The new governess did not have glasses, but looked even more dangerous than the previous one, because she had a wart next to her mouth. That wart looked very scary to me!

When Martha looked at me, I saw her body quivered. She was blushing as she hurried toward me. She stood there for a minute, hesitating. But then she did hug me.

"Kelen! Sweet Kelen!"

This is how we saw each other at the end of each school year, and in secret under the walnut tree leaves, right above the cactuses.

When I was in the seventh grade, I was growing like wheat in May. I was surprised when I saw that my clothes were getting shorter and tighter as well. Light, brown hair appeared under my nose. A few of my mates seemed to have become shorter.

At the end of the year, when I was taking my all A's report card to the castle, with my heart beating fast, a grown, beautiful woman stood in front of me in the glass hallway and appeared to be surprised. She had the mailman's yellow leather briefcase in her hand. Sometimes she was the one who took it upstairs.

She just stood there, like an azalea shrub, which turned into a girl. Her hairstyle was of the latest fashion, and her hair was no longer falling on her shoulders as before. And the color of it was no longer as light as the hair of corn; it had become a darker blond.

"Kelen!" she whispered. "Kelen."

My teacher did not come with me that time, and her governess was not standing behind her either; still, instead of giving each other a hug, we just stood there and stared at each other.

"Oh," she whispered, "how much you have grown…"

She was blushing.

We heard a servant walking toward us in the hallway. We quickly moved away from each other, as if we had committed some kind of sin. I was so confused by our meeting that I could only stammer in front of my benefactor.

"My re-reportcard… and the undeserved and your kindness… that… which enabled me to… study… through…"

He looked at me with surprise.

"What kind of a meaningless, confused speech is this? Were you not fed properly? Or did you just read Shakespeare in Hungarian?"

I was meeting with him in his library, and that confused me even more. All those walls covered with books, and there was a big calendar on his desk. Then there was a glass door to the side… I was not familiar with that room. It was in the south side of the castle. We were not allowed to go near it.

He took my report card. His face lit up.

"All A's! Well done."

He continued in a softer tone. He was talking about diligence or something like that. But I was listening toward the glass door. I was waiting for the lady, because she was the one who always let me visit Martha.

I only turned my attention to Lord Akos again, when he mentioned Ms. Ilona's name...

"You know she died during the winter. She left you the money she had saved up. It is not much, but for you, it probably will seem like a lot. You will get it from me when you become an adult. You can go now."

I was greatly surprised when he mentioned the inheritance. Ms. Ilona? The old woman, who always scolded me, left me money? Impossible! I was just standing there, as if my feet were glued to the floor.

"You can go!" repeated Lord Akos.

"The lady?" I asked timidly.

"How should I express my gratitude to her?"

"I'll tell her. She is lying in bed. She is sick."

I didn't need the lady. Martha was waiting for me downstairs, in the glass hallway. She was sitting at a small table. But there was a lady with her, whom I did not know. I could tell from her nose that she was delivering knowledge to young ladies in French and in German.

By that time Martha's eyes appeared calmer as she was looking at me. She introduced me to the lady.

"This is my friend, Kelemen. He was my childhood playmate."

If I would have heard in the dark that she called me Kelemen, I would have thought the voice was not hers, but belonged to someone who sounded just like her. But her eyes, her true, beautiful eyes were shining with the same old friendliness. And soon she called me Kelen again.

"I have changed a lot too, Kelen, haven't I?"

"You sure have Martha... I hardly recognized you. You have grown up and you are so beautiful..."

She was blushing.

The governess was astonished as she was observing us. She was even more surprised that our bodies quivered when we heard the old man approaching us and I quickly said good-bye.

As I was leaving, the only question I was thinking about was: would she have acted differently if we were alone? Why didn't she kiss me when we met? Would she have kissed me when I returned? And I felt a great distance between the two of us. As if there were a big gorge between us, and were separating us with its depth! I felt pain and tightness in my chest. I wondered if she would meet me at the back of the park, by the cactus stand, under the walnut tree, where I said good-bye to her last summer.

I knew they usually had dinner around eight o'clock and by ten they would go to bed. During the summer, Martha usually slept on the first floor, in the room with the third window. She came from there, after ten o'clock, the last time she said good bye. The window was low. It was only about three feet from the ground. She just stepped out and ran to me.

"Think about me, Kelen, think about me. I will pray for you every evening."

Those were her last words.

If she still feels like I do, she'll come out tonight. She'll feel that I'll be waiting for her.

During the summer, I slept in the school house and was able to leave and come back any time I wanted. I sneaked out to the park as early as nine o'clock. I broke through the bushes. I climbed up the walnut tree and rested my elbow on the stone wall. I kept waiting.

The evening was dark and wet. Water was dripping down from the tree every time I moved. I was terribly anxious as I was waiting. So much so, that my knees were shaking.

And I waited.

A soft wind moved the leaves around eleven. Water drops fell onto my neck, just like rain. Then the sky was clearing. I could see the stars appearing.
She did not come. My heart was aching. My hope gradually diminished as I listened toward the park.
She didn't come.

I returned home at midnight. I was very sad. I felt like a wandering king, who had just lost his kingdom.

I lay down to ponder my sad thoughts. I tried to put this cloudy situation into better perspective. Perhaps she had to stay with the sick lady. Perhaps she had to sleep on the second floor now. But what if she didn't come out because she has grown up? These thoughts weighed down my heart like lead. We had grown up and changed. Why couldn't we have just stayed children?!

Still, the next day after lunch, I wandered toward the park. I climbed up on the walnut tree and I put my elbow on the stone wall. I was on a branch which reached into the garden, as I waited with a heavy heart.

The park was quiet and I could not see anyone. It was always like that after lunch. The gardener was only allowed to work there during the mornings. The lady was wheeled out by ten o'clock in her wheelchair. She liked the quietness, as well as the songs of the birds and the buzzing of bees.

The back of the park was not any bigger than the garden in the front, but it was more beautiful. It had various trees like pines, lime trees and plane trees. There were no flowers blooming there, other than the lilies of the valley in the spring and a sea of lilies at the end of June. And the cactuses were there too, of course, right below me.

The park was white that day from all the lilies, but I could not smell their fragrance very much.

"Would she come? Would she come out," I kept asking, and my heart was sinking. If she didn't come I'd wish I would die!

I could see the shiny water of the Danube as I looked through the leaves. I could see the turn in the river, where floating bodies were stranded at times. I wished I was one of those dead bodies, without any feelings, traveling in the water, if Martha did not love me any more.

A stork appeared high in the sky. She kept circling with her wings stretched out wide. At times it seemed to me as if the bird was standing still in the air.

I looked in the garden again. I noticed a pink spot fleshed among the trees. My heart jumped. The pink spot was getting closer to me. It was not moving as fast as before, but it was getting closer. It was her. She came! She stopped. She looked toward me. I signaled to her with my hat. She noticed me.

Her face was red as she climbed up on the stairs which were holding the cactuses. She offered me her hand for a handshake.

"I knew you would come," she said bashfully.

And again she did not kiss me. I could see in her eyes that she thought about it, but didn't want to. I was so disappointed I could hardly answer her.

"I came. I was here last night too."

"Were you here? Did you know I felt it? I was thinking about it all evening… But it was dark and I was afraid."

"It was dark last year too," I said with sadness.

"No, it wasn't quite as dark, Kelen. It wasn't quite as dark."

"Yes it was."

"No. The moon was shining a little. And I was afraid then too. But now, I don't know, I was even more afraid. No, it was impossible."

I looked into her eyes.

"Tempora mutantur…"

She looked at me anxiously.

"What does Tempora mean? Why are you talking to me in Latin?"

"It means you are no longer…"

She looked at me with fear and anticipation, the way a prisoner looks, when he is waiting for the judge to hand down a death sentence. Then I told her the cause of my grief.

"You are no longer who you were."

Her body jerked, as if I stabbed her in the heart.

"Don't say that Kelen! Why do you say such things?"

"It seems to be that way."

"You are mistaken. I just don't know…"

Her body suddenly jerked. Her face became red. We were standing there silently. She was looking at the cactuses and I was looking at the moss at the top of the stone wall. I still had a sad expression on my face.

18

"Oh," she said finally. "I know you are upset with me… And I was waiting with so much anticipation for your arrival… You surprised me so much: you changed… I know you are upset with me."

"No," I answered sadly, "of course not…"

"Yes, you are upset and I know why."

"Why?"

She looked back into the garden. Then all of a sudden she hugged my neck and held me close. She kissed me. Her face remained pressed against mine. I could feel the warmth of her breath for a few minutes. Then she looked at me with tears in her eyes and her whole face was red.

"Are you still upset?"

"No," I answered joyfully.

After that, our conversation became as friendly and personal as it used to be. Martha told me she would not be sent away to attend school any more. She would stay in the house. She had taken over the keys and was in charge of the household. The only things she would continue learning were playing the piano and some languages. Then I told her about all the things that happened to me since we had last seen each other.

"I had a very bad place," I lamented. "I had to live in a shed which was converted into a room, and there was no heat in it."

She looked at me with sympathy.

"Poor Kelen; I am glad you are no longer there. Don't go back there next year."

And we continued talking, like we did years ago, as if we were siblings.

"Are you going to come out tonight?" I asked in the end.

"No," she answered calmly. "We can talk during the day. I am not kept on such a tight leash anymore. You can always come here after lunch, when the lord is sleeping. I'd better go now."

She hugged me and put her head on my shoulder, the same way she used to, when she was a child. And she whispered into my ear.

"You are no longer upset, are you?"

When I was in the eighth grade, I wrote to my teacher at the beginning of May that I needed to buy black clothes for my graduation. I also mentioned that I was too embarrassed to depend on Lord Akos' purse, so I asked him to go up to the castle and get part of the more than two thousand forints Ms. Ilona left me.

My teacher sent me fifty forints and wrote that lord Akos was annoyed. He said if I was not embarrassed to accept his money until now, etc… There were two lines at the end of the letter.

You may know that smallpox was going around this past winter, even in the castle. Poor Miss Martha, you won't recognize her!

I was shaken. I kept staring at the letter, as if I could see Martha with smallpox. Then the tears started to roll down my cheeks. Poor Martha! She was suffering in bed and I did not even know about it!

It was a good thing I was always such a good student, because in the weeks before my final exams, I thought more about Martha than about my report card.

How could I write to her? My teacher would not give her my letter under any circumstances. The letters which arrive in the castle are locked inside a briefcase by the postmaster. Lord Akos has the only other key. He would never give her the letter.

Who nursed her? Who comforted her? The stern man probably did not even look in on her. Her stepmother was no longer alive by then. Old Mr. Lukacs was also dead. New servants took over from the old ones. How well did they take care of her if they only did it for the money?

I traveled home with a heavy heart after my final exams. My teacher told me right when I arrived that our town clerk was asking about me, because he was looking for help. I made an agreement with the clerk right away. He promised to provide me with room and board, plus ten forints each month.

I liked getting the room and board the most. At least I wouldn't have to accept any more financial assistance from Lord Akos.

"You can even sleep here tonight," said the town clerk. "The assistant usually sleeps on the office couch."

I took him up on the offer.

A question occurred to me right then. How would I meet with Martha in the afternoons from now on? I would have to sit at the office until late in the evening.

The next day, as I was putting on my black coat to visit Lord Akos, he unexpectedly came into the office.

"Are you home already?"

"I arrived last night. I was just preparing to..."

"It won't be necessary. I don't like expressions of gratitude. Let me see your report card. And what was all that nonsense you wrote to your teacher. You would spend your little money, and when you step out in life, you have nothing. Your report card is good. What kind of profession are you going to choose?"

"I thought about getting a law degree."

"That is not suitable for a poor man. You should become a priest. Apply at the seminary of Esztergom."

"But..."

"Don't object to me. If I tell you to become a priest, don't even think about becoming anything else. I want you to become a priest."

And he turned away.

He was looking for the town clerk regarding his raised taxes. He was upset about it. The clerk humbly tried to explain to him that the taxes on ten acres of vineyard were higher than for ten acres of plough land. He pulled out a book to prove he was right. His forehead was sweating. Lord Akos didn't wait. He was so upset, he stormed out of the office.

"I won't leave it at that," said the town clerk. "If he gets upset, he'll get upset. I will have him see a judge."

"I will take the book to him," I answered, "I'll take it this afternoon."

"Will you take it? Well, you are a good man."

This gave me a chance to get inside the castle.

A new butler opened the door.

"I would like to speak with Miss Martha," I said, "I'd like to ask her if the lord would see me."

The butler thought this was a legitimate request. He went upstairs.

My heart was beating fast as I was waiting on the porch. I looked out into the garden, where Martha and I used to play. There were red and white peonies still in bloom. The lime trees were also getting ready to bloom. All the plants were green and thriving. The birds were cheerfully chirping in the park. But still, there was something sad in that garden. As if two happy little children were missing from it.

The butler returned. Martha appeared soon after. She looked surprised to see me, but at the same minute she became red, like the reddest peonies outside.

"Is that you?"

Tears flooded her eyes.

"Look at me! Look at me! What have I become!"

She hugged my neck and continued crying on my bosom.

"But I don't understand you, Martha," I tried to comfort her. "It is hardly noticeable…"

She sure was pock-marked, even if not as badly as some other people, but around her nose, her skin looked like someone pressed a file against it. Her redness already disappeared. Her face was white and a little thinner than before.

She didn't answer. She sat down by the window. She pointed toward a chair for me to sit on. She rested her head on her arm and cried for a while. Then she wiped away her tears.

"I know you feel sorry for me," she said. "No one else feels sorry for me in this world."

"I am only sorry this causes you anguish," I said to console her. "I cried when I heard about your illness, Martha. But the smallpox left only an insignificant mark on your face. And even that will smooth out a few years from now."

"The doctor said the same thing," she said. "He said I will completely regain the smoothness of my face. He gave me some kind of a cream. But I don't believe him! No, I don't believe it!"

Then she wiped off her tears again and asked me how my year went.

"Did you think about me every day?"

She brushed off a feather from my coat and adjusted my tie as we were talking. I did not tell her about my morning meeting. I didn't want to add to her sadness right then. I thought perhaps I would tell her about it the next day. I only told her the news regarding my employment for the summer at the town-clerk's office.

I put her hand into mine and stroked it. I already got used to her pock-marks. To me she was the same sweet, beautiful flower as before. She was still the only one for me.

"How are we going to see each other? How?"

"Well, only on Sundays," she answered and looked at me lovingly. "And in the mornings, if you attend church... Although don't attend. It would create suspicion if you did. Did you know that my stepfather was already thinking about getting me married? He just said: *'You are a grown up girl now, ready to get married. Unfortunately we don't have a female relative I could trust to help you find a husband. Well, I'll think of something.'* After my illness he stopped mentioning that *something.*"

She had a sad smile on her face.

"You see, even smallpox is good for something."

Then she got up, while I was nervously looking toward the stairway.

"Should I announce you?"

"No. We'll hear if he is coming. I don't even want to talk with him. It will be enough if I leave this book here. Are we going to see each other tonight?"

"How could we? I am even more afraid than before."

I could see that she was glad I asked.

"No, no," she said. "We cannot meet during the evenings. What would the servants think if they found out? How would they look at me?"

We heard a carriage just arrived. We looked out the window.

"An army officer," I said with astonishment, "and an old lady."

"He is Antal, my stepmother's girlfriend's son," she answered with alarm. "Did you know he became a second lieutenant?"

"Does he come here often?"

"Of course not. Not since my stepmother died... I don't know what made them come now. Although he just became a member of the Imperial Royal Chamber. He became a dignitary recently."

The guests were already opening the hallway door.

"Tonight!" I begged Martha.

She didn't answer. She was hesitating as she stood there. Then she hurried to greet the guests. She escorted them upstairs into the parlor.

"You have grown so much!" said the second lieutenant. "I was sad to hear you were sick."

And he looked at me.

I hardly recognized him. He had become tall and his legs were thin. He kept bowing and fidgeting.

Martha did come out that evening after all. And because I kept begging her, she came out the next night too. And in the end she came out every night.

I was old enough to realize that it was insensitive of me to make poor Martha climb up the cactus stand. I climbed down from the stone wall when she appeared among the trees. There was enough space between the cactus pots for me to put my feet on the stairs. Martha was shocked at first, but she got used to it.

The moon was wonderfully shining. We could still smell the fragrance of the olive trees. The park, the moon, the olive tree fragrance, and even the concert of the nightingales were all ours until midnight.

"Do you know what your stepfather wants with me?" I said to her during our first evening. "He wants me to become a priest."

She was stunned.

"To become a priest?"

"Yes."

We were silently walking under the trees and I knew what she was thinking. I stopped at the grave stone.

"Do you remember, Martha?"

She pressed close to me.

"I remember."

And then we kissed each other. And that kiss was our engagement.

Well, I won't become a priest. I will tell him in September that it was too late to enroll, and Lord Akos will have to agree to let me choose a different profession.

But how would I be united with Martha by getting married to her? That was such a distant music of the future that we did not talk about it. We did not dare to talk about it.

The next day I did not want Martha to have to walk out to the cactuses. I went all the way to the castle to meet her. Her bed was on the second floor, next to her deceased stepmother's room. She had to be very careful when she came out. She was glad if she did not have to be scared from the shadows of trees and bushes, especially if the sky was cloudy, or if the moon was not shining. She would not even dare to come out at those times.

But when I was there, I was able to mimic the sound of a golden oriole. Then she overcame her fears. The castle's white wall shined a little, even on dark nights. And we sat on a bench next to the wall. Oh, how beautiful those evenings and nights were. We saw thousands of stars in the sky, and smelled the fragrance of a thousand lilies in the park.

If the sky was completely dark, or if it was raining, we were not able to meet. But she notified me, even those times. She put a burning candle in the corner window on the second floor. *You can't come!*

One dark evening, somehow I stepped on one of the cactus leaves. The cactus turned over and knocked off another one, right below it, on the second step. Then another fell off from the first step too. I got scared. The gardener would notice it in the morning. He would become suspicious. Martha helped me to relax.

"He will think a cat did it. We never have thieves in the park, because we don't grow any fruit. But I would hear about it at lunch. If they talk about a man being in the park, I will notify you with the candle at nine o'clock: *You can't come!*"

I did not see the signal the next day. Fifteen minutes later I got into the garden and stepped on the stand. It was a dark night too. The moon was not yet up. Only the stars were shining a little.

I was careful of course. The cactuses were put back in their places and I carefully, slowly put my feet between the pots. When I jumped down to the ground, two men grabbed me.

"Who are you?"

In that moment the gardener recognized me.

"Is that you, young man? What are you looking for?"

It took me a few minutes to be able to utter something.

"My watch's key."

The next day I got a message from the castle that the lord wants to see me. What should I tell him? Should I lie? I made up a thousand excuses. But the one I liked the most was telling him that I saw a man jump over the wall and I jumped after him, to try to catch him.

The butler led me to the library. There he was, the rhinoceros, sitting in his chair. The way he was staring did not look good.

"Martha confessed everything," he said in an angry tone. "You have paid us evil for our goodness. That girl was not raised for you! Tomorrow I will give the inheritance Ms. Ilona left you to your teacher. I am not going to deal with you any longer! You ungrateful, mean rascal! Get out!"

And he stamped his feet.

When I heard him call me a rascal, my whole body shook. I clenched my fist. At that moment I became a man. Even if Romulus was raised by a wolf, after the moment he was bitten, he could not have looked toward the wolf with grateful eyes.

I don't know what I would have answered, and I don't know what I would have done, but as I lifted my head in that difficult moment, my eyes stopped on the library's inner window. Martha was looking at me from there. She was begging me with her eyes, which were full of tears. She looked just like Mary, the way she is depicted in paintings.

"Get out!" the rhinoceros stamped his feet again.

The town clerk notified me in the afternoon that unfortunately he would no longer be able to provide employment for me. I got a message from my teacher as well. He wrote that he would not be able to provide a place for me to stay and I should leave the village. He had divided my money into five parts. He advised me to study for four more years somewhere and in the fifth year I should find employment. But I must never return, because the anger of the castle is great. He gave me a little over five hundred forints. And by the evening I was sitting at the train station. I did not know the destination I should buy a ticket for.

I got on the next train that came by. I came here, to the capital. I had never seen Budapest before. I only hoped to see it after I finished my law degree.

But I was unable to find peace for weeks and months. Was I at fault? Am I truly ungrateful? Even if Martha was not raised for me, somehow I felt like I was one with her. But what if that man told me the truth? What if Martha was really born for someone else?

I would have liked to write to her. But how? The letters for the castle were taken upstairs in a locked briefcase. I couldn't write to her address directly. I didn't know anyone in the village I could trust. Most of the children who attended the village school with me became distant from me over time. Or perhaps I became distant from them. Some of them became farm workers. But even if I trusted one of them, he would tell his lord about it. But he would not be able to talk with Martha anyways. And how would Martha be able to write to me? She didn't know where I was.

I was sure she would write to me.

I only had one hope left. Some of the law students took part in political demonstrations and their names were mentioned in the newspaper. I was hoping my name would also be mentioned and she would find out about me.

There were some demonstrations in the spring and I was always demonstrating in the first rows. But I was so unfortunate that a policeman hit me and took me in, and the newspaper only mentioned the more mature law students, who were also the leaders.

There was only one feeling that gave me some comfort and strength. I thought, whatever happens to Martha and me, someday we'll be together after all. Half of my heart was with her and half of her heart was with me. We were like a pair of scissors fallen into two pieces. We only felt whole when we were together. It was impossible that we would not be united again. I would get my law degree. When I became an adult, I would go to the village and I would watch her secretly, until I had the opportunity to speak with her. And I would grab her hand.

"Come, Martha!"

Where was a forest that could hold her back? And the old man would not live forever. Martha would get rid of him sooner or later and then there would be no wall, no cactuses and no arrogance between us any longer.

I did not write to Martha. But when a High Court Justice hired me to teach his son, I put the money I had left in an envelope and sent it to my teacher. I wrote to him to add the money to my inheritance from Ms. Ilona, and asked him to take it to the castle. I would pay lord Akos back for what he spent on me. The only thing I would not pay back was his rudeness.

I did not let him know my address. To this day I don't know how he took care of my request.

I was getting to the end of my first year when on a cold, rainy morning in June, my housekeeper put sour cherries next to my coffee that I had asked her to buy. She put them there, wrapped in a newspaper, the same way she got them at the market.

As I was eating the sour cherries, I unintentionally started to read the paper. My eyes wandered to the engagement announcements.

...Martha... and K. Antal, Second Lieutenant, member of the Imperial Royal Chamber...

I immediately stopped eating my sour cherries. The room started circling. The floor was sinking. The world became chaotic.

What was the date on the newspaper? It didn't have a date on it. But why would I need to know? Did it make any difference whether it happened on a Monday or a Wednesday? It could not have happened long ago, because the color of the newspaper was still white. The main thing was that Martha left me. She put me aside!!! She put my heart aside. Was it possible? Was it possible that she left me? I felt as if cold serpents were slithering in my chest. What a disappointment!!!

I couldn't even think that she had been forced. If a girl wants to save her parents from some kind of suffering by getting married, that is her justification. But who would Martha save? Couldn't she have said to the man that she did not love him? Couldn't she have said, even at the marriage ceremony, that she was being forced?

I felt like my heart was crushed and burnt, and my thoughts were like silently flying ravens. How could I go on living? Why should I go on studying, struggling and suffering? Martha belonged to someone else! I felt like the order of the world had been turned upside down.

I don't know how I left the house. All of a sudden I was standing on the Danube's shore. My life seemed meaningless. I wanted to die. I wanted to turn my back on this world and not feel anything anymore.

A lot of people were boarding a boat. Where was the boat going? Toward Martha's house. What if I would go too? I would jump into the water. But not there, further upstream. I would swim, if my life instinct would prompt me, but in the end I would sink and the water would carry me silently. The water would take my dead body to the turn, where the dead bodies are stranded. Soon they would recognize me. She would look at me too...

But no, I would write to her first! It was customary to congratulate for the engagement. Oh, I would congratulate!

26

I went inside a post office and asked for letter paper. I wrote on it right there, on the counter.

Martha, Martha! You are not only congratulated by the living but also by one who died.

I thought I was going to faint as I signed my name. I felt like a millstone was weighing down on my chest; my breathing stopped.

"Please Miss," I whispered to the postal employee, "write this address on the letter, my hand is trembling too much today."

I put the letter in a mailbox outside.

A man was standing nearby selling merchandise. One of his goods caught my eyes. It was a big, black, rough gun.

"Do you sell bullets too?"

"No, I don't, but you can get them at the hardware store."

I purchased the gun and bullets too. I put them in the inside pocket of my jacket and I boarded the boat. I thought I'd better shoot myself in the heart before I jumped into the water.

The boat departed a minute later. I sat outside on a bench, near the railing and I watched the water; my grave.

Martha! Martha! Your name was sweet to me, like a drop of honey melting on my tongue. Today it is bitter, like poison which can stop my heart.

Martha! Martha! Your name was my sunshine until now, warm sunshine, which turns buds into flowers in the spring. Today it is a cold cloud, which makes the water's shiny surface dim.

Martha! Martha! Your name was the music of my heart. Today it is only a soft cry for help. It is a cry for help, from the depth of my heart, a cry for help, which destroyed the fairy-palace of my beautiful hopes. Its sun is burnt out. Its stars fell down. And there is only black darkness left – cold silence...

A traveler sat down next to me on the bench, and for a minute he distracted me from my sorrowful thoughts. But then I returned to them. My eyes were full of tears as I stared into the water.

The traveler spoke to me.

"What troubles you, my young friend?"

The words: *"what troubles you?"* moved me. Tears flooded my eyes and were flowing down my cheeks. Is there someone in this world who wants to know what troubles me?

I looked at him. He was a chubby old man with a gray moustache and red cheeks. He seemed healthy and full of life. Even his ears were thick and red, like the bald English hogs in lord Akos' farm. He had a yellow cane in his hand. His tiny eyes were warm and friendly.

"You are planning something foolish," he said gently. And he reached into my pocket and pulled out my gun. He just threw it in the Danube, as if it was an orange peel.

"Life has great value, my young friend. A gun is not worth much. But if you are sorry, I'll pay for it."

He put his hand on mine. He asked me in a kind voice:

"What is wrong? You are in love. I bet you are in love. Well, just confess it."

I just stared at him. I felt as if he was my father, and had the right to talk about my fate. Tears flowed from my eyes.

"It is true," I was almost gasping for air as I answered him. "But we were part of each other's lives, since we were children. And I would have never believed... I would have never believed..."

I couldn't say any more. He kept talking to me. He tried to comfort me, in a way only an old, wise gentlemen can. But I only heard his voice. I only started to pay attention to him after crying eased my pain.

"Look my friend," he said, "you will recover from this excitement if you change climates and surroundings. Who are your parents?"

I told him who I am, what I am.

"I am a dirty rag, I am nothing. I only meant something to that girl. Now I don't mean anything to myself either."

A long-necked young woman wearing black clothes walked toward us. The old gentleman directed her to go elsewhere.

"Don't sit here Eva. Walk some more."

The lady gave me a surprised look and kept on walking. The old gentleman grabbed my hand.

"Come with me," he said, "to the parlor."

We went down. He asked me a few more questions regarding the people my life revolved around in recent years. He was most interested in my excellent report card, and that I taught a High Court Judge's son.

"You must be an honest man," he said. "A person who stands the struggles of life, and stays loyal to another living person, can only be an honest man. Well look, I will make you an offer that will save you and will be good for me too. I am a land owner in Temes, and now I am traveling to Vienna. My son, Paul studies there, in a good boarding school. He is sixteen years old. Spend the summer with him. Teach him mathematics, but only for an hour in the mornings. I will pay you in gold. And if I see that the boy likes you, I will bring him to Budapest in September. You will live together. You will treat him as if you were his older brother."

"What does it matter to me?" I thought with discouragement. "What is the value of gold to me when I have lost my diamond?"

I listened indifferently to the old gentleman. His daughter, the one wearing black clothes, recently became a widow. She was only married for two months. Her

28

husband was buried the day before. Her father was taking her on a trip on the Danube, to try to help her deal with her sorrow.

The lady was walking toward us again. He waived toward her.

"Come here, Eva. Look, this young man will be Paul's teacher. He is also mourning."

The lady removed her veil. She was a charming eighteen year old girl. She was snub-nosed, but perhaps that made her face appear younger. Her eyes were red from crying. Her face was pale. She offered her hand for a handshake.

"Are you also mourning?"

"I am mourning," I uttered, "I am mourning forever!"

She sat down next to me. We sat next to each other silently for a long time. And after our pain subsided, she started to speak. She told me who and what her husband was, and how much she loved him. He was a governor. He was going to a hunt and his gun went off in his carriage and the bullet pierced his neck.

She cried again. Then she asked about me. I also told her the cause of my sorrow. And since only the two of us were sitting there, I told her the details. She paid attention to me as she listened. Her eyes were radiating goodness and gentleness.

"She was forced," she said, "believe me, Martha was forced. She loves you even now."

I couldn't answer her, just shook my head. I only looked out the window when the boat stopped. Where were we? I saw the castle of Pozsony. How fortunate that we kept on talking.

And then, as I looked at her, in my desperation I had the saving idea, that I was meant to meet her. We were going to love each other, and when I finished my law degree, I would marry her. I would also become a governor, and would not sit on a carriage with a loaded gun.

I looked at her, like a painter, who is observing a girl sitting before his canvass. She was beautiful, even more beautiful than Martha. And Eva was also deep in thought as she looked at me.

In Vienna I got to know the son as well. He was a nice, laid back child. He also had tiny eyes and thick ears.

I was in a somber mood as I went down with them to Temes. I wanted to forget! I was dreading every hour I had to spend by myself.

It was strange that I looked more for the company of women than men, even though I hated them. Serpents dressed up like flowers! – I thought. They can only be believed when we are holding their hands, but perhaps not even then.

With such a blood dripping heart, not even the beautiful widow was able to attract me to herself. We were like two out of tune strings next to each other.

Her personality was very different from mine anyway. She was very joyful and talked very loud, not like she was on the boat. She was always thinking about how she could dance, as soon as possible. She would have danced a month after the funeral. I especially did not like that she had long finger nails. Girls with long nails never appealed to me.

No, Eva was not my Eve; I thought every time I looked at her. Where was my Eve, where? How did she live? What was she like? Did she think of me when she stood at the altar? How was she able to detach herself from me? – I often wondered over the past eighteen years!

I was surprised that I had never heard of them, and life never brought me together with her husband. But I was dreading meeting with her. How would she look at me? Would she dare to calmly look at me, with her clear eyes, as she did when she was a young girl?

And every time I was attracted by female beauty, by a kind voice, or when a woman looked at me with warmth, I always thought about her. If the person I knew so much was unreliable, how could I believe someone I would never know as much?

I remained a bachelor.

I did not feel quite as bitter toward her in recent years.

I am really ungrateful, I thought, instead of thanking God for giving me such a wonderful girl to play with, who also made my youth sweeter with her love toward me, and I am only thinking about her being taken from me.

She was taken from me. She was mine until I was twenty years old. She was my joy, my treasure, but she couldn't be anymore. For some reason, she couldn't be. Life has taught me to appreciate everything God has given me and to be thankful even if I lost them.

Sometimes I thought about her during sleepless nights. I'd like to see her again. Just once more! Perhaps I would even be able to talk to her without her recognizing me. If I would have had a picture of her face, I would have put it on my desk, or perhaps I would have gotten a large size painting made from it. Even if we were separated, at least her picture would be standing in my room.

And I was able to find excuses for her. She couldn't have married as easily as I first thought in my despair. Who knows how she struggled like a poor, little, white bat, nailed to a wall? Was she tricked perhaps? Did they give her a letter that looked like it was in my handwriting? Or have they made up bad things about me? Who knows what happened.

At first I even thought it was her fault. I threw a black letter among her wedding gifts. That was an ugly deed! One thought was comforting me, that perhaps she did not receive it.

As I said, I thought about her a lot. The same way a sailor thinks about his sunken treasure. I got over her, but I always missed her. I missed having someone I could completely trust. I missed half of my heart, my heart's more beautiful half. The same way Adam would have missed Eve, if he would have lost her. And Adam surely would have kept asking the painful question until his death: where are you, Eve? Where are you?

And now imagine what happened to me the other day, on December 7th.

I always keep a flower on my desk, only one pot, not a big one. But I don't let my servant or gardener take care of it, because I never buy a flower that has opened up already. I always buy a flower that is still budding. It is most beautiful when it opens up in front of me.

I go to the flower shop every Saturday afternoon. I choose one from the budding flowers.

On that day I entered the flower shop on Rakoczi Street in the afternoon, as usual. They already know me. The woman working there smiled at me and looked in the corner to see what she should offer me.

There were two nuns in the shop, who were trying to choose from the potted flowers. I would not have paid any attention to them, but as I said something, one of them turned around. She stared at me. Her already white face became even more colorless. And I saw it was her face! But to be absolutely sure, I noticed traces of a few pock-marks around her nose...

I felt like I was hit by lightning. I just stood there and stared at her. Finally I spoke, as if I was whispering in my sleep.

"Martha!"

"Kelen," she answered, as if she was seeing a ghost. "Are you alive?"

She lifted her hand to her forehead. I noticed she started falling, and I needed to grab her. She fell onto my bosom.

"Martha, Martha, wake up!"

We took her into the room, which was used for wreath making, and poured water on her. But to me the whole thing seemed like it happened in a joyful, happy dream. I kept looking at her. Her face was fuller, compared to when she was a young girl. Her eyes moved back a little and seemed darker, but it was her! She was my white flower, the sweet, good half of my heart.

"Martha!" I asked when she came to her senses. "Didn't you get married?"

"No."

Then, after she completely regained her consciousness, she told me, in that small room, that her stepfather was visited one day by Antal, the soldier; but he was not with his mother, just by himself. They talked for a long time in the library. The man even had lunch with them. After lunch, the stepfather spoke, in his usual rough manner.

"Martha, this lunch was your engagement. You have known Antal for a long time. He is going to be your husband."

And she told me, she wasn't able to utter a word. After they were left alone, she begged the young man not to force her, because she didn't love him. But the young man just laughed at her.

31

"Don't be afraid of me so much. We'll get used to each other."

And the fine fiancé himself made the engagement known in the papers.

"Poor Martha! And they weren't able to force you..."

"No. My stepfather was so angry he put me in with the nuns, first for one year, then for another. He accomplished nothing. At the end of each year I said: no and no! And later he died and I stayed in, and renewed my vows every year."

"Martha, you will not renew them any more!"

The bachelors who were listening to him stared at him in astonishment. He was happily smiling, as he looked at them, and said triumphantly:

"Well, my dear friends, I will pay for the champagne, because this evening was my bachelor party. And now I'd like to invite you to my wedding on New Year's Eve. We'll have dinner at this table."

The bachelors congratulated him with so much joy as if they had all found their Eve in his story.

The Three Owls

The speaker was a chubby, gray, flat nosed gentleman. His rosy cheeks gave him a healthy appearance. He was a well respected lawyer. He could often be seen on Kossuth Street walking in the company of one or two volunteer firefighters. Both of the volunteers had the same round face and flat nose as he did. He could also be seen with a young man in art museums. He too looked like him with his flat nose and bright eyes. You could tell the four of them belonged together.

At the beginning of dinner he immediately announced the reason he was eating with the bachelors: the two volunteers had been transferred and the artist was traveling to Italy.

My story is like a book which was bound with the ending from a different book by mistake.

It did not even occur to me that I should get married, until I was thirty.

I was an orphan with plenty of challenges, just like most orphan children. But a child is full of energy, like a rubber ball which bounces under the pressures of life without breaking. This kind of a pressured ball existence created a thoughtful man out of me. I did not dream about women. I just considered them rivals in the struggles of life, the same way I thought about men.

Perhaps when I was a law student, my candle lit up in honor of a young lady, but the flame always went out. I was busy with life. I did not have anyone in the world except for one person, my older brother whose name was Jancsi. But the wind blew him to America from Hungary while I was still just a small child. One of our immigrant relatives took him there after my mother's death. I did not even know if he was still alive.

I finished law school when I was twenty-five. By the time I was thirty I had a great three bedroom apartment and I started to get around by carriage. But even then I was more interested in available homes than available women.

Carpets were the only passion I allowed myself. First factory made carpets, later carpets from Brussels and Persia. Once I have noticed an interesting Persian rug in a shop window. I was admiring it before I entered the store. I had been there a few times before. I knew the shop owner. He was of Armenian descent, but he was born in Budapest. He was about fifty years old. His gray beard had grown all over his face and almost covered his eyes. His hands were hairy like a gorilla. He had changed his first name from Mihaly to Mehemed. He was always serious and only laughed when he was telling anecdotes. At those times his face was distorted and became scary. But fortunately he did not tell his stories very often.

I stepped into the store. There were two ladies talking to him. One of them was wearing deep red silk; she was very elegant, beautiful. Her hat was decorated with red poppies. She had black Spanish eyes full of fire.

The shop owner left the two women and turned to me.

"Finish up with the ladies, Mr. Mehemed."

The shopkeeper was grinning.

"My wife, and my daughter."

"Congratulations," I answered.

I raised my hat toward the girl. She was smiling as she nodded toward me. Her eyes stayed on me like two burning charcoals. I have never seen so much fire in anyone's eyes before. I felt if she kept looking at my coat, she would burn holes in it like the sun could through a magnifying glass. I couldn't help to look at her periodically.

She was a fully grown beauty, thin as a robin, full of life. Magnificent, her oval face was tender white and above her beautifully carved lips there was a tiny black shadow. Perhaps that is what made her face appear so white. But perhaps it was her long earrings made of rubies. Or maybe it was because of the blackness of her eyes.

Well, those eyes were amazing. Even today I cannot tell if it was because of her strong eyebrows, or because her eyes could light up. It may have been her long, black eyelashes which caused the white of her eyes to shine so brightly. Or perhaps her pupils were larger; who knows, but she was magnificent.

I thought the carpet was too expensive. I asked the girl with the beautiful eyes and she agreed with me.

"Yes, it is expensive."

Mr. Mehemed was staring at her.

"Are you crazy, Ida?"

Then he burst out laughing. He put the carpet aside and was looking at his daughter lovingly.

"I can't believe my own daughter is ruining my deal."

Ida was smiling as she shrugged her shoulders.

"I was asked and I answered. I can only say what I feel."

I could see her white teeth as they appeared from under her red lips as she was talking.

The shopkeeper lifted the carpet again.

"Women don't know these things." he said as he was shaking his head. "Take a look at it. This is very rare, extremely unique in Budapest."

"I have six of these," I answered. "You won't fool me, Mr. Mehemed." I looked at his daughter, hoping she would be on my side again.

"I'd like to see your collection," said the girl.

"You are welcome to see it any time, immediately if you would like."

"No, maybe tomorrow I can come with my mother, if you don't mind. Or perhaps the day after tomorrow, if that works better for you."

She was blushing. Her eyes were burning like charcoals.

Her mother was looking at her in disbelief.

"I can't believe it."

Her mother was chubby and had thick eyebrows. When she was thin she must have looked like a hawk with her nose, but since she gained weight she looked more like a penguin. She was wearing lots of rings, like most of the well to do shopkeepers' wives. A gold tooth was shining from under her upper lip when she was talking.

The next day Ida came over with her mother. She did not seem too interested in looking at the carpets, but seemed even more interested in me. She was wearing scarlet colored silk and earrings made of rubies. She looked like a Venus born in the light of fire.

"Do you live here alone?" she was asking with a dreamy look. "If I would have known that you were a bachelor... It would not have been appropriate for us to come and visit you."

For a minute she was looking at the floor and appeared embarrassed.

"Well, yes," I answered. "I am like a tall well in a desert. But I am used to it; I have always lived alone since I was a child."

She seemed to feel sorry for me. Then she turned her attention to my porcelain plate collection her mother was admiring.

"These are very rare!" she said in astonishment. I was surprised to find out how much she appreciated art from the few words she said. She even made a few comments regarding the pictures on my walls.

"The moon is a little cold. These trees were painted in the summer time. During the summer even the nights are warm. The painter should have used more red color."

Then she looked me in the eye:

"Didn't you have sideburns before?"

"Maybe, sometimes I had, although..."

"But five or six years ago?"

"Well to be exact..."

"Have you often been in Paris?"

"Unfortunately I have never been there."

"Wonderful!"

She stared at me. Then she was looking at her mother, as if asking: "How is this possible?"

I did not understand why it was wonderful that I have never been in Paris. There are millions of people who have not been in Paris and nobody wonders about it.

Ida continued looking at my pictures and suggested that I hang a landscape lower. It was a picture of a plain field.

"Where have you learned these things, dear Ida?" I asked in amazement.
The girl was smiling.

"She was raised in Paris," said her mother as her gold tooth was shining. "She was in a boarding school with the children of elite families."

The girl was looking at the ground, as if she were ashamed that she was raised in Paris.

Then they invited me to look at their carpet collection. After they left, I noticed Ida forgot her handbag on my table. I sent it after them right away. But something else was left there which I could not send after them. Ida's two eyes full of fire. Everywhere I turned they were looking at me. Even at night they were looking, smiling, burning. I tossed and turned all night.

What was going on? Did I fall in love perhaps? I thought I was smarter than to let such an accident happen to me. I lit up a cigar in my bed as I was thinking.

The girl was beautiful, as if she were the creation of a sultan's fantasy. She was educated, even in Paris. She might even have been wealthy. But the main thing: she was magnificent, magnificent! A rose is a beautiful ornament of any house. Imagine having a talking rose as she was!

But as I was considering the matter with my thirty year old brain, I started having doubts. If I got tired of a rose, I could give it to my landlady, Mrs. Vice. But if I got tired of my wife, I could not give her to Mrs. Vice. And I didn't even know where her family came from.

Isn't this crazy?

The next day I visited them anyway. Why not get to know them a little closer; I thought. The company of ladies is always refreshing.

She seemed very enthusiastic when she welcomed me, as if I were an old acquaintance. The house looked great and the fragrance of flowers in it surprised me. The carpets were magnificent. The family had a parrot, piano, palm tree, lots of oil paintings and a tapestry which would have been suitable for a king's palace.

I was amazed.

Under the twelve foot palm tree there were two half-length portraits on two sides. One of them was Venus. The other was a statue of Ida in a Diana costume. I can say that Ida looked better.

I arrived around 5 p.m. and they invited me right away to have tea with them. How wonderful that tea was. I usually had tea in a restaurant called Crown, so I could tell the difference. And Ida served it to me. Her every move was so charming. It was wonderful. Her hands were just like the hands of an angel with rosy nails. She had an opal ring on her finger.

If she marries me, I thought; it will be like this during our married lives: beautiful woman, beautiful smile, good smelling tea under a palm tree, and her angel hands with rosy nails would be working with me to build our lives together.

I was astonished. I would have thought I was having tea in the home of some kind of royalty if I didn't know I was in the carpet dealer's home.

Her mother looked like a countess in her fancy dress. There was also a teenage boy there. He must have been about thirteen years old. He had big feet, thin legs and black bushy hair. He did not fit well in our company. He was Ida's younger brother called Eugene.

He did not bother us for long; he drank his tea and took off. His mother checked his pockets:

"Do you have any cigarettes?"

"No mother."

His mother tried to warn him about smoking, as he was leaving with a sinister smile on his face.

"We caught him smoking yesterday," his mother was explaining. "His father took care of him..."

Ida was smiling and she was looking at me with a dreamy look as if she was looking at a landscape in moonlight.

"Do you have a younger or an older brother?" She asked.

"Of course, I do."

The girl's eyes lit up.

"Does he look like you?"

"I don't know. We were very small when we were separated. I have not heard from him since."

"Do you have a picture left of him?"

"No."

"You must have some resemblance."

"That is what I thought. When we were children we looked alike."

"Has he perhaps been in Paris?"

"I doubt it. If he was in Europe I am sure he would have looked me up. I don't even know where he lives. But he knows Sajolad, the village where we were born. He can ask about me there if he would like to find out where I live. No, he has never visited Europe. I don't even think he is alive."

The girl was looking at her mother.

"Isn't it amazing how much they are alike?"

"It is amazing," repeated her mother.

Then they told me that a young Hungarian man was traveling with them as they were coming home from Paris and he did some kind of a favor for them. I don't remember the details...

"You must really appreciate what he has done." I said to try to please them "I am almost sorry I ruined your illusion that I was him. I should have kept you believing I was that enviable man."

Ida was smiling as she reached to shake my hand.

"But I believe you are him. You are him, just like him. Even your voice sounds like him."

I could feel her warm sympathy as she pressed my hand.

Later we were discussing the national art exhibition, especially the pictures. The mother liked Valentin's *Dying Gipsy* the most, Ida liked *The Peasant Lighting His Pipe* by Jozsef Kegyes and my favorite was Munkacsy's picture, which depicted the main group of *Calvaria*. We were talking as if we were experts. In the end Ida suggested that tomorrow afternoon we should look at the pictures together.

When I left, I felt as if I had champagne after lunch.

I went to Mr. Mehemed's store instead of going home.

"I can get a good husband for your daughter," I said to the old man jokingly. But what should I answer if he asks *how much he weighs*?

Mehemed raised his eyebrows to about the middle of his forehead as he was blinking.

"Well...if I get to choose the groom, I'll give them as much gold as he weighs. If my daughter chooses him, I'll give as much as my daughter weighs."

"What would happen if you would choose the same person as your daughter?"

"I would give them as much as they weigh together."

"In gold?"

"In gold."

I was amazed. I couldn't wait to get to the nearest bank to find out how much a pound of gold was worth. It was worth approximately 800 forints. Ida must have been about 122 pounds and I weighed about 151. And if I take into consideration that I could put myself on a weight gain diet....

But even then the main treasure was the girl. I had enough money to live on comfortably. A man can gain money lots of ways, but the angels only let one girl like Ida get to this world in a thousand years!

And there was something else that caused me to want to get married. I was so alone in the world. Do you know what the saddest spectacle is? You probably guessed a funeral procession. That is sad. Every time I come across a funeral procession I stop and take off my hat. But there is something else that is even sadder: when I see a bunch of orphan children together on the street as they are wearing their little blue caps. We think they are only orphans as long as they are wearing their blue uniforms. But the reality is they stay orphans even when they are old enough to grow a mustache. If someone does not have even one relative, he is missing something his entire life: another heart. He is searching and searching for it. The human heart revolves around others, just like the stars in the sky. The lonely man feels as if he does not fit in the order of this world.

"I am so lucky!" I was bragging to a recently married captain friend of mine, who served in the same regiment with me. I have found a magnificent girl! I will propose to her this week.

"Well, you should not rush into such a thing," he answered as he was shaking his head.

"But what if someone else takes her? She is full of promises! Magnificent promises!"

He had a wry smile on his face.

"The problem is that every girl is a wonderful promise when she is single, but when she gets married she can't fulfill the promise."

He sighed.

What he said got me thinking; there are so many divorce cases even I have to work on as an attorney. There are many people whose marriages did not live up to their expectations. Some time ago they all believed they reached the promise land by tying the knot.

Well, after all, I don't have to take an express train to the promise land!

The next day I visited them. We were going to look at the art exhibition, as we had discussed earlier.

"We shouldn't go there today," said Ida as we were sitting in a carriage. "Instead let's go to Margaret Island. It is less crowded."

We ended up walking on Margaret Island.

They invited me to look at a vacation home located on Svab Hill the next day, but I had a few clients scheduled for that afternoon.

"It's impossible," I said. "I am truly sorry. Wouldn't it be possible to do this a day later?"

It was possible.

"But tomorrow evening you could at least come with us to the theater."

The next day I accompanied them to the theater on Gyapju Street, where Mrs. Blaha was the lead actress at the time. I also accompanied them on the following days, sometimes in the afternoon, at times in the evening, but the girl always thought of some place where I could be with them.

Of course there was always a fourth person with us when we were going out of the house. Most of the time a woman came along who was visiting with them, but never the same person. When there were no women available, the youngster Eugene trudged along.

Even today I cannot tell if I was the one she liked so much. Or was it my double from Paris? But she seemed crazy about me.

During the second week she already started to ask where I was at certain times of the day, what I was doing, with whom I spoke. The third week I felt it was necessary to tell her everything. She was very inquisitive. By that time I even disclosed my financial situation to her.

"I have a little house on Nagy street, approximately five thousand forints in cash, and if I consider the value of my practice…"

She was listening with bright eyes. Her mother was too. When I started to appraise the value of my clientele her mother stood up and left the room. She must have been sure that by the time she returned, Ida would be blushing and would give her a big hug.

But I still did not declare my love for her. There were moments when I would have, but in front of the mother... Who knows, mothers can be so prosaic! Like a loaf of bread next to a short cake. When we were alone, Ida was looking at me with so much admiration that I thought it was unnecessary to declare my feelings for her.

I don't even know what was holding me back. Perhaps the reason was my rental agreement, which did not terminate until November and it was only June. I thought I would not be able to marry her until then, and in August we would look for a place together.

At the end of June they rented a vacation home on Svab Hill. I couldn't visit them everyday any more. It was an hour and a half round trip on carriage and I had to stay there for at least two hours. I did not have three or four hours of free time every day.

I did desire to see her very much. I did not sleep well if a day passed by without me seeing her. My eyes and my heart were hungry for her. I felt sick if I did not see her for two days in a row. She was even more distraught. She looked at me with so much reproach at those times!

One of those times a town clerk visited me from Sajolad in the morning. He came up for the art exhibition. I did not know him from before, but he was from the same village and I felt I needed to spend the afternoon with him. A person who grew up as an orphan is always glad if there is anyone in the world who can somehow be associated with him.

I got home at midnight. The woman, who was in charge of the gate of my building told me someone came by and asked if I was sick.

"Who was she?"

"Didn't say a name, just said she was from Svab Hill."

The next day I went there. She was waiting by the fence peaking through a jasmine bush. You could tell that she had a restless night.

Of course, on Sundays her father was home. He was wearing Turkish slippers and smoked out of a long pipe. He too got used to me being part of his family. Otherwise he was a boring man. He was always talking about Smyrna, where he spent his youth, and about money, how carpets were the best investment. I was certain that even if he had given me my weight in gold, he would have first removed my keys and watch out of my pockets.

One July evening, the three of us were sitting on a bench under a tree overlooking Budapest below. Her mother got up and went inside to take care of dinner preparations.

Ida was silent as usual. Her warm, beautiful eyes turned to me expecting something. There was silence around us.

"What a beautiful evening," I said. "I wish I could stay here."

At that moment I really felt the harshness of my life. Thirty years of laboring hard, thirty springs without seeing their flowers and now fate had brought me a magnificent human flower. I just had to reach out for her to become mine for good.

I felt I had reached the big turning point in my life. The girl was looking at me with a dreamy look and said quietly with a warm, sweet voice:

"You should rent a vacation home near us."

"For myself?"

She closed her eyes. I could tell she didn't know what to say. In our silence the quietness seemed even deeper. We could only hear some kind of a bird in the distance as if she were trying glass whistles.

"Why didn't you get married?" she asked me in a faint voice.

And then I started to move to grab her hand and answer: why didn't you come into my life sooner, you sister of fairies! But then the big footed prose appeared: the youngster Eugene. And he scared away the excitement of that fairytale moment.

The driver was getting restless.

"Kalman, I only offered to stay until 7," he said.

I stayed a few more minutes. Then I reached to shake Ida's hands:

"You see, I always stay longer than I plan to."

She squeezed my hand as if she wanted to squeeze her soul into it:

"This is life," she said with a sad smile "even the drivers interfere in our affairs."

"Not this time!" I raised my head as I answered.

"Eugene, my friend, here is a ten forint bill, give it to the driver. I don't care about him! I will stay until eight regardless of what he says."

"You'll stay for dinner too!" said her mom as her gold tooth was shining.

"Well, maybe not for that..."

"Yes, you will stay!" Ida was pleading as she grabbed my hand "My dad will be home soon. We'll go up to the station to meet him.

She was holding my hand with her two hands. Then she started clapping, she was so happy.

The youngster Eugene ran away. Her mother went back into the house to set the table for dinner.

Again we were left alone.

"I am so happy," she said, "finally you are spending an evening here. Thank you!"

And she held out her hand.

"I am happy whenever I am with you," I answered with a passionate voice.

I lifted her hand to my lips.

She hugged me. Then I hugged her even tighter.

"Ida, dear Ida…"

"Say it once already…" she said softly and hugged my neck.

"Why? You know it."

We were already holding hands as we were going to meet her dad.

A lot of things happened to me that year. Once I was sitting on a horse drawn bus, which was departing from Christina Town. I was sitting right next to the entrance. At the end of Chain Bridge a pale woman wearing wild pigeon colored clothes stepped on the bus. She had blonde hair, tired blue eyes and lacquered shoes. She seemed too elegant to ride on a bus. She was about thirty. Her nose was a little short and her chin was sharp. I think I can even say she was attractive. She was holding a grey leather handbag in which she was carrying papers. Her bag was hit as she stepped up and her papers fell out and scattered all over. They were mainly letters, all kinds of old yellow papers.

"Wait a minute!" I called out to the driver.

And I was picking up the papers.

"Oh no," the lady said in anguish, "if only one of them is lost…This case does not start well!"

"Rest assured ma'am," I was trying to comfort her, "we will not move until all of your papers are gathered."

The lady gave me a grateful look. She sat down next to me. After a little while she said:

"I am much obliged. You are a very kind gentleman. Would you be able to recommend to me a trustworthy attorney?"

"Trustworthy? I'd be glad to."

"I'd like to find an honest one, the most honest."

"I can recommend one. I happen to have one of his cards."

I gave her the card.

She stepped into my place in her wild pigeon clothes, two or three hours later. She seemed surprised when she reached my door. I hurried to welcome her and smiled as I was apologizing.

"I don't know a more honest lawyer than myself."

It turned out she was an impoverished baroness from Transylvania. Her husband was a patient in Elizabeth Hospital. He has some kind of a spinal fracture. They wanted to file a lawsuit regarding one of their relative's estates.

I looked through the papers. They were regarding two thousand acres of land. The letters were proof that the previous owner wanted his adopted daughter, the baroness, to inherit the land.

The woman told me the case in her words. I calmly listened to her lengthy story which included many details that were not pertinent. I thought her case was very promising. She gave me a worried look at the end:

"Well, what is your opinion? Will you accept it?"

"I cannot tell you yet today."

"So it is doubtful!"

Her eyes revealed her anxiety.

"I didn't say that. But I have to read through all these letters. If I see that the case is doubtful I won't even take it on."

"That is the kind of person I was looking for!" she exclaimed with a joyful expression on her face.

"Other attorneys would have accepted it without reading the letters, just so they could make me pay them. We'll give you twenty percent, or twenty five percent of the value of the property."

"I will only accept ten."

She seemed grateful and her eyes were shining with joy as she was leaving.

The baroness often came to see me from that day on.

I had been engaged for three weeks already, when Ida asked me about my women acquaintances in Budapest. I smiled at her question.

"If I could list them all."

"Just the ones you know well, the ones you talk to the most often. You know that I am interested in everything. But don't tell me. It's better if I don't know. I will get to know them in November anyway."

We were planning to get married on November 7th. We couldn't do it any sooner. The old man was very busy with the increased business which was generated by the art exhibition. His wife helped him during the afternoons. She even spent Sunday mornings in the old man's store.

"As you wish," I answered, "although I know very few women I can introduce you to."

I thought the only reason she asked me was to find out if I knew any well respected women she could get to know. She was raised in Paris. She was used to high society. She wanted to live among them in Budapest as well.

"Just tell me the name of the woman you know the best," she was interrogating me even further, "the one you speak to the most often."

"The most often? With whom do I speak the most often? I most often speak to the woman at the tobacco shop where I buy my cigar in the morning."

She slapped my head with her fan. A few minutes later she asked again:

"Still, what kind of families do you know?"

I told her. She paid careful attention as she listened.

"And do you have visitors?"

"Do I have visitors? I am a single man and I usually talk to my friends at the coffee shop."

She was searching my eyes.

"Who is the high society woman usually visiting you at four in the afternoon?"

"Me? Let me see."

"She wears wild pigeon colored clothes and her hat is decorated with flowers…"

"Now I know: she is one of my clients."

And I told her about the baroness. I started wondering:

"But how do you know about her?"

"Our maid happened to be in the area."

I smiled. It even pleased me that she paid so much attention to me.

Not long after that I had to travel to Zala on behalf of a bank. The property of a bankrupt gentleman was auctioned off and he owed the bank a lot of money.

I thought I'd take a look at Heviz as I was passing near Keszthely. I had an acquaintance there, the baron. He was trying to recuperate from his spinal malady.

I spent the afternoon with him. Of course his wife was there too. Her sick husband was getting better but he couldn't stand the lodging and its restaurant. It was a pitiful little place back then.

The baron's doctor recommended that they should rent an apartment at Lukacs Bath. The next day the baroness joined me on the train. She wanted to select and negotiate a price for a place at the bath.

I had not seen my fiancée for four days. The first thing I did was to visit her.

I was surprised how pale she looked as she stepped in front of me. That was the first time I have seen her pale. I have never seen anyone in my life change so much in color. She looked as if I was looking at a marble statue of her, dressed in her clothes. But even for a live marble statue she looked hideous. As if her eyebrows were drawn above her eyes with coal dust. And the little shadow above her lips, which was so appealing before, looked more like a mustache.

She was ugly when she was pale.

"Ida!" I said to her in an alarmed voice. "What is the matter?"

"Nothing," she said with a smile. "I am just not feeling well. I will have my color back in less than an hour."

But her mother also looked like a bristled up turkey. She kept looking at her daughter with her round eyes.

I was concerned about Ida's condition.

"But what is wrong, dear Ida?"

"Oh, let's not talk about it."

And suddenly her eyes flashed on me as if she wanted to charge at me. They stayed on me like two cold daggers.

"Who was the woman traveling with you?"

I was amazed.

"The baroness."

"The baroness?"

"Her. Do you doubt it? And how do you know? I just arrived."

She closed her eyes.

44

"One of my girlfriends sent me a telegram."

Then she suddenly hugged my neck and started laughing.

"I scared you, didn't I?"

"Is that why you were sick?"

Then I told her about the baron's bath problems.

She calmed down. Her color returned. We spent a nice, joyful evening together in their home.

The next day we looked for a four room apartment together near Elizabeth Square and Museum Street. It was her wish for us to live near a wooded area.

We found a suitable place on Joseph Square. Ida especially liked that she could see the beautiful square from the window.

"I will put my sewing table here," she said. "I will enjoy the scenery from the window."

And she clapped.

I did not even negotiate the price. I just gave the agent a deposit.

From there we walked together to a nearby pastry shop. My carriage followed us slowly. Ida was happy. She chose a couple of pastries. We were discussing wallpaper colors we were going to use for the different rooms. All of a sudden she became quiet. She became disheartened.

"Can I say something, my dear lamb?"

"Of course, just say it, my little angel. You can be open with me."

"I am not questioning that."

"Well, just say whatever it is."

"I don't really like that apartment."

"Why not, my angel?"

"I don't want to be constantly staring at the back of Count Joseph's statue. We should leave that place at the end of February."

"Okay, we'll leave."

"We should have looked by the Danube's shore. There we can see ships, the Gellert hill and the King's Castle. I think we would have found a better and cheaper place there. Let's look. Even if we don't rent there we should at least look, my dear lamb."

We sat on the carriage again. We searched near the Danube and found a beautiful four room apartment across Rac Town.

"You see," she said. "We rushed into it."

I shrugged my shoulder.

"We can easily take care of this. I will even get my deposit back. I will give ten forints to the agent and it will be taken care of."

And that is what happened.

But Ida was nervously playing with her engagement ring as I was getting back my money.

"My dear lamb, I'd like to say something... but don't get upset."

"I am not upset. Just say it, my angel."

"I think it would be better if we stayed here after all, my dear lamb. The ships can blow a lot of smoke, just like factory chimneys."

I laughed. I told her father and he laughed too. He thought it was ridiculous. He slapped his knee, held his belly and shook his hand as if he was choking. And he was shrieking:

"I can't believe how whimsical women are!"

Ida shrugged her shoulder and smiled. Everything made her appealing. Or did she just appeal to me so much?

I don't even have to say that I was burning for her like charcoal. There has never been a longer summer. No one has ever waited with so much anticipation for that rainy and windy November, like I did.

But she did too.

"What would our lives be like, if we would have never met?" She asked.

"You would have married someone else."

"Never! I believe at times an angel is leading us. We were led together by a good angel."

"If your father offered me a cheaper carpet, I would have bought it. We would have never exchanged words and you would not be my fiancée."

"The carpet was expensive by providence. We exchanged words and got to know each other. And now I could not live without you anymore!"

She lowered her head like a dying pigeon and rested it on my chest.

I also felt I could not live without her. The only thing I did not understand was why she still doubted me.

We had a very windy Sunday in September. The wind in the capital is always ugly. It blows dust, papers and all kinds of trash back and forth. I was sitting at home in the afternoon waiting for a clergyman client of mine from out of town. There was a military band marching outside. I had never seen them on University Street before. I stepped to the window and looked outside. I had to look sideways to be able to see anything. I did not see very much of the band, but on the other side I had noticed the youngster Eugene, as he was standing by the gate of a house across the street. The kid was cheerfully smoking as he was stretching his neck toward the music.

I was surprised to see him there. They did not live close to me. I had never seen him in the area before. But I thought maybe he was visiting one of his pals. Perhaps he had permission. I would make things a little uncomfortable for the little brother-in-law for the smoking. He needed to honor his parents by obeying them. They had clearly told him he was not allowed to smoke.

I sat back down to my desk. I heard the doorbell ring after a little while.

A young woman entered through the door instead of the clergyman. She was wearing black clothes and her coat was decorated with tiny pearls. Her face was very pale, as if she was sick.

She said the baroness recommended me to her and she wanted a divorce from her husband. Her husband was a station master at a good place, but he got angry and violent very easily.

She spent a couple of hours at my place. She told me all the details regarding how she had met her husband, and all the promises he had made to her in the moonlight at Korond Bath.

I just let her wheels turn. I figured they were turning for me. A few hundred forints were worth the listening.

We agreed. I asked for three hundred forints. Getting a divorce done was easy work back then.

I visited my fiancée at seven o'clock in the evening. Their maid gave me a dirty look in the hall.

"The miss is sick. She laid down."

"Oh no! What is wrong with her?"

"I don't know."

The family was sitting together with somber looks on their faces. They were staring at me.

"What is the matter with Ida? Can I go in to see her?"

"No, you can't."

"Has she seen a doctor? I hope it is nothing…"

At that moment Ida staggered out of the inner room. She was wearing white clothes with pink print on it. She was pale. Again she was ugly like a marble statue with a mustache. Her hair was let down all the way to her hips.

"I got up," she whispered. "I couldn't stand it…"

She hugged me as usual, held her cheek for a kiss and looked me in the eye.

"What kind of a cheap perfume do I smell on you?" she said as she was sniffing around me. "It smells terrible."

I knew right away that the youngster Eugene got me in trouble, because there was no perfume on me.

"Be honest," I said to her and started laughing, "you are suspicious again! That is the reason you are sick!"

"Well, who was that lady in black clothes?"

From that day on she often dropped in unexpectedly when I was meeting with women clients. She gave the women a cold look and then stared at me, to see if I got nervous. Only then would she start smiling.

"I was in the neighborhood and thought I would pop in quickly to give you a kiss."

This started to get on my nerves.

I still remember the tenth day of October that year. It was rainy and cold outside. I had the fireplace burning. The lights had to be lit long before five o'clock.

My servant put three letters on my desk. One of them was from Sajolad. I didn't have anything or anyone there, but that was the one I opened first. I found two letters in it. One of them had three lines from America. I could hear my heartbeat as I was reading it. It was an official inquiry to find out if I was still alive, where I lived and about my circumstances. The other letter was from the town clerk informing me that he responded to the questions with three lines on the tenth of last month.

I have never in my life had so many feelings whirl in me.

My brother! It could not be anyone else, only my brother, the Jancsi! Finally I would find out where he lived! I would go to meet him! I would go to see my brother! My very own brother! The only person whose heart belonged to mine even without knowing him, just like half of an apple to the other half.

There were thousands of questions in my head: Why didn't he write himself? Did he perhaps not speak Hungarian? Was he so rich that he had someone else write everything for him? He was used to it. He probably just told people what to do. I had my assistants write everything for me, if I thought about it.

But he might have been poor and that might have been the reason he was asking about me, because he was needy. What if these three lines were a cry for help. A cry across the ocean to Europe.

I was shaken by this thought. Oh, my poor brother! I would wire him money. I would send him a thousand forints. Then I would divide my wealth and would take half of it to him. The trip would only take me about three weeks.

Who knew what kind of a life he had. What if he was treated like a dog? Did some unkind people put him to work when he was still small? Did he know how to read and write? Was he a day-laborer, or a bum smelling like brandy, or perhaps even a prisoner? Oh, poor Jancsi! My poor dear brother, Jancsi!

But he could not be in misery after all. He was my blood. I was also tossed around in life and always got over it. A hard working and smart man always gets through every trouble and suffering, especially in America. How many times had I heard that every diligent person finds wealth there. He was most likely a wealthy man. Richer than me. Maybe he was going to give me half of his fortune. That could be the reason he was inquiring.

I was walking up and down in my room.

What kind of a person could he be? What kind? Would we recognize each other if we met on the street?

He was six years old when we were separated. I could still picture his round head with his short brown hair. We looked alike. He too had a short neck, flat nose and bright eyes.

I stood in front of the mirror.

I wonder if he still remembers the little poem our father taught us:

Once there was a little castle,
In which lived a little rabbit,
The little castle fell to pieces,
The little rabbit ran to safety.
He is running this way, this way….

As I was musing about this I heard the baroness ask for me in the hall. I hurried to greet her:

"Welcome ma'am. But in such weather…"

"I came by carriage," she answered cheerfully. "Good news, very good news!"

And she shook her skirt to get some of the rain off of it. Then she went to the fireplace. She was warming her hands by the fire.

"What awful weather. Please let me first warm up a little."

I pushed an armchair next to the fireplace.

"Please have a seat."

I put her file and a lamp on a small table nearby.

Her lawsuit was primarily revolving around a will. The grantor wrote the will but did not sign it. We needed a witness and the baroness found one. That was her good news. The man she found was worth two thousand acres for her and about four thousand forints for me.

We were cheerfully sitting around the fireplace. I even made some tea quickly. I put another small table between us and put the tea and a lamp on it. I poured a cup of tea for me too so the baroness would enjoy hers more.

The fire was cheerfully crackling. The tea smelled wonderful. The baroness was telling me with a joyful expression how she found the witness and how willing he was to prove in front of the court that the will was valid. When she got to the most important part as she was talking, the door burst open. Ida came in. She was looking at the baroness with yellow circles in her eyes. I was paralyzed with fear. She turned to me and with a tragic move pointed at the baroness:

"Who is this woman?"

I got up and turned to the baroness. I had a somber look on my face as I turned to the baroness:

"Please allow me to introduce my fiancée. She is a little jealous…"

I noticed the baroness became a little pale, but she was smiling and nodded toward Ida.

"I am sorry," Ida whispered," but I did not think that in such a late hour… And you are having tea during client meetings…"

The baroness lost even more of her color.

"But Ida!" I said to her in desperation.

The baroness closed her eyes. She swallowed. Then she turned to me with a painful expression on her face:

"If you please…"

She nodded toward Ida and left in a hurry.

"What have you done?" I said when I returned from walking her out. "You insulted this important woman. She may even take her case away from me."

Ida collapsed into the chair. Her eyes were full of tears. She took out her handkerchief and started sobbing:

"How they are trying to play a comedy! You must really think I am a fool. How well you are acting!"

"But Ida!"

"I know; she is your old girlfriend… Every man has one… The true one only gets the leftovers… the leftovers!"

"But look, here is her file. Read it!"

"You just put it there to use it as your lightning-rod. You can't deceive me! I am not that simple! How you are trying to pull wool over my eyes!"

She was sobbing.

It took us an hour with my staff to convince her that the woman was truly the baroness. Then she buried her face in her hands. She was very embarrassed. She was begging me not to be upset with her. She was going to visit the baroness to ask her forgiveness. She was going to make everything right, as long as I was not upset with her.

I took her home and had dinner with them. I told her parents what happened. I recommended that we should not wait until November 7th with the wedding. There must be one Sunday when they could close the shop. Ida and I could stay in my apartment on University Street until we could move into a bigger place.

The parents discussed it. They agreed.

"So a week from now," I said. "That will give me enough time to get an exemption from having to announce the wedding. We don't have to have a lot of guests. Let's keep everything simple."

Ida was happy and gave me a hug:

"Well, a week from now."

"And until then," I answered, "you can visit me every day at four in the afternoon. That is when my letters arrive. You can open them, so you can sleep well this week. Start tomorrow. I'll be waiting for you at four."

"No," she answered and appeared repentant, "I won't come any more. Even actresses can visit you this week. Although tomorrow… I'll be there at four. But the reason will not be to open your letters. No. We will go to see the baroness. I will bring her a nice bouquet of flowers. I will get down on my knees when I hand it to her. That is how I will ask for her forgiveness."

And she got down on her knees as if she were already in front of the baroness. She had tears glittering on her eyelashes. She was magnificent.

"That is a beautiful thought, Ida. I have to kiss you for it!"

Just as we were discussing letters, I remembered the letter that came from America. My brother, the Jancsi; I was telling her the news with joy. I pulled out the note from my pocket and read it to her. Ida was clapping.

"You found him, you found him!"

She was as happy as if she found her own brother. Only the old man seemed to be deep in thought as he was blinking.

"Why didn't he write himself?"

He probably did not expect much from the inquiry. Who knew what kind of a high position he had. He just thought of me. He told his clerk to inquire about me.

"A millionaire!" shouted Ida. "I am sure he is a millionaire. He owns an oil well. What a lucky day this is!"

"Perhaps." nodded Mehemad. "People are quiet when they are struggling. They are embarrassed to admit they are poor. But when the bread becomes large, they say: well, who should I slice a piece for?"

"One day he will just show up," Ida continued with joy. "Oh, if he would happen to come to our wedding! What a celebration that would be! What a celebration!"

This thought made me happy too. What a lucky day indeed! Every good thing was coming my way, like a shower of flowers from the sky.

I felt great as I was going home.

"Paul, I said to my butler," if someone comes from America when I am not home, take him in the parlor. Tell him to sit down. Be very kind to him. Have him sit next to the fireplace. Put some cigars in front of him."

I had to be at a banquet the next day. I was away until four. I hurried home because I did not want Ida to worry about me, if she was there already.

My butler opened the door with his usual sleepy face.

"Is my fiancée here?"

"No, but," he continued as he was helping me take my coat off, "we have some visitors from America. I took them into the parlor. They just arrived."

My heart was beating loudly. I noticed a couple of yellow suitcases in the corner of the hall. I took off my coat and entered the room.

There was a woman in the middle of the room with a humble look on her face and there were three young boys standing next to her. The boys' faces seemed identical.

They were standing there with wide brimmed hats in their hands. All three of them had dark, short haircuts. The oldest was perhaps six years old, the youngest maybe four.

They were staring at me with their round eyes. They seemed fearful and anxious, like three little owls.

I was also staring at them in amazement.

"Who are you?" I said finally and I was almost shaking with excitement.

The children pulled even more together when they heard my question. They seemed even more worried as they looked at me.

"We are looking for the attorney gentleman," said the woman in a quiet and humble voice.

"That's me."

"These boys are your brother's children. And I am his maid..."

"His children? And where is my brother?"

The woman was blinking. She was silent. I noticed tears on her eyelashes. She lifted her handkerchief to her eyes.

"Is he dead?"

The woman nodded. The three children were getting teary eyed. They were looking at me through their tears.

All of a sudden I realized why they came. I don't think I would have been as confused in that moment if lightning would have struck the room.

I was just standing there and I was staring at the children with their big shoes and large hats. The wind had blown three little owls back from America instead of my brother.

What should I do with them? What would Ida say? My wedding was in a week. Should I start my marriage with three children?

Then I remembered our childhood, when I was five and he was six. We were orphans, just like them. We were being looked at with similar cold eyes as we were quietly waiting to find out what would be decided regarding our future.

"Come to the window!"

I sat down. The three little owls stood in front of me in a row. All three of them had flat noses, round heads and short dark brown hair. They reminded me of my childhood picture.

"Do you speak Hungarian?"

"Yes, we do," the oldest one answered quietly and fearfully.

I was moved when I heard his voice. It was as if I heard the childhood voice of my little brother. It was as if he was looking at me with the eyes of this boy.

The maid spoke up:

"They can speak English too."

"Do you speak English?" I shouted at them with a loud voice.

"Yes." all three of them answered.

I hugged them. I felt that all three of them were my blood. They were the fruits of the same tree I came from, only from a nearby branch.

"Don't be sad," I said in a softened voice.

"Do you know who I am?"

"Uncle Kalman," answered the oldest with a smile.

I pulled him close to me and kissed him. Then I kissed the second one and the third one.

"Yes, I am uncle Kalman. Put down your hats and take off your coats."

I helped the little one unbutton.

"What kind of a carrot smell do you have? Where have you been?"

"We came on a ship which was carrying vegetables on the Danube," answered the maid. "The little ones slept among the baskets."

After they took their coats off they stood in front of me in nice checkered clothes.

The smallest one put his hand on my knee and looked up to me.

"Uncle Talman," he said to me, "I'd like to eat."

"Are you hungry? Oh you little starving children. What should I give you?"

"Chocolate milk," answered the little one.

Just then the door was opened by my fiancée. My butler probably already told her that I had visitors from America.

"Can I come in?" she asked and her face was shining with joy.

"Come in!" I said. "Look at the three children God sent me."

"Are they your brother's children?"

And she came in.

"How beautiful they are!"

She kneeled down and kissed them.

"How beautiful they are! What is your name, dear?" she asked the smallest one.

"Gyulu."

"And you?" she asked the oldest one.

"Jancsi."

"And you?" she asked the middle one.

"Kalman."

I felt a warm wave around my heart. So he named his second son after me.

"She is going to be your mother, children," I whispered and my eyes were swimming in tears. "She is going to be a good mother. And she is a beautiful mother, isn't she?"

"Why, don't they have a mother?" Ida asked with surprise.

The maid lifted her handkerchief to her eyes again.

"They don't have one."

Her tears were flowing as she told us that the children's mother was hit by a car on a street. The father was sick in bed with heart disease when it happened. When his wife was brought home in blood after she died, he jumped out of his bed, fell on the woman and died.

"He loved her very much," said the maid at the end.

"She was English, but did not have any relatives."

Ida looked as if she turned to stone as she was staring at the maid. Then she looked at the children and finally at me.

She said in a quiet, thoughtful manner:

"Where are you going to put them?"

"They could stay with us," I answered as if I was in a dream. "We will have more room after we move into the bigger apartment."

I turned to the maid:

"What was my poor brother's occupation?"

"He was a cashier in a factory. He was a very good man. He mentioned you at Christmas too."

"My poor brother. So the family died out. And these poor children are orphans. How did you come over? Who paid the expenses?"

"Well, I had a little money saved, four hundred dollars. I thought someday I will get it back somehow..."

"You can be sure of that. Was my brother very poor?"

She raised her shoulder.

"They had a few things. The furniture was sold. You will receive papers regarding it."

Ida stood up.

"Continue your conversation," she said. "It is almost 7 o'clock..."

"But today we will not be able to go to the baroness..."

"Let's leave it for tomorrow. You don't have to take me home. I came by carriage. You have a lot of things going on here, just take care of them."

She kissed the children. They kissed her hand after the maid quietly instructed them in English. Then I walked her down to the carriage.

As I was coming back I remembered that the children were hungry. I sent out my butler to get chocolate milk and pastries.

"Well children," I said and again I pulled them close to me, "the chocolate milk will be here soon. Cheer up!"

"Do you know the poem which goes like this:
Once there was a little castle..."

"We know." the children answered with excitement.

The oldest one continued:

"In which lived a little rabbit..."

Then all three of them:

"The little castle fell to pieces:
The little rabbit ran to safety..."

My eyes welled up with tears again. My poor brother. He must have been thinking of me when he taught his children this poem. And now I had lost him. I would never see him again, never!

The children quieted down and became serious when they saw the tears on my cheeks. It felt as if there was a shadow of mourning floating around us in the room...

I turned to the maid:

"Do you at least have a picture left of him?"

"Yes, I do," she answered. "It is packed with the children's clothes."

She brought in one of the suitcases and pulled the picture out of it. I hurried to the lamp. My heart was trembling as I was looking at his picture. I saw a smiling twenty year old young man, with flat nose, bright eyes and short neck. It was as if I was looking at a flawed picture of myself when I was a law student. I kept looking at it.

In the meantime the butler arrived with the chocolate milk. The children sat down to eat. The maid tied napkins around their necks. It was as if I was seeing my own mother, when she did the same thing to us…

The children started eating with healthy appetites. The maid stayed behind them.

"Why don't you join them, dear," I said. "Don't you usually eat with them?"

"Yes, I do."

She sat down and put the youngest one on her lap. I joined them too. It was a pleasure watching them eat. All of a sudden the youngest one turned his eyes on me:

"Uncle Talman…"

"What do you need Gyulu?"

"Are you our daddy from now on?"

"I am, dear, I am."

A person taking an oath couldn't speak more from the heart than I did when I said these few words: I am, dear, I am.

Then I turned to the maid:

"What is your name?"

"Julcsa."

"Well then Julcsa," I continued, "what are your plans? Are you planning to return? Or…"

"I am not going to return," she was staring into her cup. "I would like to find a place here in Budapest. Somewhere near."

And she continued in tears:

"I was the nanny for all three of them… I would like to see them every day."

Of course I was glad to keep her with the children.

The next day I was waiting for Ida. The kid Eugene came with a letter instead of her:

My dear,

We have guests. I am sending you my kisses: Ida

I looked at the boy. I noticed the sides of his mouth were stained yellow.

"Eugene," I said, "you smoked."

He turned red.

"No, I did not."

"It is useless for a cat to deny she drank the milk, it is on her nose."

He was embarrassed as he was staring into the distance.

"Well," he said trying to make an excuse," Ida gave me…"

"Ida? Impossible! There is not one cigarette in your house."

"She gave me money."

I was carefully examining the kid's cunning expression.

"Eugene," I said, "who are you visiting on this street?"

He was surprised.

"Nobody."

"Think about it."

"I don't have to think about it."

"One of your friends?"

"None of them live around here."

"Then why were you standing by the gate of the house across the street when you were looking at the marching band?"

He turned red and started sweating.

"Well, just tell me. We'll keep it to ourselves."

I gave his shoulder a friendly tap.

"Just tell me. I'll give you something."

"Ida asked me…"

"To spy on me?"

"No, just on the women."

"Were you also at the railway station?"

"No…"

"What did you get for spying? Well, just tell me. I'll reward you."

"I got a six filler coin. I got six fillers for every woman and five for the baroness."

"What about the railway station?"

"I got one forint for that."

By that time he was pale and had a worried look on his face.

"Don't be afraid," I said," I find all this amusing. I'll make you a better deal. When Ida sends you spying again, just come up here. She'll give you six fillers and I will give you five. We'll laugh about it. But please don't smoke. It is harmful, even if you are used to it."

I went over to Ida's place at seven o'clock. They did have three guests who were just leaving.

"It's too bad," I said. "We should have visited the baroness after all. It would have only taken half an hour. Your mom could have kept your guests entertained until then.

Ida shrugged her shoulder:

"I am really sorry. But I'll take care of it in a letter. You can rest assured, I will write such a nice letter that the baroness will forgive me. I'll write in French. You know, that way it is more elegant and touching. She will answer and later we will visit each other."

"Well, that will be good," I left it up to her.

Then we were talking about how nice and healthy the children were.

"I wish they would have come later," Ida said.

"They are not going to bother us," I answered with a smile. "Julcsa will take care of them and they are used to her."

There was a pause in our conversation. Her parents were silently sitting at the table. Ida was staring at the lamp.

"What if you were not alive?" she said. "Where would the children end up?"

"In an orphanage or perhaps with relatives of their nanny. I can't even think about it. But it is wonderful that to me it feels like they have been with me for a long time, as if they were my own children."

The next day they were talking about one of their bishop relatives. He was coming to visit them in December from Asia Minor. It was her dad's wish that he would perform the wedding.

I looked at Ida. She was calmly playing with her opal ring.

"December!" I was horrified. "That is like a hundred years!"

Ida glanced at me:

"Well, what can we do if this is her father's wish? Just think about it, could anyone else perform our wedding if there is a bishop in the family?"

No bishop was ever thought about with so much resentment as I thought about that unknown bishop. But I felt I needed to respect their decision. This kind of a family celebration is more spectacular if a bishop performs it. Even today I don't know if Armenian bishops are as dignified as Romans, but weddings performed by a bishop are truly magnificent.

What I did not understand was why the following ten days neither she nor the youngster Eugene came to see me. She should have at least visited the children. But then the defense attorney spoke up in me: a bride has lots of things to take care of. She is sewing, shopping. She wants a lavish dinner for the bishop's sake.

She really had so many things to do that she even forgot to write to the baroness. I was embarrassed, but made some excuses for her in front of the baroness.

The baroness was a wonderful woman. She even wished to see the children. She asked me to take the little Americans to visit her. I took them in the carriage. She was so nice and motherly to them that the next day they asked:

"Are we going there today?"

It was unbelievable how much my home had changed because of them. I stopped attending the restaurant. I ate lunch with the children. I bought them a rocking horse, a sword and all kinds of toys. I put the oldest one into school. It was a great feeling to buy him a backpack, school supplies and walk him to school. It felt as if I was seeing myself when I was small.

I told these little things to Ida in the evening. I kept cheerfully telling her:

"You'll see how much you are going to love them."

Ida smiled.

She was wearing dark sour cherry colored silk close and she had red Turkish slippers on her feet. The light from the lamp's red shades made the wrinkles on her clothes look purple. Her earrings, necklace and bracelet were made of rubies and had a burning purple color, like the grandeur of a beautiful sunset. It seemed as if her eyes were also the color of red rubies.

I was enchanted when I looked at her as my sleepy body was stretched out on their sofa.

"It is beautiful how much you love them," she said day-dreaming. "Other people would have looked for a good family or a reputable orphanage house..."

"Perhaps," I answered. "At the first second I had similar thoughts going through my mind as well. But then when I felt my brother in Jancsi, and when I felt myself in Kalman, and when the little one said, 'Are you our new daddy from now on...' You should see how excited they are when I get home! And the little things that make them happy. After all, only children can be truly happy. Ida, I did not know until now how much seeing happy faces can relieve the pressures of life! All children have happy faces."

Her eyes were half closed as she listened. Then she lifted her hand and held it toward me.

"You are a good man."

I kissed her hand and kneeled down next to her.

"You are so beautiful, Ida! You are always beautiful to me, but today you are a miracle!"

She hugged my neck, pulled me close and looked me in the eye.

"Do you love me?"

"How can you ask such a thing?"

"How much do you love me?"

"As much as it is possible to love you."

"If I were a beggar, would you marry me?"

"Without question."

"If I wished for you to become a beggar..."

I was shocked.

"Don't wish such a foolish thing."

She smiled.

"But if I wished."

"Well good, you know that I would do it, even if it was an insane wish."

"But what if I asked you a smart thing, something big, but perhaps not big, but smart? Would you do it?"

"I would be glad to, especially if it was something smart."

"Swear to me! No, don't swear. Just do on your own what I ask you. Well look, there are very good boarding schools out there. Even children from elite families attend them. You should have seen where I was educated…"

"I understand," I answered with a heavy chest.

We did not continue. Her mother stepped into the room.

"Well come, the dinner is on the table."

All of a sudden I remembered the three children. When I left I promised them I would be home for dinner. Julcsa probably even baked something special. The children usually had milk in the evening. It was already eight o'clock and those poor children were waiting for me…

I said good bye:

"I can't stay today."

I was stunned as I was going home. It is true that there are good boarding schools, especially in Switzerland… But who knows how they would be treated? I have heard horror stories even about nuns. Not to mention the boarding schools for boys. And those poor little creatures cannot protect themselves, especially if the parents live in a different country.

Children are not only raised on bread but also on love. Oh, my chilling childhood! I was tossed and kicked around. The North Pole is not as freezing cold as some hearts. An orphan is like a stray dog.

Then I thought about Ida. I understood her anxiety. But she could not be serious about her wish. Even if she were, she might still change her mind. So far she had always changed her decisions. But what if she stayed stubborn regarding this one thing?

I reached my street. I looked up at my apartment's window. The three little owls were peaking outside. The little one was playing with his hand shadows. He started to play with hand shadows every time the lamp was turned on.

I hurried upstairs and entered my apartment. The children were shouting with joy as they rushed to greet me.

"Uncle Kalman! Uncle Kalman!"

Two of them grabbed my hands. Gyulu only had my leg left to hold onto. They walked me to the table this way. Julcsa was smiling as she brought in the steaming dish.

"They have been watching for you through the window for an hour."

The next day I did not visit Ida. Who knows what was holding me back.

The following day I got a letter from her:

My dear lamb!

You are probably worried about the expense. But I was just recommended a very good boarding school near Vienna. The children are raised by monks. Come over so we can discuss it.

I was getting ready all afternoon, but kept delaying it. In the meantime the evening came and I ended up staying home.

The next day was All Saint's Day. I knew they were going to the cemetery. Another day passed without me seeing Ida.

The following day I got a short letter from her. She wrote that she was home all afternoon and waited for me. She saw that I was reluctant to do what she asked me. But I had to choose either her or the children.

I only wrote one word as my answer: *the children.*

Seeing Ethel

Steven Olajos is a cellist. He plays in a Gypsy band, although he is not a Gypsy. But the big war has reduced the size of most bands. Where there was a violinist left, he tried to put a band together any way possible.

Olajos played as a cellist in Budapest before the war. He was in a band of the blind. That is because he was blind himself. But he got a letter from home telling him that the violinist Csurka was asking about him, whether he would be willing to join his band. He was recommended by the wife of the cymbal player. She has a blind son in Budapest. He lives in the house for the blind. His name is Kalacsos, but the Gypsies just call him Csuta. He told the violinist about Steve. Csurka lost both of his cellists to the army. It is too bad, because as he has sworn, "this was a great time to be a musician! In my band musicians earn ten times as much as other places."

"That may be Gypsy math," said the letter, "but you could get at least twice as much. And if you end up disappointed, you can always go back. You won't lose anything. It is possible that the Russians will invade us and then you would be left alone. But even if there is no war, we would still like you to come home, if you can. We would like you to have a little family life at least, our dear Steve, while we are still alive."

Terka, the blind man's sister, wrote the letter.

"And you should come home," she wrote at the end, "because mother is sad that your younger brother was drafted into the military. I have to work at the post office and she is by herself a lot."

Someone of course was reading this letter to the blind man, but Olajos heard it as if he were listening to Terka's high pitched voice and as if he could hear his mother's good, bagpipe voice at the end.

"Come home, my Steven!"

So Olajos moved home.

He was already twenty eight years old, but he looked younger. He had black glasses and long curly hair. He was a master of his profession.

"You play in such an aristocratic manner," said Csurka during a break. "Make that cello cry!"

Olajos would not make his cello cry; he played every note clearly, shorter or longer, as was needed, as he learned in Budapest. But of course he was still careful, because in Budapest he played mainly classical music, marches, opera openings and waltzes. The conductor quietly tapped the beat with a baton. They also tapped their feet secretly, quietly. They only played Hungarian folk melodies at home for their own enjoyment.

Still, Olajos shook his curly hair and answered with a smile.

"The Gypsy school is different, Csurka! The music school is another thing too. I am trying to play music, not cries."

Well, good.

The band leader made his violin cry according to Gypsy school and Olajos accompanied him with deep tones, according to music school. The café was always very busy in the evenings. Even if bread and meat were scarce, there was plenty of money floating around. Sometimes Olajos took home as much as thirty or forty koronas. One Sunday he took home as much as sixty five. Well, his family was very happy about that when he got home.

"Sixty-five koronas," Terka said with excitement. "In Budapest you would have worked a whole month for that much. We will hire a guide for you, a smart boy. He'll have to live here, so he can guide you wherever you want to go. Or would it be better if we hired a girl so she could also be our maid?"

Olajos shook his head:

"What would I do with a guide? I know my way around. There is only one spot that is difficult, near a construction site."

Their mother spoke:

"First we have to have nice black clothes made for him."

"Elegant clothes!" Terka said cheerfully. "A tuxedo!"

"Not a tuxedo, no. He needs clothes he can wear on the street in May. The Gypsies wear black clothes in the band. You don't fit in with your tobacco colored clothes. And we also have to get you some new shoes."

"Elegant shoes," whistled Terka kindheartedly. "White shoes. They are very popular these days. After all, you will be walking with me at times... Now I know a lot of people in the town."

"He can get whatever he wants," piped their mother. "He earned it. It's his money. But I would say white shoes are not very practical. He may get some mud on them, or coffee, or perhaps some ink, or a drop of oil... No, no, just nice black clothes and regular dark shoes."

Mrs. Olajos was a widow. Her husband had been a clerk in a village. She especially loved her blind son. He had lost his sight when he was an infant. He had an eye infection. His eyes looked completely normal after his illness, as if he could see. He did not see a thing.

"My clothes are still good," he waived his hand with a smile. "I sit at the back of the band. My shoes are still good enough too. Let's just save my money. I don't need a guide either. That is expensive. And why would I need one in the winter? During the spring perhaps, when I walk among the fragrant trees in the sun. I like the trees a lot and the grass too, the smell of the grass. I like to listen as the insects fly by and the birds sing. I can use help when I am outside in nature during the spring. I don't need a guide in the town."

62

One sunny morning in November he was walking slowly on Main Street without anyone leading him. He was going to visit Csurka. They were going to learn some folk melodies and practice them. Previously there was a young boy guiding him there, but the schools opened in mid-September and he was no longer available.

"I don't need help to get there," said Olajos.

He kept his stick moving in front of him as he slowly walked. He already knew every house. He knew there was a hat store next, followed by a bookstore, then a tobacco shop, a pastry shop, then a house without a store in it. On a sunny day there were a couple of yards of warmth next' followed by cold again, then a store with a sewing machine. They sold gramophones too. Then a house again which was big and old and smelled like beer. There were loud carts going in and out of its gates periodically. He was walking slowly and kept moving his stick in front of him. The asphalt was wet. The smells coming from the nearby houses kept changing, right then smelling like cigar smoke. He kept walking.

"The tobacco shop is next," he said to himself, "then the spice store."

And he passed the tobacco store. He walked slowly. Two children ran in front of him. One of them made a neigh sound. They were acting like horses. Olajos stopped as they galloped next to him.

"Gee!" one of them shouted.

Their steps were behind Olajos. He continued his walk. When he had barely taken ten more steps, a hand softly grabbed his arm and a female voice said to him:

"Be careful. There are some boxes here in front of the store."

"Thank you," Olajos said gratefully. "Thank you."

He was walking more confidently as the woman held his arm. They got to the edge of the sidewalk.

"Step down here," said the female voice.

After about five steps she said:

"Now step up to get back on the sidewalk. Can you find your way from here? No, I will go with you to Kazinczy Street."

"Thank you, Miss."

"How do you know I am single? Can you see?"

"From your voice."

"From my voice?"

"From your voice. You would make me very happy if you told me your name. If I know your name, when I get home I can think about how grateful I am to you."

The young woman was silent.

Olajos continued.

"That even without knowing me…"

"Oh, not without knowing you." said the girl. (And he could feel from her voice that she was smiling.) "But I do know you."

"You know me?"

"Yes I do. I know you and your dear sister. I also live on Baratok Street."

"Well then, please tell me your name."

"Ethel. Now we step down. And again up. Good… Now up. But now can you go from here? Are you going to the Gypsies' house? I know you are a cellist and people say you are very good at it. I heard it from someone who listens to you every day at the café. She knows a lot about music. She plays the piano, when she has the opportunity. She said you play well, Mr. Olajos. God be with you."

She softly pressed the blind man's arm and left him. Olajos stood there for a while and was still all ears. Then he continued his walk. He calmly and carefully kept moving his stick in front of him.

*

"Tell me, Terka," he said around noon after he got home, "who is the girl you know here on our street called Ethel?"

Terka was thinking.

"Ethel? On our street? I don't know anyone called Ethel."

"Do you perhaps know her as Ethelka?"

"No, I don't know an Ethelka either."

His mother shook her head:

"We don't know anyone called Ethel or Ethelka."

They had been living in the town for about a year and a half. Olajos' younger brother started law school at that time and that was the reason they moved there (and because Terka wanted to also). It had been four years since she turned twenty nine, but she was still hoping to meet a man. There are all kinds of single men in a town. She regretted many times that she did not whisper yes to Barsay, the veterinarian, when she was eighteen, and to that Eugene Kocsis, the teacher, when she was twenty. She was waiting for a man from the town, because she wanted to live there. She was still an attractive girl. She was blond and a little proud. She liked to look at her hand. She was a little worried when she looked at her blouse, because her hair seemed to be thinning, mainly above her right shoulder blade. She planned to learn sewing, or hat making, but they read an ad which was looking for someone who was a good writer, for the post office. Terka applied. She told them that she practiced writing in a clerk's office and that she could even type. She was hired with fifty koronas pay per month.

Olajos was calmly stirring his soup.

"She is thin, or at least she is not chubby. She is quite a bit younger than you. And her voice has a gentle ring to it."

"Her voice?"

"Yes, as if she had a sweet sounding flute in her mouth."

"A flute?"

"And she is just as tall as I am. She did not wear gloves. But she is single."

"She didn't wear gloves? She is single?"

And Terka pouted her lips.

"Some kind of a maid. I don't know any maids called Ethel or by any other name. Why are you asking?"

"She is not a maid. Her shoes had rubber heels. She may have worn gloves, but took them off right then."

"Rubber heels?"

The two women seemed curious as they looked at each other.

"Yes," continued the blind man, "and she is full of life, although her face and eyes are sad. She uses almond soap."

The two women laughed.

"You even know that?"

"I could smell it. The soap is the easiest to smell. But I think she must be a poor girl after all. She was carrying tomatoes home this morning. I could smell them. She is probably the daughter of a craftsman like a cobbler or someone who makes leather goods. The wind from Kazinczy Street blew some leather smell toward me. She has a very nice voice, very nice."

The two women spoke at the same time:

"She is cobbler Kaszab's daughter!"

"Of course she is," Terka pouted with her lips. "I wonder why we could not think of it. Of course she is. My yellow shoes needed mending this summer. She brought them home. She talked a little. She complained that the book binder apprentice who was courting her was drafted into the military. She was sad about it. But she wore shoes with rubber heels! She probably put on a rich woman's shoes for an hour. Why are you asking?"

Olajos shrugged his shoulder.

"You know how people try to help me. She is a good girl. Thank her for me if you speak to her."

And he calmly dipped his spoon into the soup.

*

From that day on they had cobbler Kaszab do all of their shoe repair. They had him make little adjustments. They asked him to come out even when Olajos wanted warmer shoes for the winter. The cobbler came, he measured.

"But I cannot do it for less than twenty eight koronas," he said seriously.

He was a serious, small, stocky man with red hair and a mustache. He pulled in his neck, as if it were raining. Even when he walked on the street his neck was pulled in as if it were always raining.

"No, I can't do it for less then twenty eight," he said very seriously. "Leather is expensive, and if I were not doing it for someone blind..."

Olajos moved:

"Being blind is no trouble for me. I see even through my elbows. I can even earn a better living than a lot of people who can see."

65

"Well," apologized Kaszab. "I didn't mean it like that... but in today's world I can't do it for less than twenty eight. And it will be ready by Sunday."

Terka smiled.

"It won't be ready."

The cobbler was surprised.

"Why wouldn't it be ready?"

Terka shook her head.

"I've never known a cobbler who delivered the shoes in time."

"But I am such a cobbler," said Kaszab and moved his finger under his nose. "And now that leather is expensive I have less work. As I said, even this work cannot be done for less than twenty eight koronas."

Olajos nodded.

"Okay, good. We don't expect you to do it for less. I completely trust that you are an honest man. Someone who has as nice of a daughter as you can only be an honest man."

"My daughter? You know my daughter?"

"Yes I know her," Olajos nodded, "dear Ethel, she is very nice. I hope she will be happy with her fiancé."

Kaszab was surprised and shook his head.

"She did not yet have a fiancée. And now she won't have one. We read in the paper that he died."

"He died?"

"Yes. He was a brave soldier. It is too bad. He did not drink and did not play cards either. He could have supported himself by the spring."

He sighed and grabbed his hat.

"The shoes will be ready by noon on Sunday."

After he left, the blind man began to speak.

"Tell me, Terka, what kind of a girl is Ethel?"

Terka shrugged her shoulder.

"Turkey egg."

And she laughed.

"Don't say that," said her mother.

Then she turned to her son.

"She has a pretty face and her eyes are smiling. She is a very kind girl. But you have taken a better look at her."

Olajos was sitting on the couch deep in thought.

*

Olajos was still sleeping at noon on Sunday. Cheerful guests often had them play music until almost morning. Olajos took home over seventy koronas. And he said they should not wake him up. The band was not practicing on Sundays anyway. Olajos was woken up by women's voices. He heard his mother's good, bagpipe

66

voice, Terka's hoarse, duck-like voice, and a well known, sweet voice. The voices came from the kitchen:

"We are sorry," said the sweet voice, "but Mr. Steiner, the shopkeeper ordered three shoes all at once. One of them was for his wife, to be delivered by Saturday, and two of them were for his children to be delivered by Sunday morning. My father is very embarrassed that he could not get the shoes ready. He is very, very sorry, but you know, this was the first time the shopkeeper ordered from us. And he has a large family. There are eight of them. If they like the shoes they will order more in the future."

Olajos was all ears.

"I am disappointed," said Terka's harsh duck voice, "if something is already promised..."

"It is no problem," sounded his mother's calm, pipe voice, "Steve will not be upset about it. He is not going to be upset with Ethel's father. Your name is Ethel, isn't it dear?"

"Yes it is. We were very surprised Mr. Olajos knew about me when my father was here to take measurements."

"Oh," cheerfully piped the mother, "my son sees a lot of things better than those who have two eyes. But please sit down, sit down dear..."

The chair made a quiet squeak.

"Oh, thank you."

"Our Steve can see better," Terka was bragging too. "He even told us that you used almond soap that day."

"Unbelievable! It is true. But how did he know?"

"He saw," said the mother with satisfaction, "many times he sees things we don't even see. And he sees many other things which we think he does not. For example, when he passes a house he can tell if it is old or new, tall or short, what kind of shops or workshops are inside of it. And when someone passes him, he can tell if the person is an aristocrat, or a peasant, or a craftsman. If he is a craftsman, what kind of a craftsman he is."

"Well, I have never heard of anything like this! I saw right away that he is a very smart man. And he is very nice. It is a pity..."

"He doesn't feel that way."

"Still, it is a pity. He is a handsome young man. He has a very nice complexion. I like his long, curly hair. It is amazing... because it is true that I use almond soap. Poor Kulcsar bought it for me, or he actually won it. He won it at the fair."

"Your fiancé?" asked Terka.

She sighed.

"He was not yet my fiancé. We were not engaged. But perhaps we would have been. After all, he has only been at our house maybe four times. But he already told me about his feelings for me. He told me the third time he was there. And he asked what my feelings were. Well, I wasn't going to hug him right away. To tell you the truth I did not even like him that much yet. His face was full of pock marks. You could hardly see his eyebrows. He had no mustache or beard. But despite of that, he was a handsome boy, but you know, you had to look at him from a little distance, kind of like an artist's painting. Did you happen to see the exhibition last year? Well, looking at him like that, he was even attractive. He had red cheeks. I thought I would get used to him from close as well. The next time he came he started questioning me again. He was already wearing a military uniform by then."

"'Who knows if I will return?'

"I gave him a short answer:

"'Look, you don't know me yet. I promise I will pray for you every day, but please be content with that much for now.'

"He was satisfied. Since the fair was on that Sunday, we walked out to take a look. My mother was with us of course. Kulcsar paid my ticket to see a couple short movies. One was about an American crocodile hunt. Then I won a mustache trimmer. He won an almond soap. He gave me the soap. I was very confused. I didn't know if I should give him the mustache trimmer. Then I thought I had better be up front with him.

"'Look,' I said, 'you may be able to exchange this for a cigar or for something else.'

"He did exchange it, but he did not get a cigar. He got another almond soap instead and gave it to me. He was a very good boy. But he did not earn very much yet. He barely earned eighty koronas a month. His food was also provided by his employer. He was a very polite, good boy."

And her voice became emotional.

"It is true," sighed Terka, "life has been difficult for single girls even until now. I am already twenty nine years old but I have not met anyone I really liked. There are thousands of girls nowadays who become widows even before they have a chance to get married."

She sighed.

"You are still a young lady. You could find someone even ten years from now. Nobody could tell you are twenty nine. You have a nice, clear face. And you are so elegant… This checkered skirt looks especially good on you, very elegant. But what can a poor girl like me expect? What can I expect if I don't have money, beauty or a checkered skirt? There was only a bird that ever loved me. It was a raven. I bought it from the children in front of the Taithy shop. One of her feet was shot. She was dragging her wings and one of her eyes was shot as well. She was hopping around on her one foot. She was happy when I put her on my lap, and looked at me gratefully with her one remaining eye. It is true that there was a child who also loved me. He was an orphan who was placed with our neighbor. His name was Elemer. He was taken away because my neighbors beat the poor boy every day, even though he was only five years old. Then a dog tore my raven to pieces. The poor thing followed me onto the street one day. Then I had nobody left. That was the time I got to know Kulcsar. Now he is also gone."

"You may still find someone," Terka tried to comfort her.

"You are a good woman," the mother also said. "Goodness is also beauty. It is the most lasting beauty."

"Goodness is on the inside, but most men only look at the face. For this boy it did not matter. It is true that people behind us would have said that the pockmarked married the freckle. There are some people who are unkind. But he would have married me. He was a very good boy. I cried for a week after I found out that he died. Even now when I think of him, that he will never come back..."

And her voice became very emotional.

"Well now," the mother was comforting her, "every girl is beautiful if she is healthy. And you are so kind. Not every boy will stay away. They will come home after the war. Only a lot of them will be crippled."

"I wouldn't mind that," the sweet voice was ringing with all of its warmth. If he lost his arm, I would be his arm. If he lost his leg then I would be his leg. If only he would not come home without his head."

"Are you sure he died?" asked Terka with sympathy.

"His parents received an official letter."

And in a little while the sweet voice said quietly:

"I'd better get going... Have a nice day. The shoes will be ready by Wednesday."

And her sweet footsteps could be heard as she left.

*

Olajos usually did not talk much. The reason may have been that he was always listening and smelling the air. He mostly just talked at the table if he had a question or some news to share.

He just nodded that day when they told him the shoes would not be ready in time.

"It's okay. It is not urgent."

After lunch he said:

"Tell me, Terka, what kind of a girl is Ethel?"

Terka thought about his question and started to laugh.

"She is a turkey egg. I already said that she is like a turkey egg. It is interesting that you are asking me about her the second time already."

"Calm down," said their mother.

"Well, I could also say she is an almond soap," Terka said jokingly, "a simple almond soap."

"She is pretty and kind. She is a good girl," their mother corrected her.

"Pretty, pretty," the blind was wondering, "but still..."

"She has smiling eyes."

"What else?"

69

Terka laughed.

"Interesting, you have never asked about anyone before."

The blind man's eyelids fluttered.

"Her voice is so gentle. I have never heard such a gentle voice. I have heard a similar voice only once before, in Budapest on Andrassy Street. I just stopped, as if the ground grabbed hold of my feet. I will never forget it. But that voice wasn't any gentler."

The two women were surprised.

"I did not even pay attention to her voice," their mother said with a smile as she shrugged her shoulder.

"I have not noticed anything particular about her voice either," Terka was wondering, "only that she talks too much."

"That is also a sign of kindness," nodded the blind, "if someone talks a lot. But that girl's voice... If she were talking nonsense all day long, I would still be glad to listen to her. Like something... well, like something wonderful."

"But what is wonderful? How is it wonderful?"

"Well... I can't explain it to you. It is impossible to explain a voice. It feels as if she were a large, beautiful flower and I could hear her voice."

The two women laughed.

"You are saying a lot of strange things."

"I am surprised too. But I am a musician. The female voice is the most beautiful music. Her voice is especially nice. It is like the fragrance of lilies of the valley, among other smells. When we walk at the bottom of Janos Hill, we can smell the grass, the bushes, even the ground. We can also smell the leaves on the trees, then all of a sudden the fragrance of lilies of the valley. We have to stop there, whether we want to or not. Please tell me once more, what is she like? What kind of a girl is she? Start from the top. You have plenty of time. The post office is closed today."

He got up and sat on the couch and leaned on his walking stick.

"What is she like?"

Terka looked bored. Their mother signaled to her to start talking.

Terka thought about it.

"What is she like, what is she like? Well... She has blond hair. She has bumps on her forehead. We already told you about her eyes. Did we not? Well, her eyes are the same as most eyes are on this world. She has a harp chin. Her nose could be a little bigger. To be honest with you I did not take a good look at her."

And she laughed.

"Please just tell me more about her."

"Well... What should I say? Her mouth is like... as if she were getting ready to blow out a candle."

"Nonsense," said the mother. "You should have said her mouth looks as if she were whistling. As if she were whistling without making a sound. She is a pretty, kind girl. It is not polite for you to say anything unpleasant about her."

"But I did not say anything unpleasant about her. She is a pretty girl, pretty, but just like a simple postcard among letters; there is nothing interesting about her."

The blind man was resting his elbow on his walking stick. He was looking upward like a goose.

And he did not ask any more questions.

*

Olajos usually sat next to the cymbal player in the band, on the cymbal player's right. The Gypsies got up during breaks. They went in and out and had conversations. Csurka, the violinist, sat down at some of the friendly guests' tables. Olajos was the only one who always stayed in his seat quietly. But that evening he spoke. There weren't many guests, so they took a long break. Only the cymbal player remained at his seat from the band. He leaned over his cymbal and tried to tune it.

"Csuta," he said quietly to the cymbal player, "have you ever seen a turkey egg?"

"I even drank one," answered Csuta. "I drank one when I was a child."

"What was it like?"

"What was it like? Well, it was good; what would it have been like?"

And he continued to tune his strings.

Olajos thought about it. After a little while he said:

"Tell me Csuta, how much less is a turkey egg worth than other kinds of eggs?"

"Worth less? Who said such a crazy thing? You should try to buy one on the market. It is very hard to come by."

"Is it more expensive?"

"Of course it is more expensive. One turkey egg is worth more than thirty regular eggs."

Olajos' eyes blinked. He shook his head.

"Then why do people talk about it as if it were not worth much."

"As if it were not worth much?"

"I was told about a girl that she is a turkey egg."

"I see. I understand now. Her color is like that. Because a turkey egg is like…"

Olajos waved his hand:

"I am not interested in colors."

After a little while he spoke again:

"Tell me Csuta, have you ever seen a man with a pockmarked face?"

"A man with pockmarked face? Of course I have seen one. All I have to do is look in the mirror and I see one right away."

Olajos smiled.

"Well, what is that like?"

71

"What is it like? Well, what is it like? Here is my face; touch it with your hand and then you'll know."

Olajos touched it. He shook his hair.

Csuta leaned over his cymbal and tried to tune the higher notes. He was carefully putting the key on the nail. Those high notes can be very difficult to tune.

"Tell me Csuta…"

"Please stay quiet already!"

"Just tell me one more thing. Is a turkey egg somewhat similar to your face?"

"Yes it is. But be quiet now."

And he continued to listen to his strings. Olajos thought about it and shook his hair. Then he started to rosin his bow. The cymbal player felt guilty that he misled the blind man.

"Listen," he said with remorse, "a turkey egg is not like this. Turkey egg means she has freckles. Pockmark is like having pits. Freckle is just a color. Now you know."

"I am not interested in colors," Olajos responded.

The door of the café was opened more and more often, and many conversations could be heard, along with the knocking of chairs. The cigarette smoke was getting stronger, but the smell of coffee too. Once in a while the smell of tea was also felt and the smell of rum too. During one of the music breaks, Olajos felt there was a woman nearby who was selling flowers, or perhaps he heard her bargaining. He called her to himself when she passed him to leave the room.

"Just a second, flower lady! Let me see."

The woman held her basket toward him with a smile. The blind man smelled into it. He touched every flower softly, as if he were touching sleeping faces. He was smiling and sniffing.

"All carnations?" he asked, "all carnations? Well, they will do. Do you know the Kaszabs on Baratok Street?"

"No I don't know them, but I can find them."

"Will you find them? Not now, tomorrow morning. Cobbler Kaszab. You'll probably see his name on his sign. Well, how much do these ten most beautiful carnations cost, here on the side?"

*

Terka came home at noon on Wednesday. In the morning she ran into the cobbler in front of the leather store. He said he was sorry, but he wouldn't be able to deliver the shoes that day either. He was so embarrassed, he was almost sweating. But he said it would be ready by the next day. Even if he had to work on it part of the night, it would be ready.

Olajos' face remained as if he were expecting to hear something more. But Terka did not say anything else regarding the matter. She took off her coat and removed the needle from her hat. She put it down.

"It is really cold today," she said. "I was worried that Steve might slip and fall somewhere. Did you have any problems today?"

Steve shook his head that he did not.

Their mother carried the soup into the room. Terka took care of the rest of the meal. They cooked beef and ate it with horseradish. They had crepes for desert afterwards.

"Talking about Kaszab reminds me," said their mother after she finished her soup, "do you know Steve what I thought about last night? I was thinking Kaszab's daughter would be good for you. She seems like a kind girl. And she even guided you once. You said that no woman who wore a hat ever helped you. She does have a hat. Nobody could tell that she is not a well to do woman. Everything she wears is inexpensive, but fits her well. And she is a good woman."

Olajos' soup went down the wrong pipe. He became red and started coughing. Just then Terka put the beef and horseradish on the table.

"Isn't it true, Terka?" the mother piped with emotion in her voice, "Kaszab's daughter would be good for our Steve. I thought about it last night."

"Nonsense!" said Terka.

The blind man heard their mother raise her hand. He knew this move signaled a warning. Terka pouted as she continued.

"Having such relatives... the Olajos family never had anyone smell like shoes in it."

There was silence. The blind man felt that their mother shook her head and Terka was embarrassed. Their mother's voice was soft when she spoke again.

"I thought about it the first time she was visiting us. When she said: 'If he has no arm, I would be his arm. If he has no leg, I would be his leg.' I almost said: 'and if he has no eyes?' But we know what her answer would have been, even without asking her. Believe me, she would make a good wife."

Terka shrugged her shoulder:

"If Steve would like her..."

Olajos' eyelids moved rapidly. His face was still red from coughing.

"This is not a melody," he said seriously.

"Not a melody?" the two women looked at him.

"What do you mean it is not a melody?"

"Marriage is not a melody," Olajos shook his head, "not a melody I can just quickly play."

"Of course it is not a melody," nodded their mother, "but who said it was a melody? You'll have to get to know each other; first you have to know her. Then if you like her, you'll marry her; and if you don't like her, you don't like her. There will be plenty of girls after the war..."

Terka sighed. Her mother also sighed.

"I was only just thinking of it," she continued, "because we are doing fine today. But Terka works at the post office. Today she is here, tomorrow she is there, wherever she is placed. And if I... when I am not going to be around any longer..."

"Please don't say such things," Terka whispered. "Would you like some more beef Steven? We still have plenty of meat left.

Steve shook his head.

"My appetite is not good today. Please pour me some water."

Olajos never drank anything other than water.

"If you want," said their mother, "we could make up a reason to invite her, and then you could talk to her."

Olajos shook his head.

"No, that would not be appropriate. What if she would figure out why we invited her?"

Terka raised her head.

"And if she figures it out? What if she does? A girl like her just gets tossed around in life like an unaddressed letter at the post office."

"An unaddressed letter?" Olajos wondered.

"Yes, an unaddressed letter. It would be considered lucky if someone put a name on it."

Olajos looked as if he had just blown dust out of his nose.

"An unaddressed letter. Aren't you also like an unaddressed letter? Every girl is an unaddressed letter! Some of them have gold in them, some have silver. But others... Every one of them has some kind of flower in it too."

Then he shook his head with a smile on his face.

Terka laughed.

"It is a good thing you did not say that some of them are empty inside. But thankfully some of them at least have flower in them, almond blossom, almond soap."

And she laughed as she leaned back in her chair.

Olajos blinked.

"Why are you laughing about almond soap? I like the smell of almond soap. We used to wash ourselves with it at the institute."

"I am just laughing," Terka tried to make up an excuse. "After all, we also washed ourselves with it when we lived in the village. But you know I was just thinking about that girl. She could consider herself lucky if we invited her and you even talked to her. After all, you even have money, eleven thousand koronas. We have not touched it until now and we are not going to touch it in the future either. And your musical talent is an even bigger value. It will provide you with dependable income until you die."

She was trying to please her brother, but she had the same mischievous smile on her face as before.

Olajos blinked again.

"That is true. I haven't even told you that I am teaching the band the Eva waltz, even the cymbal player, and the double bass player as well."

And he laughed.

"They are all learning from me, from the blind man. I am teaching them the things I learned in Budapest. None of them can read written music."

Then he became serious.

"Still, it would not be proper to invite her like that. No, no, I won't let that happen. What is she like? Tell me once more."

"I already told you, she is like…"

The blind man felt his mother's warning signal.

Terka continued with a laugh:

"She is pretty and kind."

"Tell me the details. What is her hair like?"

"She has blond hair."

"Please don't tell me colors. They don't mean anything to me. And please stop laughing because it makes me feel like you are making fun of me. And I can't tolerate that."

He shook his hair, the same way a dog shakes his head when a fly lands on his ear.

"Please don't get upset," the girl asked him. "Ask me whatever you want to know."

"Her forehead?"

"Her forehead is bumpy. Her mouth looks as if she…"

"As if she is whistling," finished their mother, "as if she is silently whistling."

"Her hands and feet?"

"Her hands and feet? I didn't look at them. But she has an attractive figure."

"She is beautiful, slender, light," said their mother seriously.

Olajos listened with a smile on his face. He rested his chin on his walking stick. He thought about her and his face was just like a dreaming child's face.

"The tailor," he spoke fifteen minutes later. "Let's ask the tailor to come over. I'd like him to make black clothes for me after all."

The shoes were ready by noon the next day. The cobbler's eyes revealed that he had to work on them part of the night. But it was ready.

"I am very sorry, Mr. Olajos, very sorry," he apologized. "But it was impossible to get it done sooner."

"No problem, no problem," said Olajos kindly, "the main thing is that it is ready now."

"These shoes are very good quality. Please try them on. They go on your feet as easily as slippers. And their shape would be elegant enough for a count, wouldn't it Miss? Oh, I just remembered, my daughter would like to thank you for your kind gesture, Mr. Olajos. But she will come over this afternoon. You are going to be home, aren't you? She would like to thank you personally. She was so happy."

Olajos became red.

"She is welcome," he whispered, "she is welcome."

"That day was full of joy for her," continued the cobbler. "We got news that her fiancé did not die. No he did not. We read in the newspaper that Janos Kulcsar is among the prisoners in Russia. He is alive, thankfully. He is a very fine boy. He doesn't drink or play cards."

And he pulled his finger under his nose.

Olajos did not speak any more. His face was colorless and emotionless as always. His mother paid for the shoes.

"What was he thanking you for?" asked Terka.

"Nothing, nothing," the blind man answered and seemed annoyed. "It is unbelievable how much the two of you can talk!"

The two women were silent. Steve never scolded them before. They thought perhaps he was upset because he thought the shoes were too expensive.

"Steve is upset," they whispered outside. "We should have told the cobbler ahead of time to tell Steve the shoes cost half as much. We should have known..."

The blind man sat on the couch, and he held his walking stick as usual. At home he never put it down. At times he leaned on it; other times he just held it. He sat there silently. At three o'clock Terka mustered up enough courage to speak.

"The tailor is coming at four, Steve."

"What for?" the blind man asked.

"Well, to make you black clothes... You asked for him."

"Send him away. Tell him I am not home. We'll buy one if we need to. I am already used to the clothes I already have. And I have something to discuss with the violinist."

He reached into his pocket and pulled out his pocket watch. It was given to him by his father when he was taken as a child into the institute of the blind. The clock was quietly ticking. It signaled every quarter hour with a double click.

He really did get up and leave and did not come home for dinner. He was away at night as well. At dawn two Gypsies were leading him home. The two women were surprised to see that Steve could barely stand on his two feet. His hat was all dusty. He was not wearing his glasses.

"He was having a good time," the Gypsies explained, "even threw some glasses at the wall."

*

Olajos got up slowly that afternoon. The two women seemed worried as they looked at him. The Gypsies must have made him drink, or perhaps a drunkard guest. Poor Steve! Nothing like this ever happened to him before. But, the whole thing did not seem quite as tragic after Steve got up with red cheeks, and the first thing he asked for was water.

"More," he said, "more."

And he drank. He poured water down his throat.

"More. Don't give it to me in a glass. Please give me the whole pitcher. And why is it so hot in here? Don't put so much wood in the stove."

He drank all the water out of the pitcher. Terka was worried as she looked at him.

"Are you sick?"

"I only have a headache. Please give me some more water."

"Well," said Terka, "you got yourself mixed up with bad company."

His mother also scolded him as he was getting dressed.

"Don't you have enough common sense? You should have said: 'Thank you, but I don't drink.' If they tried to force you, you should have said: 'Please, if you want to be kind to me, don't offer me a drink. I only drink water.' Did they try to force it on you? There are pushy people. They tried to force you, didn't they? That's why you threw the glasses at the wall."

"What about your money?" Terka said. "Do you have your money?"

Olajos did not answer her question. He sat still as usual. His clothes were not as well organized as they usually were, but the two women helped him get dressed.

The two women were upset.

"You also acted like a fool," said their mother. "The more they try to force you, the more you need to resist them."

"Thirty fillers?" asked Terka, "there are only thirty fillers in your pocket. Those criminals!"

"And your glasses? Where are your glasses?"

Olajos wrinkled his forehead and his face twitched.

"Let it go already!" he waived, "I don't like when you talk too much."

And the mother signaled to her daughter to stay quiet.

"It is not his fault," piped the mother kindheartedly. "Steve never acts like a fool. Somebody led him astray. Why shouldn't he have a good time, if he feels like it. It is no problem, Steve, no problem. I am just glad you were not hurt. You will be more careful next time. What would you like to eat? Would you like to have lunch with us, or should we give you some coffee?"

"I'll have lunch."

They found him some food.

Terka tried to cheer up her younger brother with more pleasant conversation.

"Well, you should be sorry you left early yesterday. Ethel came by. She wanted to thank you for sending her flowers on her birthday. She said she was very touched that someone thought of her. She has never gotten any flowers on her birthday. I think she did not get flowers any other time either. But how did you know?"

"I didn't know. I just sent them to her," Olajos answered nonchalantly.

"Well, you happened to send it on her birthday. We didn't know you were such a generous man."

"Perhaps it is better this way," their mother also said. "At least she had some happiness on her birthday."

"Because we congratulated her," continued Terka, "we congratulated her regarding the good news about her fiancé. Then she told us they were mistaken. When they looked in the paper they did not realize that the Janos Kulcsar listed there was from a different regiment. Someone they know in the military told them that he could not even have been a sergeant yet."

The blind raised his head:

"A different Kulcsar?"

"Yes, a different one. She is sure her Kulcsar has died."

Olajos raised his eyebrows.

"Is she mourning him?"

"No, only her face is a little sad when she talks about him."

Terka went outside to get a vegetable dish. Her mother continued talking.

"I really like this girl. You know, I even mentioned my thought to her."

The blind man dropped his spoon into the soup.

"What? How?"

"'Well,' I just said, 'you are a very kind, good girl, Ethel. You are the kind of girl I would like to find for my son.'

The blind man leaned back in his chair. His eyes were wide open.

"And... and..."

"Well, she blushed and smiled."

"And then?"

"Then, let's see, what did she say? Oh, yes. She said: 'but Mr. Olajos doesn't even know me yet.'"

Olajos shook his head.

"I know her. I know her! You should have said I know her!"

"That is what we said: 'If my son talked with someone only once, he knows that person. He can pick her out from a hundred people if he hears her voice.'"

"But did you notice anything about the way she was reacting? Did she seem reluctant?"

"No. She said: 'Mr. Olajos is a very nice man. It is a pity...'"

Olajos was tapping the side of the table with the palm of his hand.

"It is not a pity!" he almost shouted. "Why didn't you say, 'It is not a pity'? There is nothing wrong with me. I don't miss my eyes. It is foolish to think that I cannot see. The blind can see better than anyone else! Only the colors... But what is a color? Nothing! A wall is a wall regardless of whether it is red or blue! And the ground is the ground, regardless of whether it is blue or red. When the Gypsies want to find out if a coin is real, they ask me. I just put it in my hand, and I can tell them right away. It is really hot in here."

Terka brought in the food. She stopped at the door, so she could close it. The blind man was excited as he continued.

"Terka is standing at the door, and I already know what she is bringing. People with eyes can't tell from this far what she is carrying. She is bringing savoy cabbage, isn't she? There is some smoked meat in it too. And you are baking small cakes in the oven. Aren't you?"

"It is true," said Terka as she put the dish down. "It is amazing that you can tell."

The blind man did not eat. He just sat there thinking, and he tapped on the arm of his chair. His face was red. His eyes were wide open.

"Would she marry me? Did she say she would marry me?"

"No, we couldn't ask her like that!" Terka said and now her voice was compassionate as well. "We can't break down her door so suddenly. But if you want, I can visit them; the heels of my shoes seem to be getting worn. I will do it for you, I will do it. I will talk to her too. I'll do it."

"What? How?"

"Well, I will just tell her that you would like to visit her."

"Good, that will be very good!" said Olajos. "And then we will know right away."

"Yes," continued Terka calmly, "if she seems very surprised and does not answer right away, then you will not visit her. But if she tells me right away that you are welcome…"

"Then I will visit her!" Olajos tapped the edge of the table. "Then I will go."

And he got up as if he was ready to go.

"I will visit her. I will. But when, when? After lunch. Take your shoes to them right after lunch, take them."

He sat down on the couch. His face was red, even his ears. He smiled as he held his walking stick with his two hands. The two women looked at him. Terka left to get the small cakes. She put them on a plate and set them on the table.

"No, we cannot do this in such a thoughtless manner," their mother said in an anxious voice. "Even if that girl does not dislike you, we cannot do this so suddenly…"

Terka was also thinking:

"Of course, she was just here yesterday. Should I already run over there today to tell her that Steve would like to visit her? The heels of my shoes are not even that worn, they are just starting to…"

"This is not a good strategy," piped their mother. "It is not good to show that we want her so much."

"That we think we would be lucky," pouted Terka. "We should see that she feels lucky. These cakes are a little burnt."

"Steve likes them a little burnt. After all, Steve makes as much money as an attorney. And he looks like a gentleman. Artists are all gentlemen and Steve is an artist. But come, eat some of these cakes."

"You are a good girl," Olajos said joyfully. "You are a good sister. Come here, let me kiss you. And I will give you my eleven thousand koronas. It will be your wedding gift."

"You are so good," whispered Terka. "I cannot accept your money. If a man will not marry me for who I am, he should not marry me for my money. And nobody should marry me for my cakes either."

"I was thinking," piped their mother. "I should have new soles put on my slippers. The girl will probably bring it home and then we'll invite her in for tea."

Terka laughed.

"To have new soles put on your slippers? Kaszab will tell you it is cheaper to buy new ones, Mother."

Olajos raised his head.

"The tailor!" he said anxiously. "Terka, please run out and get the tailor!"

*

Terka led Olajos to the entrance of the café at eight o'clock. She didn't like to lead him during the day, but she went with him during the evenings, if the road was slippery or snowy. On that day the snow was melting around noon, and it was getting icy in the evening.

The guests started to arrive at nine. The band stopped tuning and started to play. The violinist looked over the guests and their tables. They only ordered coffee and beer yet. Most of them were regulars in the café.

A teacher drank tea. An old engineer played chess in the corner with the town's doctor. The man in charge of making the coffee yawned and played with his watch. He wore a signet ring on his gold chain. There was boredom in the café. The elderly cashier put some sugar cubes into a holder.

"One tea please," could be heard at times.

"One tea without vanilla please, Ms. Kornel."

Around ten o'clock four guests arrived who were not regulars in the café. The violinist was excited to see new faces. He looked back at the band and they finished playing a Viennese melody. The violinist started a Hungarian folk melody with a long note.

The new guests did not even look there. They ordered red wine in bottles and seriously poured it into each other's glasses. The words "cattle and pigs" could be heard from their conversation: "lean cattle, fat cattle, lean pigs, fat pigs, fat cow, ox, brewery," and other words like these. One of them seemed to be a farm owner. The top of his head was bald. His two eyebrows were separated by a deep wrinkle, which seemed to divide his forehead into two. His face looked very stern because of it.

80

"The dogcatcher should take it!" he kept saying at times.

Or he would just say:

"The dogcatcher!"

The Gypsies rested for a little while. Then the violinist started the Eva waltz. They had just learned it a few days before from Olajos, who was their instructor now. Their previous teacher was taken into the army. At one point the violinist seemed a little unsure. Olajos felt it right away and took over the lead. The cello became the lead instrument for a minute in the band.

The stern farmer looked at the band briefly. The Gypsies looked at Olajos. The violinist found the tune and took back the lead. Olajos' play mixed in with the rest of the instruments.

The four strangers continued their conversation:

"Lean cattle, better to feed. Fat cattle, better later. The pigs bring in the most profit."

The Gypsies rested. The violinist kept his eyes on the strangers.

"Champagne!" said the stern farmer.

The waiter quickly ran to the cashier.

"Champagne, Ms. Kornel, Champagne."

Ms. Kornel pulled out a silver bucket from under the cash register. The man in charge of making the coffee straightened out and looked toward the table where the strangers were sitting.

The violinist felt energized. He tapped the top of his violin with his bow. The cymbal player quickly played through all his strings. The leader started: *I love you my only flower...* And the whole band started to play that wonderful folk melody, with the expectation of a generous tip.

The stern farmer turned around.

"Let the cellist lead the band."

The Gypsies felt like someone had just poured water on them. Olajos' body jerked suddenly. All the instruments stopped at once. The double bass player put a chair in front of the band. The cymbal player grabbed Olajos' hand and led him there. Olajos touched the back of the chair and sat in it. His face was red. He touched the four strings and started to play his cello's beautiful baritone: *I love you my only one...*

The café quieted down. Ms. Kornel leaned on her elbow by the counter, and she held her powdered face with her powdered thumb. The guests looked at the long haired cellist wearing dark glasses. The cups were quietly rattling. Even the man making coffee turned to look at him. Only the two chess players continued their game seriously as they leaned on their elbows by the chess table.

The cello's sound rose and then fell into the depth sweetly. Olajos leaned forward at times, and his hair fell forward; then he leaned back and shook his hair. His lean fingers ran through the strings like spider legs. He pulled out long notes

81

with his bow. At times he slammed down forcefully and the cello trembled as it was singing in a melting sweet cry: *The harsh winter's snow is melting away...*

The Gypsies were amazed and quietly accompanied him with their instruments.

"I can't believe it," the violinist tried to please him at the end. "You did learn from me finally, didn't you?"

*

Olajos stood by the side of the road. There was construction on Main Street, in front of the bookstore, where he usually crossed the street to get to the sidewalk on the other side. He could not hear the steps of the people in front of him from the wheelbarrow squeaks and construction noise. Some of the pedestrians were held up under the brick smelling scaffolding.

He just stood there.

He tried to listen to the noise of the traffic and waited for it to die down. He hoped a kind person would help him get across the street. He didn't always find someone willing to help. But at times he was offered help, mostly by gentlemen. Some of them smelled like cigars, others like cologne. Women seldom offered to help him. If they did, they were usually from the village. Children never offered to lead him.

The weather was mild that day. The sunshine dried up the sidewalk. The road was still wet and had an unpleasant smell. But it was always like that. In the summer it smelled like dust and in the winter like mud. But it always had a horse smell.

Olajos continued his walk again when the noise of the traffic died down. But he stepped on a barrel cork and it confused him. He stopped. In the meantime he heard a carriage which came from his right, where the theater was. It took about five minutes for the carriage to get where he was. He could have gotten across the road by that time, but what if there were more barrel corks on the road?

"I will turn back," he thought, "I would rather cross the street by the construction scaffolding."

He hesitated for a little while before he turned back.

"A black eraser please," he heard a child's voice when the door of the nearby bookstore opened.

"...I will wait for the carriage to pass by," Olajos thought.

Then he felt that someone approached him.

"Good morning, Mr. Olajos!" sounded the kind voice.

The voice's owner grabbed his arm. She was slightly out of breath. She was either in a hurry or she may have run.

"Good morning," she repeated softly. "I saw from the other side that you wanted to cross the street. And in such a big traffic! How do you dare? Well, you can come with me confidently. But I am so glad we met. And I can thank you for the carnations. It was a very nice surprise. I don't even know what I have done to

82

deserve it. You are very generous, a very generous man, Mr. Olajos. Are you satisfied with your new shoes? My father paid special attention to it when he worked on it. I told him to do his very best. And I waxed its sole. It is more durable that way, you know; the water does not get through it as easily. My father chose the finest leather, and he used copper nails at the heels. Now please step up. Good, we are in the middle of the sidewalk now. It is quieter in this area. I would be glad to go further with you. I would be very glad to go with you all the way to the Gypsies' house. But my mother is waiting for me. By the time the bell tolls the soup has to be on our table, and I brought some cabbages from the market. It takes a long time to cook those. God be with you, Mr. Olajos. Oh, I wanted to tell you that the cashier from your café, Ms. Kornel, lives in our house. Do you know her? She said the guests did not want to listen to anyone else but you last night. She said it is amazing how wonderful you can play. I was glad to hear it. Well, God be with you Mr. Olajos. The cabbages are almost screaming from my basket."

Olajos blushed and smiled. He could not say a word. Only at the end was he able to whisper:

"God be with you, Ethel."

*

Terka had to go over to the cobbler that afternoon with her shoes and thank Ethel's thoughtfulness. The blind man made her go. And she wanted to invite Ethel for tea.

Kaszab started to work on her shoes right away. He wiped off a chair in the workshop for Terka.

"We are sorry," he said kindly, "but our living room is full; my daughter is ironing."

Ethel looked out from the room.

"Oh... Well... Please come in here. I am ironing. We are washing clothes today and there is some steam in here."

"No problem. I would like to talk to you, Ethel. I would like to invite you to come over to our house for tea."

"For tea," Mrs. Kaszab was flattered. "But today..."

Kaszab pulled out a pair of slippers from a pile of shoes.

"Please put these on while you wait."

The living room was full of freshly washed clothes, and steam. The pictures on the walls were almost sweating. A picture of Lajos Kossuth almost moved to take off his parka.

"We would have liked it so much," Terka seemed disappointed. "Steve will be home too. He is always waiting for the opportunity to thank you for your kindness."

"My kindness? I have to thank him for his."

They moved some underwear from a chair. Ethel was embarrassed. Her mother seemed very happy to have Terka there.

"I am sorry," she said, "but I have to wash some more clothes, and the daylight is very short. And today is Saturday. I can't leave it for tomorrow."

The two women were left alone.

"Steve said you were very kind, very kind…"

"Don't mention it, Miss," Ethel said. "I saw that he wanted to cross the road. Anyone would have done the same thing. It is a joy for me if I can help someone unfortunate."

"No, he is not unfortunate," interrupted Terka. "Please don't say this word in front of him! It bothers him a great deal when people feel sorry for him."

"Is he bothered by it? I had better be careful then. But between you and me, I feel sorry for him. It is a pity. He is handsome, noble and calm. And today when I helped him, I looked at his eyes. They looked like there was nothing wrong with them.

"No. Sometimes, when he opens his eyes, he looks like a person with normal sight. But he always talks as if he could see. When he came home today, he said:

"I saw Ethel. She was going home from the market. She carried cabbages, meat and leather for her father."

Ethel was amazed.

"It is true. I was carrying cabbages and meat and enough leather for two pairs of shoes. Well, he must be able to see something then."

"He sees, but not with his eyes. On the street, he always knows what kind of person passes him, lord or peasant, woman or man, child or a woman carrying a child. He can even tell whether the person is young or old. When he was a child we still lived in the village. He could always tell who walked by our house, even though there was no asphalt sidewalk or road. Mr. Bota walked by. Mrs. Czapek walked by. Or Jani Szucs ran in front of us. We often asked him: 'how do you know? After all, Jani Szucs walks barefoot.' He just shrugged his shoulder: 'I don't know, I just know.'"

"Strange."

"Yes. And that is why he does not understand why we feel sorry for him. I only heard him ask one time for a description of what something was like. He asked about the sound of the violin. We laughed. He thought the music sounds were beautiful things we could see, flying back and forth. He was just an eight year old child. Our neighbor sometimes played the violin. And since he could hear even the butterflies, he thought the violin sounds are something similar. After we told him we could not see those sounds, and our neighbor could not see them either, he was never jealous of our ability to see. Although recently… Recently we heard him ask us to describe someone for him. He is asking about you, Ethel."

Ethel stopped ironing. She smiled, blinked and seemed surprised.

"Is he asking about me?"

"Very much so! We had to describe you to him in detail. Of course he was not able to touch your face. If he touches someone's face with the tip of his fingers, he sees that person better than a person with normal eyesight."

Ethel shook her head. She smiled.

"Interesting. But what did you tell him, what am I like? Did you tell him that I am ugly, freckled?"

She leaned over the iron with a sad smile on her face.

Kaszab opened the door and had her shoes in his hand.

"Here you go."

"How much do I owe you?"

"Nothing. I don't charge my favorite clients for such a small thing."

"Thank you very much. Could Ethel come over today? You would let her, wouldn't you?"

"If her responsibilities will let her..."

And he looked at Terka. He pulled his finger under his nose. Then he hurried back into his workshop.

"No, I cannot possibly go now," Ethel apologized, "thank you, but I cannot go today. You can see..."

"What about tomorrow? Tomorrow is Sunday."

"Tomorrow?" Ethel blinked, as if she had never heard the wonderful word, tomorrow. "No, I cannot go tomorrow either. If the Miss would not have said that he kindly asked about me... No, I can't go now..."

She had a shy expression as she raised her shoulder.

"What if he came for you? If he escorted you to our house?"

Ethel quietly ironed.

"I don't know," she said finally, "but no, I can't. If the Miss would have not said that Mr. Olajos asked about me... No, I can't... It would not be proper for me to go there. But you did tell him that I am ugly and have freckles, didn't you?"

"Of course not. We told him you are beautiful. What are you talking about, being ugly?"

"I know what I am like. It is unfortunate that especially my face... Take a look at my arm. There is not one freckle on me except for my face."

"You can put some powder on it, or even some cream."

"Powder and cream would be the last things needed in our house. We are glad when we have enough to eat. Didn't you tell Mr. Olajos that I have freckles? You had better tell him."

"What does he care? He only sees your voice. Finally his wish to see voices became reality. But please be honest with me, Ethel. You are reluctant... because he is blind."

"No, I am not!" said Ethel. "To me he is a very dear gentleman. How could you say that Miss? The first time I met him I felt as if he were my poor raven. Oh, excuse me… not my raven, I just thought about my raven right then. Or not that I thought about him… I just feel everyone is my brother if he is…"

And she shook her head and laughed.

"I got everything confused in my head today."

Terka looked at her like a watchmaker at the inside of a pocket watch.

"Well then," she said, "let's say, your brother, our Steven would accidentally stumble in here… let's say tomorrow afternoon around four o'clock. Would he find you home?"

"Well," she said with a smile, as she looked in front of her, "why wouldn't he find me home?"

Olajos played even better that evening. There were no cheerful guests, but the Gypsies offered Olajos the chance to play solo twice. And there were indications that this was going to be repeated every evening. If the guests feel like it, they should have the opportunity to hear the talented cellist.

Olajos was unable to sleep well that night. He got up earlier than usual.

"Please give me warm water," were his first words, "and my razor."

He usually shaved himself. Not in front of a mirror of course, but flawlessly.

"My black clothes!" he said after shaving.

"Terka, please run over to the store and buy me a nice silk tie, the most beautiful one, the softest one, the most expensive one. Terka, buy some flowers too. Go inside the flower shop. They do sell hyacinth already. Buy a nice bouquet of hyacinths."

"What are you thinking? It is not proper to take her flowers yet. This is the first time you are going there, and you want to take hyacinths. They don't make bouquets out of hyacinths. But even if they did… What if they don't welcome you as gladly as you think?"

The blind man was surprised.

"They won't welcome me?"

"It is possible that they won't welcome me. But I am sure they will welcome me."

Olajos walked up and down on the room's carpet. He listened to the clock.

"You should have talked with her parents too," he said sternly. "You forgot about that!"

"Well, don't worry," answered Terka. "After all, her father seemed very pleased when I said I would like to invite his daughter for tea."

"But, what about her mother?"

"Her mother seemed flattered."

"What kind of a woman is she?"

"She is simple as a mud scraper."

Olajos shook his head and he smiled.

"Well, your tongue is sharp! If you were married to a tailor, your husband could use it instead of a needle. Well, don't they mind that I am blind?"

"Please, don't be so narrow-minded. You are the only one who would mind."

"I don't mind; only when I am walking outside, sometimes I wish my shoes had eyes. But I don't know anyone who has shoes like that."

Something flew by his ear.

"Are there flies already, early in March? It was probably brought in with the wood basket."

He only spoke again at lunch.

"Atilla Horvath is blind," he said as he thought out loud, "and he is a world famous pianist. And Illes Edvi, he is a famous lawyer and writer. And Milton was also blind. Have you read from him, Terka? He wrote a very famous book. I have not read it either. But Milton was a very famous poet. He might have also been an attorney as well."

Around three o'clock he asked if the clock in the tower was too fast.

At three he rose.

"Moustache curler!" he shouted, as if he were screaming fire. "Please give me a moustache curler!"

The two women laughed.

"You don't think that we use a moustache curler?"

"Didn't my brother have one?"

"No, it is not popular any more. How did you think of it?"

"My moustache is messy."

"It is not messy. You don't have a big moustache. But if you want I can curl the ends of it with my hair curler."

"Yes, curl it."

He kept feeling his moustache with his hand until four o'clock, and also his necktie, and his hair. Then he asked: "Are there any feathers on my clothes?" He listened to his pocket watch every minute.

"It is almost four o'clock."

The weather was cloudy that day. The snow from the end of February had melted a few days earlier. The smell of wet pavement could be felt in the air. Olajos stepped carefully, because he did not want to get any mud on his shoes.

"It is too bad I could not bring my cello," he said on the way.

And after a little while:

"She'll make music. Her voice is like music."

And again after a little while:

"I should have brought some flowers after all. Proper or not proper, my feelings say it is proper."

"It's not proper!" answered Terka confidently.

Olajos only spoke again at the gate.

"Do I look okay?"

He felt his gloves, to make sure they were buttoned. He felt his moustache. He sniffed. He was able to smell the smoke coming from the yard, although no smoke was visible for someone with healthy eyes.

Terka opened the gate.

"Be careful, we'll step down here into a hallway."

The blind tapped his stick in front of him and he stepped down. In that second the door opened and Ethel flew out to greet them.

"Welcome Miss! Welcome Mr. Olajos."

She softly pressed the blind man's hand.

"I will lead him from here," she said with her warm voice. "I will, I, I."

And she put the blind man's arm into her hand.

"Come confidently, Mr. Olajos. We'll step down at the doorstep. This is the kitchen, and..."

"I know," said Olajos joyfully, "I know. The stove is over there, and the door to the workshop is that way. I have never been in here, but I would find my way into the living room."

"Wonderful," said Ethel enthusiastically, "Wonderful. It is unbelievable."

Her mother was the only one home with her. She apologized that her husband had to go to the trade guild. Leather became so expensive, and they were constantly discussing what to do about it.

"Please sit down on the couch," Ethel offered the blind man. "Please sit down Miss."

"No, you sit next to my brother. After all, he likes talking to you. But please call me by my first name from now on."

And she kissed Ethel.

"It will be hard for me to get used to," Ethel said shyly. "You are so good. And I can see goodness in Mr. Olajos' face."

Olajos sat on the couch and smelled the air. Ethel took away his walking stick, and this confused him a little.

"No," he said and shook his hair, "only you are good, Ethel. I felt it right away the first time we met. Because I knew there were boxes there. The boxes smell. I can smell the labels on them. They use tar or something like that to write on them. I felt and knew that after about six steps I would have hit those boxes with my stick."

He never talked that much. But that day he just kept talking. His face was red, and he turned toward Ethel.

"But getting help from you made me feel very good. And today I wanted to bring some flowers, but..."

"The flower shop was closed," interrupted Terka. "It was already closed."

Olajos was surprised. He blinked.

Ethel blushed as she looked at him.

"Oh, thank you," she said softly, "thank you for the thought. I did not deserve those beautiful carnations the last time either."

Olajos smiled. He looked toward Terka to figure out how to respond to what she said. But Terka was silent and there was a pause in their conversation. The clock's tick was the only thing that could be heard.

Olajos felt his moustache with his hand.

"It is amazing," said Mrs. Kaszab, "how some flowers bloom even during winter in some places."

She got up and went to the commode. She put a bottle of red wine on the table. And she smiled graciously.

"Thank you," Terka said, "but my brother doesn't drink."

"No," the blind shook his head, "only water. Water is the best. Atilla Horvath does not drink wine either. Atilla Horvath was my teacher. He is also blind, but he is a well respected artist. He is a world famous pianist. Princes and counts listen to him when he gives a concert. He is not bothered by his blindness. There is also a famous attorney in Budapest who is blind. He is a lawyer and a writer, Illes Edvi. Have you read his articles?"

"My husband probably reads them," said Mrs. Kaszab. "They read politics at the trade guild. My husband understands politics very well. He is always talking politics at home too. Isn't that true, Ethel?"

"Then he must read them," Olajos nodded with joy.

"But how?" Ethel was wondering, "How can Illes Edvi write? How does he put his pen into ink? And how..."

"He uses a typewriter."

"On a typewriter," Terka confirmed it. "I write on a typewriter too."

"Of course, of course," said Ethel. "How did I not think of it?"

Olajos shook his hair.

"But it is possible that he does not use a typewriter. He could write with a pencil too, or even with ink. The ink doesn't have to be touched. I can tell you keep some ink in this room. There is a commode here on the right, isn't it?"

"It is true!" Ethel said with surprise.

"We just brought in some ink this morning," said Mrs. Kaszab. "My husband wrote a letter to one of his friends because he is seeking an apprentice."

"And there is a candle," the blind man pointed toward the mirror. "We had one too when we lived in the village. And this table is new here. I know without touching it."

"It really is!" Ethel was amazed.

"And there is a window behind me, overlooking the back yard."

"Unbelievable!"

"And there are two other windows in the room," continued the blind man triumphantly, "and in the window on the other side you have a flower pot, and you planted geranium in it."

Everything was as the blind man said, and Ethel was truly amazed. Her mother was too.

The conversation that followed was very pleasant and warm. Olajos was red and alert, like a child playing ball. He told them about Milton and bragged about Rudnyansky.

"He wrote such beautiful poems. The bishops shook hands with him and a cardinal too."

"But how did he know?" Ethel was wondering. "How did he know which one was the cardinal? Did he touch their faces? Because Terka said... Yesterday she said that... That is how they do it... those who are without sight."

Olajos raised his eyebrows with surprise.

"Is that how they do it? The blind are not particularly interested in the size of people's beards."

Terka moved.

"I only said it because I thought... because you asked about Ethel so much. After all, you did touch the statue of Lajos Kossuth with your fingers."

Olajos blushed.

"That is altogether different. Ethel is different. If a blind person would like to get to know someone close... Didn't I touch our mother's face many times? And yours too. Our mother has wrinkles and she is wrinkled under her chin too and she has a mole on her neck. Your face is smooth and your eyebrows feel like silk. I was allowed to feel them."

He shook his head with a smile.

"But I wouldn't dare to have done that with Ethel. What would she have thought?"

"I wouldn't have thought anything bad," answered Ethel confidently. "I know that blind people see by touch. And if once... if you would like to see me Mr. Olajos, you can touch my face too. Please touch it, what am I like?"

She moved closer on the couch. She held her face and had a playful smile.

"Here you go."

The blind man blushed.

"Thank you," he whispered gratefully, "thank you very much. But... Isn't it unpleasant?"

"No, if you would like."

"I would... If you let me..."

"Gladly. I would also like to find out... But tell me the truth about what I am like."

"I know anyway that you are beautiful. But if you allow me..."

"Please go ahead, go ahead."

Olajos smiled and his eyebrows trembled like leaves. He carefully lifted his hand and touched the girl's shoulder... I am most interested in your shoulder."

"My shoulder?"

Olajos nodded with a smile.

"Yes. Ethel, you are so kind... It is impossible that you don't have wings."

"Oh," the girl was flattered. She shyly pulled away her shoulder.

"I've never heard anything like that."

"Even if you don't have wings, I am sure I can feel where they were," Olajos persisted.

"Oh, you are very kind, Mr. Olajos," the girl blushed, "but my face, here is my face. What do you think about my face? Let's see, what is it like?"

And she held her face toward him.

"If you allow me," whispered the blind man.

His hands trembled as he lifted them. He first touched the girl's forehead, as if he were trying to bless her.

"How beautiful," he whispered, "how beautiful!"

He felt her eyebrows.

"Yours also feel like velvet, but yours are longer. Your eyes are beautiful, big..."

He was in awe. He touched the girl's face gently, the same way he touched the carnations before he bought them.

"How beautiful!"

Then he touched her face with his two palms, as if he were stroking a child's face.

"Oh, how beautiful!"

He felt her mouth and chin too.

"How beautiful!"

His finger stroked her neck.

"How beautiful!"

Then his hand was on her shoulder again.

"It is amazing that you don't have wings."

From her shoulder he stroked her arm and ended up by her hand.

"I already know your hand."

And he rested his hands there. He held her hand tenderly, as if he held a little bird."

He was in awe. He closed his eyelids.

"I am not too interested in colors," he said with a joyful smile.

And he pressed the girl's hand to his lips

Forget Me Not!

Imrus Kovacs was a fifty year old man. His face was shaved and looked as if it was carved out of stone, like the people who sat in the English Parliament. Even his clothes were tailored according to English fashion. He smoked a pipe instead of a cigar. It almost sounded strange when his name was called.

Imrus Kovacs

"Why didn't you get married, Imrus Kovacs?"

I don't even know. I forgot. Or I didn't want to. Or I didn't have time. Or I forgot, didn't want to, and did not have the time. I don't even know what the true reason was. But it is odd that every time someone asks me that question, to me it sounds as if I am being asked in French.

I always think of an artificial flower called forget me not and a little water color picture. I would give thousands for that fine little painting, when I think about it. It was a magnificent little picture painted with colors of dreams. It was kept in a red silk case. It depicted a smiling blond girl. That smiling blond girl... I am surprised even today that it was the portrait of two different women.

The story is a little unusual. But even today I could not tell if it was my fortune or misfortune. It caused me heartache until I was thirty. I smiled at it for a long time even after that.

My story started at the time when I went abroad after I finished high school. It was my father's will that I should study philology in Switzerland. Our priest encouraged him. I knew even then that it was not the right path for me. I would have liked to become a painter, although I only painted ornaments which were popular back then when I was educated in drawing.

But I couldn't oppose my father. He was a hard man who liked to smoke long pipes when he was a governor's assistant. He raised six children on his little salary and made sure they all got diplomas.

It is true that only my oldest brother, Peter got new clothes. When his clothes became too small for him the second oldest inherited them. By the time I ended up with them my mother had already turned them twice inside out and left my coat long so the patches on my pants could not be seen.

Oh, that coat really made me bitter. I sure wished I wasn't the sixth child born in the family. I felt that way even more when I finished my elementary education and started high school! I got to sit next to my father until then. He put the best parts of the meals on my plate. The chicken's liver, the cock's crest. But as soon as I started Latin school I had to move down to the end of the table at home.

"You are a big boy now. It is important for you to respect your older brothers."

And I had to constantly respect my five older brothers. I always ended up with what was left at the bottom of the dish, with the smallest apple, with the wormy walnuts and with the hazel nuts with holes in them. I had to respect my older brothers. I didn't have a younger brother, so nobody respected me.

We lived like this. We always had to feel that there were a lot of us, a lot!

My brothers did contribute some money toward my school tuition. My father even owed some money by that time. Not much, but it bothered him a lot.

"You will pay this loan off, kids!" he kept saying. "There are a lot of you, and you need a lot!"

"I won't get married unless I find a girl whose money will be brought to me in a cart drawn by four oxen," grumbled one of my older brothers once!

But we lived decent lives. My father did not spend money on anything. He did not go anywhere. His only enjoyment was getting together with our priest during afternoons. They played cards against each other.

I can still picture the sausage shape of that little priest as he watched the cards with a hunter's eyes. He became red from being upset when he lost five krajcars and he screamed with joy when he won four.

The crazy idea that I should be sent to Switzerland was born in that priest's mind.

"Teachers who speak French are well paid!" he said, "It will be as if he got two diplomas when he graduates, and two diplomas bring double pay."

He had some kind of a distant relative professor at the School of Technology in Geneva. He just called this relative Kelemen Mikes. He immigrated to France after the 1849 Hungarian revolution in fear of persecution and never returned. The priest wanted him to take me under his wings as I continued my education.

My father of course did not understand his good intention.

"Have you lost your mind, Matyi? Don't you know that..."

"Well, tomorrow..."

And the next day he showed up with a little bag of money. It was full of krajcars...

"We have been playing cards together for the past twenty six years. I won all this money from you. Two hundred one forints. It will be enough for the boy to travel there and cover his expenses for the first month. He can find himself a child to tutor or some other type of employment during that time. He won't die of hunger. Diligence is the main thing."

We were dumbfounded.

"But there is one more problem. The boy has to know French to be able to understand lectures."

"He'll learn. He'll learn by September. I will teach him myself."

And the priest took me into his house for those two months. I had to be with him nonstop. He spoke to me in French. He started with greetings and short sentences. I had to write down everything I learned during the day while he was playing cards. I was able to speak some French by September.

I put some weight on during those two months. My brother who was a doctor hardly recognized me when I came up to Budapest.

"What a strong young man!" said one of his friends, "I can tell he was raised on the wheat fields of Bacska."

I was very proud as I traveled to Geneva, Switzerland. I found the priest's relative, the professor. He was a sixty year old, calm man, with sleepy eyes. He had a lot of books around him. His head was sunk as he sat in an armchair. I couldn't have imagined him fighting with a sword during the revolution.

He calmly read my letter of recommendation. Then he looked at me from under his red eyelids with a bored expression.

"Do you understand the language well, son?"

"I studied it throughout the whole summer."

"The whole summer?"

He asked me in French too. He shook his head and gave me a French book.

"Read it out loud and translate what you read. I'd like to find out if you understand what you are reading."

I read it. I did not understand any of it.

"Just go home, son," he said indifferently, "you would not be able to benefit from listening to lectures."

I just stared at him. I felt what he said was smart. But how should I go home? Should I put my poor priest to shame?

"I won't go home," I uttered, "I'd rather sweep streets for a year until I learn the language fluently."

The old man looked at me. He started to smile.

"I like your attitude." he said, "A person who is willing to sweep streets is ready to take on life's challenges. Well, okay. Where do you live, son?"

"In a sched. St. Victor Street 10. I rented it for six franks."

He wrote it down.

"What do you know besides sweeping streets?"

"I know how to draw and paint. I was always first in drawing. I didn't want to study philology, but I wanted to be a painter instead, or at least an engineer."

He nodded.

"I will try to look for something, so you can support yourself."

He sent for me three days later.

"Well, look," he said, "there is a wallpaper factory here. At times they need a young man who can draw and paint. They advertised for some help. You'll get forty franks per month. You can live on that much through your first year here. Speak French nonstop and read it too. Here is a list of textbooks. Buy them in a used bookstore and spend all your free time reading them. Then you'll be able to enroll in school in a year."

And he looked at me.

"Well, what is the matter?"

"I don't dare to let my parents and the priest know about this."

"Okay. I will write to them."

And he took down the priest's address.

I went to the wallpaper factory.

I had to work next to an old designer. My job was the coloring of all kinds of drawings. I had to watercolor the drawings ten to twenty different ways. They were evaluated. The most suitable one was chosen. It was carved into a wooden mold and the picture was pressed on paper by a roll.

The old designer's name was Lupen. He was a short French man with broad shoulders, and his long hair reached his shoulders. His short legs and face reminded me of a dachshund. He had a cheerful, honest personality.

I still don't understand how he was able to be so cheerful all the time. But there are people with such a happy personality. If he was able to drink a glass of beer at ten o'clock, it was evident that life was full of happiness for him, even though he wore shabby clothes.

His annual income was five thousand franks, a large sum at the time! And still, the bottoms of his pants were threadbare... He wore the same top hat for ten years and the same beige coat perhaps throughout his whole life.

When I was introduced to him he asked me so many questions that I felt like he was a police captain. He wanted to know who my father and mother were and what their occupation was. He also asked if I had any brothers or sisters. What did the wallpaper factory have to do with my family tree?

But he was a very nice man. He always made jokes and was enthusiastic about life. Sometimes he would pat me on my shoulder, and pretty soon I would get a raise. That was an encouragement to me.

The large room we were in was constructed with iron beams and had a glass roof. It was full of drawing boards on large tables. The factory's very strong glue and starch smell entered our space, but I got used to it in an hour. I got used to it so much that even today when I walk in front of a bookbinder or a woodworking shop and I smell the glue, I stop for a minute. I close my eyes and inhale as if it was a wonderful smell.

I saw only a young Italian man when I got settled in. He was an agile man who whistled constantly. He always stood toward my back and painted different flowers on large sheets of paper: violets, apple blossoms, anemones and everything that came to his mind. I can still picture his dirty, quick hands, his bright black eyes, his wide rimmed hat and his brown cloak with wings which flapped. He looked like a scarecrow when he was out on the streets.

The old man left the shop. I remembered right away that I needed to practice my French. I said to the Italian:

"Are there only the three of us who work here, monsieur?"

"There are four of us, monsieur."

And he raised his eyebrows with a smile, as if he just said something funny.

"And who is the fourth person?"

"The gattina."

And he raised his eyebrows in an even more peculiar way.

He spoke worse French than I did. He mixed French words with Italian. I didn't understand him.

"Gattina? What is a gattina?"

He pulled out a wrinkled, dirty little book from his pocket and looked into it.

"A cat. A beautiful cat! Mr. Lupen's cat."

And he laughed. I started to smile as well.

We did not continue our conversation, because Mr. Lupen entered the room. He grabbed his pencil and started to work. It was his job to draw ornamental frames around the Italian's flowers.

I had been working there for five days already when all of a sudden a girl who wore a white batiste blouse joined us. She was a seventeen year old blond girl. She had sort of a daffodil shape, kind of like the pictures decorating the storybooks of English children, except her face was round, instead of being long. She had curly hair, a baby nose, and a little mole in the middle of her left cheek. My eyes stopped on her. So this is gattina, the cat!

The girl walked straight to my boss.

"Bonjour Papa."

She kissed his hand. They exchanged a few words. She took off her hat and put down her parasol.

Lupen turned to me:

"My daughter. Her name is Georgette. She works here too. But her mother was just sick, Monsieur Kovaks.

Of course, I was Monsieur Kovaks. A wonderful feeling tingled inside me when I realized I got such a beautiful girl as a colleague. She shared a double table with me and was right in front of me! I thought I was really going to practice my French.

The girl took off her white silk gloves which reached her elbows. She pulled out her drawer and quickly took out a little ivory hand mirror and looked into it from left and right. Then she held a pencil with her thin fingers and started to draw lines with skilled eyes and confident hands.

The Italian turned around and looked at us. He winked at me and started to laugh.

She is truly a cat, I thought; a white cat, but a wonderful cat!

The girl lifted up her face when her father left.

"Excuse me, Monsieur Kovaks, but your name is so strange... It isn't French and it isn't German either. And she smiled. She had wonderful dimples when she smiled and her little sour cherry color mole was right at the edge of her dimple.

"It is a Hungarian name," I answered joyfully.

"Hungarian? I see, Austro-Hungarian."

"No, just Hungarian."

This is how we started to get to know each other.

My pulse however was beating twice as fast as before. I was feeling poems, and my heart turned into a musical clock. It played a soft tune every fifteen minutes. Of course I was the only one who could hear it. I looked at the Italian right in the first hour to see if he showed any interest in gattina.

I was relieved to see that he had an engagement ring on his finger. He was either already married or engaged. All of a sudden I felt great sympathy toward the entire country of Italy.

At ten o'clock the servant brought in a glass of beer and a glass of milk. He put the beer on Mr. Lupen's desk and the milk on Georgette's.

I tried to keep my eyes on her to see how she drank the milk. She took tiny gulps and licked it periodically.

Truly a cat!

The third day after lunch, as I walked toward the factory, my eyes stopped on a basket out of which a woman was selling flowers. One stem of rose... can't be expensive... if Georgette would find it in her water glass...

My musical clock was playing melodies.

"How much does a rose cost?"

"Only ten satims, monsieur."

"Only?"

My musical clock became silent. Ten satims meant a meal for me. Could I afford to buy a rose when I only made forty franks a month?

I kept walking.

To have dinner or not to have dinner? That was the Shakespearian question.

Finally I said:

"Not to have dinner!"

Fifteen minutes later the stem of rose was in her water glass.

Georgette came. She always came with her father, just as she returned home with him. She took off her little coat and removed her long gloves from her thin, white hands. I looked at her. My musical clock played a triumphant march.

Georgette turned toward the table and her eyes lit up with joy when she noticed the flower. All of a sudden she looked at me. Of course I cast down my eyes. We were silent for a few minutes.

"You?"

"Me. I hope you'll accept it."

"Thank you, Monsieur Kovaks."

She said my name with a sweet whisper and she looked at me with her warm, blinking, cat eyes.

My musical clock played nonstop that afternoon, but no composer ever wrote such melodies like the ones ringing inside me! What a wonderful idea it was from the priest that I should continue my education in Switzerland!

When Georgette finished work she took out the rose from the glass, wiped its stem off with a paper towel, and pinned it on her blouse. On her blouse! And she gave me a warm and grateful look. She stepped in front of me and offered her hand for a handshake.

"Bye, Monsieur Kovaks."

She looked into my eyes, and the magical dimples appeared on her face.

I felt the way she pressed my hand even at night. I gave up dinners from then on.

"What is a dinner good for?" I thought. "It is a useless invention."

Once, when she drank her glass of milk, it occurred to me that perhaps she would accept a bar of chocolate to go with the milk. She did accept it.

From that day I told myself that breakfast was also a useless invention. But hunger tormented me at times. But a question tormented me even more: would Georgette's musical clock start up as well, to play along with my clock?

I spent sleepless nights thinking about this! When I thought that Georgette would come to work with an engagement ring on, tears flooded my eyes and my musical clock played the Raquiem. No, Georgette could not belong to anyone else!

By that time I could not think of anything else other than Georgette. She was my only thought, day and night.

Her face radiated joy like a lamp radiates light. The room with the iron beams smelled bad until she arrived. But after she entered, all of a sudden it seemed to turn into a ball room decorated with lights and flowers. The air became full of wonderful fragrances, and relaxing music seemed to be playing around her.

I did not dare to talk to Georgette when her father was around, and she was also silent. But when Lupen left the room, I always practiced speaking French with great enthusiasm.

"This Italian is so happy!" I said to Georgette.

"Why, Monsieur Kovaks?"

"He is engaged. He is over the age of twenty and he is allowed to get married."

"Here we can get married earlier than that, Monsieur Kovaks."

"But my age would probably still be too young."

"How old are you, Monsieur Kovaks?

"I am eighteen."

"It is possible. In Switzerland it is possible, Monsieur Kovaks."

And she looked at me so sweetly that if someone looked at Mont Blanc like that all the snow and ice would have melted from it and the world would see green peaks instead of white ones.

It took me a few minutes before I was able to speak again.

"Please allow me a question, Georgette."

"Speak freely, Monsieur Kovaks."

"Do you have someone... special?"

"Oh," she answered and turned peony red, "how can you ask me such a thing, Monsieur Kovaks?

"I don't mind even if you get upset with me," I said, and my face burned as well, "but please answer this one question, please answer."

She smiled and closed her eyes.

"I don't have anyone."

Minutes passed again before my wildly playing musical clock allowed me to speak.

"Wonderful," I said, "wonderful!"

Georgette smiled. She looked at her palm and then at me and all of a sudden she became serious.

"There is nothing wonderful about it," she answered calmly. "I cannot get married for a long time, Monsieur Kovaks."

"Why not?"

"While my uncle is alive... I can't get married."

Her Papa stepped into the room.

I wondered all night about her mysterious uncle. Why couldn't Georgette get married while her uncle was alive? But I was glad he was still alive because I could not support Georgette as my wife on a forty franks per month pay. The truth is she ate a lot of chocolates. It didn't matter how big of a piece I put on her table, she never left any of it for the next day. And if I married her I was sure she would eat even more. I am not saying this to complain, because my heart beat with joy when she arrived in the morning and looked at the chocolate in silver wrapping.

"You brought me chocolate again, Monsieur Kovaks? Thank you."

And she put it away until her milk arrived at ten.

My pay was raised to fifty franks in November. But by that time flowers become more expensive too. I had to pay twenty satims for one stem of carnation and I couldn't stop. She got used to getting some chocolate in the morning and a carnation in the afternoon.

I don't know whether from the chocolate or from the carnation, but it was evident that she was gaining weight. I noticed her arms and face were getting rounder.

I ate lean meals at lunch which cost only one frank, even when the weather was freezing outside. I had to sew my bottoms closer and closer every week and my clothes were getting looser and looser on me. My size sixteen collar become enormously wide by December. I was almost terrified when I tried smaller sizes at the store. The shopkeeper thought size fourteen and a half would fit me.

By that time Lupen suspected or knew something about my musical clock, even though I had not even declared my feelings to Georgette. How could I have declared them; her rich uncle... my pay had to be raised to five hundred franks per month to be able to reach her uncle's shoulder.

But Lupen felt in me the five hundred frank pay too. I noticed several times that he kept an eye on me and had goodwill toward me. He even complimented me.

"He is an honest, diligent young man! He is magnificent with colors! He will get a big pay raise next spring."

I looked at Georgette joyfully. Her dimples appeared on her face.

One Saturday the Italian did not work. He asked for the day off for his wedding. Finally I was able to speak to Georgette the way I wanted to.

As soon as Lupen left, both of us stopped working. I looked at Georgette with devotion. She got up and came to my table as if she wanted to look at color samples.

She smiled at me.

"Aren't you happy, Monsieur Kovaks? You'll get good pay. Perhaps I will too."

"I am happy even without that," I answered, "if I can see you Georgette. Oh, Georgette," I said to her with my heart trembling, "Oh, Georgette, if you knew..."

She turned red and kept staring at the floor. She was touched.

"I did not even suspect," she answered, while she was still red, "I did not even suspect, Monsieur Kovaks..."

And she held out her hand.

Oh, what a beautiful hour it was. I felt as if wonderful organ music filled my heart and white apple blossoms rained on us from the heights.

I said it was an hour even though it only lasted for about three minutes as I got up, grabbed her hand, lifted it to my lips and pressed it with both of my hands while I practiced the most beautiful pronunciation of Georgette.

"Oh, Georgette... sweet Georgette..."

She closed her eyes in response and whispered with a red face:

"Oh, Monsieur Kovaks..."

Then she anxiously looked at the door and pulled back her arm. We went back to our seats.

"Tell me, Georgette," I said after a few minutes, "your uncle... Tell me something about your uncle."

"About Uncle Anri?" she answered with faint happiness. "Oh, he is a great man! He is a very distinguished man. When the spring arrives..."

She was still red. She glanced at the door.

"When the spring arrives, "she continued, "we'll walk to the cemetery and I will show you his crypt. You'll see, Monsieur Kovaks, that there are only one or two other crypts like that in the whole cemetery."

She pulled out her little ivory hand mirror and looked into it.

"Is he no longer alive?"

She looked at me cheerfully from behind her mirror.

"Of course he is alive! He just had a crypt made for himself. It is made of black marble and has a life size marble statue of an angel pointing toward the sky in front of it."

"It must have cost a fortune!"

"It cost thirty-six thousand franks, Monsieur Kovaks. He is a rich man, Monsieur Kovaks. He is a great, smart man. He sent that money from there."

"From where?"

"From Australia."

"Is that where he lives?"

"Yes."

"Is he a manufacturer?

She smiled.

"Not exactly, but something similar. He raises ostriches. He has five, six hundred ostriches, or perhaps thousands. We don't know. We have not heard from him for ten years."

Lupen stepped into the room.

Georgette continued her work with her red face cast down. I tried to hide the excitement from my face as well. I worked diligently. I thought to myself that it wasn't wise to put one's wealth in ostriches. They could catch some kind of an epidemic like foot and mouth disease...

But it didn't matter. The main thing was that he was rich and Georgette had already chosen and she had chosen me!

I looked at her in secret. She looked back at me. Her Papa was dipping his brush into paint indifferently.

I was living on even less from then on. I had to buy clothes and ties, even though I was really sorry to spend the money. Even then I bought a carnation and a piece of chocolate for Georgette daily. I wasn't sorry to spend the money on those.

When Lupen came to work on a day about a week before Christmas, I hardly recognized him. His eyebrows looked like they grew together and his nose seemed larger. He barely paid attention to me when I greeted him.

I was shocked.

Georgette also had a long face as she followed him, and gave me a sad look.

Well, I surely felt like a dog in a snare. Georgette must have told her parents about us and they didn't like it! They would surely fire me from the factory today!

My musical clock played confusing minor chords. I felt a tragic cold blow in my spine. My legs trembled as much as if I stood under a gallows tree.

I couldn't wait for Lupen to go over to visit the factory workers because I wanted to talk to Georgette. Finally he grabbed his worn top hat and signaled to the Italian to join him in the roll room.

Georgette did not even wait for my question to look at me. She seemed so sad as she looked toward me, like the sun looking through the rain clouds in the fall.

"Sad news, Monsieur Kovaks."

"What, Georgette?"

"He died..."

"Your uncle?"

She nodded.

Then I realized this could be good news for me even though it is sad for her.

"Please accept my condolence," I whispered finally while I was feeling some relief from my anxiety.

"Thank you," she answered in a faint voice. "We are not truly mourning him. He deceived us. He deceived us, Monsieur Kovaks. Oh, what a misfortune!"

She pulled out her handkerchief and pressed it to her eyes. Pretty soon wet spots appeared on it.

"Oh! Oh!"

"Georgette," I said as I hurried to her, "don't cry my dear. I don't even understand..."

And I grabbed her hand, pressed it and lifted it to my lips.

Georgette stood up and hugged me as if she wanted to shed her tears on my heart.

"Comfort me, Monsieur Kovaks! Comfort me, because my heart is breaking!"

I was glad to hug her and my heart trembled.

"But how should I comfort you, sweet Georgette? Didn't you just say that you are not mourning your uncle?"

"No, no," she answered while she cried violently, "I am mourning us. You see... my uncle... died in a poor house in Sydney. Oh... comfort me!"

The news shook me as well, but still I tried to comfort her. I thought since she hugged me I could kiss her cheek. I kissed her forehead. I also kissed her wet cheek under her eyes and kept saying to her:

"Don't cry, little Georgette, don't cry. As long as I live..."

As I hugged her I noticed with terror that Lupen was already in the room. It was strange that he acted like he didn't see us and kept pacing up and down the room with an anxious face.

I got scared and pulled back my arms, but Georgette stayed next to me and I couldn't even step back, because the way we were standing the desk was behind us.

"No doubt," Lupen said as he stood in front of us, "this is a great misfortune to us, Monsieur Kovaks. Oh, what a worthless drunkard! Good for nothing! He was my daughter's only hope."

When Georgette heard this, she collapsed into her chair and continued to cry on her table.

I was stunned as I stood there.

"Miss Georgette is not poor," I stuttered, "not poor."

"Not poor?"

"No" I answered with confidence "anybody who is young and beautiful and is able to work is not poor, Mr. Lupen."

Lupen's eyes cleared up for a minute but then became cloudy again.

"A poor house? Do you know what a poorhouse is?! Disgrace! Drunkard pig! And the will... Did my daughter tell you what the will says?"

"She didn't tell me, Mr. Lupen."

"Well, his will says that his only possession was the crypt in Geneva and he wanted to have his body brought home at my expense... Should I be the one to get him home? Me, a poor beggar?"

"This is really an impolite and unreasonable wish," I answered when I was able to get some air, "because the crypt is an asset and it can be sold."

Lupen's eyes became large.

"Well! We didn't even think about that."

Georgette was so surprised at my idea that she took her handkerchief from her face and her eyes stuck to me with interest and admiration.

"It can be sold," I repeated even more boldly. "There is no dead person in it, so it can be sold. It is an expensive building, so it is a house. It is an inheritance because it is a house. The deceased had no children, so you are the beneficiaries."

The girl looked at her father. The father looked at his daughter. My idea almost stunned them.

Lupen moved finally. He stepped to the desk and picked up his pipe. It was a short little pipe. He lit it and walked up and down the room while he was thinking.

"This is not a bad idea!" he kept saying, "Not bad. You are a smart man, my friend Kovaks."

He said to me when the bell rang for lunch:

"Join us, young man. We can walk together."

I was glad to walk with them through the bridge and the streets until we got to their entrance.

We talked constantly about the crypt during the next few days. Lupen talked with several attorneys. They all had different opinions on the matter. One thought the crypt could not be sold as an inheritance; another thought if the diseased was already buried then the family could dispose of the crypt; only the state had to approve it first. A third one said the crypt stayed in the deceased name for fifty years and if he did not move into it during that time then the beneficiaries could ask for it.

Lupen arrived with good news one day and with bad news the next. He felt I was part of his family already and he started to tell me the news as soon as he arrived.

"Good news, good news, Monsieur Kovaks: the crypt is ours."

Or:

"Bad news, bad news, Monsieur Kovaks: the crypt belongs to the deceased."

He shook his hair when he was upset, the way a dachshund shakes his ears.

He surprised me the day before Christmas by inviting me to have dinner with them Sunday night.

I was happy. I washed myself three times in the afternoon on that memorable day and spent hours with the little, tiny, blond hair under my nose which heralded that my moustache would soon be arriving. I tried to make it darker by paint. But the paint stuck to my skin of course. That is why I had to wash myself so many times.

It was true that the inheritance worth millions was gone, but Georgette herself was a treasure! And still she may have some dowry perhaps. A family with such rich uncles... And perhaps the reason old Lupen wore an old top hat and threadbare pants was so he could provide for Georgette. He was a frugal man. What did he spend his large salary on?

But, would I be able to take home Georgette, my beautiful, live treasure? Or would we be working happily together for a while by the double desk?

I left my place at seven o'clock and felt like I was going home.

I would surely sit next to Georgette. I knew she had siblings. Once a sluggish, young student joined us and they introduced him to me as Georgette's brother. Another time I saw two little girls with her and Mr. Lupen on Rosseau Island in October. I only saw them from the bridge and didn't have the courage to join them. The two little girls had thin legs, as if they were made out of reeds and they were joyfully running around Georgette.

She did have brothers and sisters, and they would be my brothers and sisters. What a great feeling! I was far from my homeland and a loving family was waiting for me along with the calmness of a warm and happy Christmas Eve.

I almost stumbled on a basket of oranges that were placed in front of a delicatessen store.

Well, I thought, the children probably have a Christmas tree. I should give them something to put on it. I thought about what to do. I couldn't take them oranges. They were ordinary and cheap.

I noticed in the shop window two little lambs made out of sugar. They seemed more suitable.

"How much do they cost?"

"Half frank."

I was stunned. If the two of them were one frank... that was exactly the price of a lunch. Should I not eat lunch right on Christmas day?

The money I brought from home was gone already. I had to supplement my forty franks I had coming in per month. The books I purchased were expensive too, especially because I had to buy a dictionary. I had spent the last pennies of my little wealth I brought from home just the day before.

I kept going.

Then I stopped again. I couldn't go there without a gift! And I would get dinner there, a holiday dinner. Perhaps I would even upset my stomach with it, so I wouldn't have any appetite the next day.

I bought the two lambs. Then I stopped before a flower shop. There were some magnificent lilies of the valley in a glass, among ferns, azaleas and rhododendrons. There was a small wreath made out of fresh forget-me-nots around the glass and the fresh, dewy lilies of the valley seemed even whiter in the little blue wreath.

Hm! How foolish I was when I bought those two sugar lambs so quickly! I wasn't thinking! I had to bring flowers to Georgette. It was impossible for me to go there without them.

"How much do these lilies of the valley cost?"

"They cost twenty satims per stem, monsieur."

I almost collapsed. I had to take at least ten stems, which would cost two franks.

The lady who sold the flowers already lifted them out of the shop window and put them in front of me. What a magnificent fragrance! I couldn't help it, I had to buy it for my little... wife!

"Can you sell them to me for less?"

"I can give you six stems for a frank."

I bought six stems. I carried them in wrapping paper. I had to get my stomach upset for two days. And still, I was happy. My musical clock played Christmas music.

It was seven o'clock by the time I rang their doorbell. I heard loud rumbling from inside, kind of like when a regiment marches through a bridge.

"Come back! Come back!" I heard Georgette scream.

The door opened the next minute and Georgette's rosy face smiled at me with her adorable dimples and bright, beautiful, clear eyes.

"Welcome, Monsieur Kovaks!"

The smell of roasted meat coming from the kitchen was wonderful.

I kissed Georgette's hand and looked at all the children around her with surprise. All of them had the same black eyes.

So there were more of them! And I only brought two lambs.

In a little while a door was opened and even more black eyed children appeared. Lupen's dachshund figure was among them. He held a barefooted, serious baby, who wore a little shirt. He too had black eyes.

"Please go away, my children!"

I don't know what I said, and I don't even know what I thought or how they took off my fall coat, which I called my winter parka. All of a sudden I stood in a room among lots of children.

I was introduced to a woman who had a thick waist and wore an apron all the way to her neck and a head scarf.

"My wife," said Lupen.

The woman with the jowly face and thick waist kindly shook my hand.

"I heard many good things about you, Monsieur Kovaks."

I have never seen such a big white headscarf, such a big face, and such a big egg whisk like the one she held in her hand.

It was strange that she resembled Georgette. She even had a mole on her left cheek, but it was the size of a penny and hairs were sticking out of it.

I felt like I walked into some kind of a school, and Lupen and his wife were the school teachers.

"You are surprised, aren't you?" shouted Lupen joyfully. "I have a lot of children, don't I? Many beautiful children! Look at this one…"

He lifted the barefoot child who sat on his arm.

"Have you ever seen anything more beautiful? Has Murillo ever painted a more beautiful angel?"

And he wiped the angel's nose.

"But this one…"

"No, not all of them are mine. This one with the pear shaped head is not mine. He is a relative, but we love him as if he was ours."

And he shouted at the children.

"Line up, children!"

The children lined up in a minute like the pipes of an organ. There was a three year old at one end of the row and at the teenager I had already met was at the other end.

"One is still missing!"

The missing child ran in. She was a fourteen year old girl, brown like her father. She wore an apron and carried a wooden spoon. She got in the line. Georgette followed her. It was evidently not the first time they had lined up before their father.

"Shout: Vive la Hongrie!"

The children shouted. Lupen introduced them to me one by one. There were fifteen of them, including the child he was holding, so fourteen of them were his.

I still had the two sugar lambs and the flower in my hand.

"Forgive me," I said to Lupen, "I didn't know you have so many children and brought only two lambs."

And I gave them to him. I figured I would let him divide them among the children, if he could.

"We will cut them into small pieces after lunch. Let's hang them on the lamp here until then."

I handed Georgette the flower. She was touched.

"Oh, how thoughtful, Monsieur Kovaks," she whispered happily.

She smelled the flowers, kissed them and looked at them with pleasure.

"Well, but now let's set the table!" Lupen stamped his feet. "Let's put some wood in the oven."

He led me into a nearby room, which smelled like tobacco. It was his bedroom and had a worn desk and a drafting table too.

"Aren't they beautiful children?" he said joyfully, "and all of them are healthy. Light up a cigarette, dear Kovaks. Or do you prefer a pipe? I just purchased some new pipe stems. Wait, I put them in the drawer because the children were blowing bubbles with them."

And he turned to his drawer.

"Please hold the baby for a minute."

I have never had such a lively child in my hand. I held him as if he was made out of glass. And I must have given him a strange look, because he became even more serious and started to scream and wiggle. I was barely able to hold him.

Loud noise could be heard from the other room too, including some cries. But the screams were louder than the cries.

"I will lick it too! I want to lick it too!"

Lupen opened the door. The little ones were all on the top of the table. One of them kneeled on it and licked the sugar lamb. The rest of them followed him.

"Quiet," shouted Lupen at the door.

The children quickly got off the table. They looked toward us fearfully.

"Gil," said Lupen, "take this screaming baby!"

Gil was busy setting the table by then. She was unfolding a long, white table cloth with Georgette in the middle of the room.

"We have order in this house," Lupen bragged. "I just shout once and there is quiet in the house. Oh, I just remembered today is Christmas Eve. Children, come make a circle! Let's sing a Christmas song before dinner."

And he lifted his finger and the children started to sing.

For dinner we had cherry soup, mutton in onion souse and soufflé at the end.

The fourteen year old daughter served the food with the help of a sleepy maid who had red eyes. All the children quickly devoured their food. The little ones faces became messy.

"More! More!" they kept saying nonstop. "Only this much?"

Lupen shouted at them.

"Quiet!"

He slapped his hand on the table a few times and the plates danced.

It did not escape my attention that the plates were made of cheap porcelain and were not even the same color. Two of the children ate from yellow plates and one of them from a green one. The silverware was also mismatched.

It was impossible to fulfill my plan of eating so much that I would upset my stomach, even though Georgette kindly encouraged me to eat more.

"Monsieur Kovaks…"

"Thank you, Georgette, but I had just enough."

Her mother sat down in front of me. The little baby was in her lap. She also kindly offered me the food.

"Monsieur Kovaks, please feel right at home."

At the end of dinner the old man poured hot sugar on fruit to make desert. He put raisins, cinnamon and almonds in it too. A couple of the children burned their mouth and screamed. Then they became sleepy and their mother and one of the older sisters carried them out one by one. I still don't know where they took them.

Lupen lit up his pipe.

"Well," he said joyfully, "we still have a surprise for you, Monsieur Kovaks. Gil, here is the desk drawer key. Please bring in the picture here. We are going to laugh at you, Monsieur Kovaks, we will have a good laugh!"

And he laughed already. Georgette mysteriously smiled at me.

Gil returned with a red book like object. Lupen opened it. It had a red silk case inside of it covering a picture. He put the picture in front of me.

I really was surprised.

It was Georgette's picture. It was a beautiful water color. It depicted Georgette in white batiste clothes as she rested her elbow on a stand next to her while she smiled.

The charming dimples were on her face, even the small mole above her left dimple... And her figure was very light, like a fairy of an English story book.

"Superb!" I said with honest astonishment.

"Truly superb!"

And I glanced at Georgette.

"Well, this is a very good picture of you."

They all laughed.

Her mother entered the room. She saw that I was looking at the picture. She sat down among us again and laughed so much that her jolly face shook.

I didn't understand what they were laughing at.

Finally Georgette spoke while she bashfully smiled.

"This is not my picture, Monsieur Kovaks."

"Not your picture?"

They laughed even harder.

"This is mother's picture. It was taken when she was young."

I kept thinking as I was going home. I couldn't believe that woman with her large face and headscarf was just like Georgette some time ago; so light-figured, with such thin arms, clear eyes, silky hair with lips of a fairy.

At night my head felt like I had a storm of Lake Balaton inside of it. Troubled waves. I could see children with black eyes. I kept hearing noises and from time to time a loud shout of a man.

"Quiet!"

Then the waves quieted down. A rosy face of a fairy smiled at me from the clouds.

I was almost sick when I sat down to work the day after Christmas. I put the usual chocolate on Georgette's table and I kept mixing the paints indifferently.

A lot of snow had fallen during the holiday. It was snowing almost nonstop. I was not getting proper nourishment. I was living on carrots, like a canary.

But as soon as Georgette stepped in the room, all my troubles disappeared. I felt like sunshine filled the room. My musical clock started up and it played a song of greeting.

She wore a Persian lamb fur coat. Her hat was also made of the same Persian lamb fur. It looked great on her curly, beautiful, blond hair! And there were three lilies of the valley in her hair, above her forehead, from the lilies of the valley I gave her.

She smiled at me while she was still far away. She gladly allowed me to take off her fur coat. She took off her gloves as well and shook my hand only after that.

"How did you spend your holiday, Monsieur Kovaks?"

"Joyfully," I answered. "I kept thinking about you the whole time."

She smiled.

She sat down at her desk, took a long glance into her mirror with the white handle, and organized her rulers. She kept smiling the whole time.

And we worked as usual.

At times I looked at her as if I was examining her.

...Her mother was just like her when Lupen fell in love with her. It would have been impossible for him not to have fallen in love with her! And perhaps Lupen sat in my chair and perhaps his wife sat in Georgette's chair. So everything is repeated in the world! Everything! This meant that everything would happen with Georgette and me the same way it happened with Mr. and Mrs. Lupen...

A lead mountain weighed down on my chest. I looked at her and shook my head.

No, no. Fourteen... that is many!

When Lupen went to visit the factory workers, Georgette got up and came over to my desk as usual. And she looked at me with a friendly smile, as if she said: Come and hug me! Kiss the dimple of my cheek and smell the fragrance of my hair. This is our minute.

And I got up, hugged her, kissed the dimple of her cheek and smelled the fragrance of her hair.

"Dear Georgette," I whispered to her, "you are the only one, the only one!"

She hugged my neck and bashfully whispered:

"I love you so much, Monsieur Kovaks!"

And she kissed me on my lips.

"I love you so much, Kovaks!"

She had never said this before and she had never kissed me, except for that one time. I became so excited that the brush still trembled in my hand an hour later. "She is mine!" I thought triumphantly. Mine! It was true that she would be like her mother, but that would be a long time from now. And it was not certain that she would have a lot of children. There are a lot of women who don't have children, even though their mother did.

And I kept glancing toward her joyfully while I kept working. She also looked at me as well.

"Tell me, Georgette," I said softly. "Did your mother work here as well, in your chair?"

"Oh, no." she answered, "My mother can't draw."

This statement had completely cleared the last cloud from my sky.

"I will marry her," I thought. "I will marry her as soon as they'll give her to me!"

In the same hour I heard a familiar voice from behind the door.

"Monsieur Kovacs!"

He said my last name as Kovacs. The voice was very familiar. A minute later the door opened and the old Kelemen Mikes trudged in.

"I was in the neighborhood," he muttered. "I thought about you... Well, how are you, my friend?"

"Like a blossoming tree," I answered happily.

"Please have a seat."

"I am glad. I am glad. Well, that is why you don't visit me, but it doesn't matter."

And he also glanced at the girl with his sleepy eyes.

"Well, how are your studies coming along?"

"I am zealously practicing the language."

"But the books, the books..."

"The books?"

"Did you buy them?"

"Unfortunately I did."

"Why unfortunately?"

"I have no use for them. I am not going to become a teacher. I can make a living doing what I am doing now. It is possible to live like this. They keep raising my income. I have a bright future ahead of me."

The old man nodded.

"Well, that is good too."

"And , well," I continued triumphantly, "I am going to get married too."

"What?"

"Yes, I will."

"While you are still so young?"

"It is possible in Switzerland. This is a wonderful country."

"That is true."

And he glanced at the girl.

"Is she the one?"

"You guessed it."

"Hm. Does she have anything?"

"Isn't herself enough? Just take a look at her."

"Well, she is pretty, pretty. Whose daughter is she?"

"She is my supervisor's daughter."

Lupen was working with his back toward us. He glanced at us when he heard the word supervisor. Mikes nodded toward him. He nodded back. Then we continued talking in Hungarian.

"But he is a poor man!"

"You are mistaken. They even have a crypt."

"A crypt?"

"Yes. They inherited it recently. A millionaire uncle left it to them."

And I told him what a strange millionaire that uncle was.

Mikes was amazed and sleepy at the same time. He shook his head.

"How many siblings does the miss have?"

"How many siblings? Well... fourteen."

"Hm."

I was getting bored. I kept looking at my paint brush. The old man got up and shook my hand.

"Well, congratulations," he said kindly. "Please visit me sometime, my dear friend."

And he trudged away.

I walked Georgette to the entrance of her house at noon. Lupen told me confidentially that a welcome surprise was waiting for me in the New Year. He looked into the directors' book; a big raise, big!

I understood. He recommended me to the directors and asked them to show their appreciation toward me.

Georgette glanced at me with her eyes shining with joy. I looked back at her happily. So Lupen would give her to me! To me! Perhaps this spring already!

But we didn't get through half of the winter when a mailman stepped into our factory. He put a telegram and one hundred franks on my desk.

I was frightened as I read the telegram.

> *Your father is sick. Come right away!*
>
> *Your mother.*

Georgette turned pale.

"Is something wrong?"

"Yes." I groaned. "My poor father."

Georgette's eyes welled up with tears. She pulled out her handkerchief.

Old Lupen was deeply moved as he stood in front of me.

"Be brave, my friend," he said to comfort me. "I will ask the directors to give you a month off from work."

Both of them came with me to the train station. Georgette hugged me while we stood on the platform and cried as she kissed me.

"Don't stay too long! Don't stay long, my sweet Kovaks!"

She put in my pocket a lock of hair and an artificial forget-me-not, which were wrapped in tissue paper.

I was teary eyed when I answered her:

"I won't stay long, Georgette, no..."

"Mr. Lupen, please take good care of this girl... Our relationship is obviously not a secret to you, Mr. Lupen."

Lupen gave me a warm handshake.

"Don't worry, my son. You will find Georgette when you return."

I cried all the way through Switzerland, Tirol, Corinthia and from Pagerhof until Zombor in Hungary. I loved my father very much. The thought that I would arrive for his funeral made my heart despair.

When I opened our home's door I saw my father was in the middle of playing cards with the priest at the table.

"You rascal!" he shouted with joy. "Well, I am glad to have you home, rascal!"

What I suffered after this could not be painted with the paint of nine wallpaper factories.

"My married son," my father kept saying.

"The crypt owner," the priest kept saying.

"The father of fourteen children!" my brothers kept saying.

I sure was angry at Kelemen Mikes of Switzerland. I cried. I bought a pistol with my leftover money and went to the park at the edge of the city to shoot myself.

I was eighteen years old... And who shoots himself after lunch? I just sat there like a sick chicken, in the shadow of a willow tree and I mourned. The sky was blue. The ground was full of life. A mayfly played in front of me in the air. Should I be the only one to die? I took out the lock of hair and the forget-me-not. I felt as if the forget-me-not spoke to me:

"Live, work and don't be sad. Fight for your life, like I do. Just don't forget, just don't forget!"

I sold the pistol the next day. I used the money to buy a gold plated silver locket. I put the lock of hair in it. I hooked the locket on my watch's chain.

I wore it for a long time.

My sorrowful, great grief gave birth to only one poetic letter. I wrote to Georgette that I was deceived and my heart became the subject of a cruel game. I asked her to be steadfast. I would study in Budapest to become an engineer. Four years is not that long. The flames she started in my heart would be burning during that time. I ended my letter by writing: Just don't forget me! Just don't forget me!

Georgette tried to comfort me in her response. She wrote that the flames would continue burning in her heart as well, and I should write to her from time to time. She ended her letter by writing:

Yours always:

Georgette

I did study, and wrote to her from time to time. I wrote to her that I carried her lock of hair and the forget-me-not under my heart, and perhaps we would see the wonderful day when not only her lock of hair would be mine, but the blue forget-me-not would be placed into the silk case with the picture they showed me.

She responded, and it was evident that she was touched. She assured me that the rest of her hair would not belong to anyone else and she would be the one who inherited the portrait in the silk case, because surely nobody else could inherit it.

Then I had to study a lot. Great opportunities opened up to me. An outstanding engineer hired me to work with him and took me to England for four months. When I returned I saw even the stars in the sky with the eyes of an engineer.

Later I realized that my locket became worn. The gold plating wore off. It looked like an ordinary tin merchandise. I opened it. The lock of hair and the forget-me-not were still in it.

I mused as I looked at them. My musical clock started to play soft moll chords. "Don't forget, just don't forget!" I put the locket in the same box I kept my report cards in. I wanted to write to her, to apologize, to ask some questions, to let her know that I was thinking of her. But something came up and I left the letter writing for the next day. Then on the next day something else occupied me...

Then the time went by. It slowly took away all the flowers of my youth and took the music of my music clock as well.

In the end the only thing I had of little Georgette was her lock of hair and the forget-me-not.

Lucky day.

I turned twelve years old today and my good father gave me a newly minted five korona coin and he said to me:

"On this day make a wise resolution. I will leave it up to you what. And let your resolution shine in front of your eyes for the rest of your life."

I spent the five koronas on chocolate filled bonbons and a Japanese box which had a key. I locked my diary away from the girls. And I thought for a long time about what my wise resolution should be. I didn't want to make a resolution which is too hard to keep, but I wanted something that would shine in front of me for the rest of my life. Finally I made the resolution that I will never get married.

Unlucky day.

I got an 'F' in Latin and even though I told my teacher that my birthday was yesterday, that meant nothing to him! I still had a little money left, twelve fillers, and on my way home I spent it on raisins so I would feel better. And as soon as I stepped in the room, Emma said to me:

"What happened to you?"

And Ethel also said:

"What happened to you?"

"Nothing."

"You cried! I can tell from looking at your eyes!" said Emma, "You got another 'F', didn't you?"

And Yolanda also made some comments.

"Silence," I said, "or I will mess up your hair!"

And they would have told my parents about what happened to me, but luckily Mrs. Iza came with Martha and she wore new pink clothes which made them forget about me. It was a good thing that Mrs. Iza stayed for lunch with Martha. Their visit made my sisters forget about my troubles. And we ate cooked cabbages and my good mother put more on my plate than she usually does. And my good father said to me:

"Why are you picky? You will eat it!"

And I ate it.

And Ethel looked at me and seemed to be rejoicing at my suffering. And Emma did too and Yolanda also. Nice sisters! But even my cousin did the same thing. Nice cousin!

And I saw on my good father's face that he felt sorry for me during my suffering and kindly said after I finished the cabbage:

"Erno turned twelve years old yesterday."

Mrs. Iza wished me a happy birthday. Martha also did and she kissed me. If it didn't happen at the table I am sure she would have bitten my ear.

And my good father said:

"The resolution?"

"I made one," I answered.

"Well, and what is your resolution?"

I hesitated, but finally I made the decision to tell them.

"My resolution is that I will never get married."

And they laughed at me.

Only my good father approved of it and that was satisfying to me. Then Mrs. Iza started to interrogate me:

"Why?"

"Because," I answered, "because I know what women are like."

And I looked at the girls with disdain.

Lucky day.

We had pineapple parfait at lunch. We were at the Veszprem's home in the afternoon. Miklosh got some oil paint. I got to see how he paints with it.

Well, it is neat to have all that paint, canvas and easel, but it is not practical, because the paint drips on the painter's arm. And we decided to become artists.

It is nice for them. All of the five children in the family are boys.

Unlucky day.

I got an 'F' in Latin and in geometry as well. My good father reprimanded me and told me I should make Emma my example and my younger sisters, because they are such good students. I didn't say anything, because he wants me to stay quiet at times like that, but Ethel begged me in the afternoon to do her homework in writing. The topic was:

What can our nation thank Janos Hunyadi for?

"Would you like me to write it?" I said with bitterness.

I am a bad student, the donkey of the family and I should be the one lending my brain to my shining examples! They can flatter me all they want...

"Good," answered Emma. "Tomorrow I will bake the almond pastry and I won't put a lot of jam in it!"

And I did not do her homework, despite of what she said.

Ordinary day.

I did write Ethel's exercise. And the girls put their new spring clothes on for the first time. And Emma was still in a bad mood, because I told her:

"You are pale like an unbaked loaf of bread."

She didn't believe it, but Ethel also said:

"Even your lips are colorless."

My good mother sent us to sit on the balcony to get some fresh air. Emma's color really did return on the balcony and she turned red like a red lobster. And as we sat on the balcony a soldier walked toward us with a dull face.

"Look," said Ethel. "It is the Zulu."

And she laughed.

First we didn't understand what she was laughing at. Then she explained it.

"Don't you see? Our butcher's dog... he joined the army."

We laughed because he did look just like Zulu.

Emma was upset with us. She said:

"That is not nice!"

But we didn't let her educate us in manners.

And I said Zulu must have stomach cramps and that is the reason he keeps looking up toward us so bitterly. And we almost burst from laughter.

"Bark down to him!" Ethel encouraged me. "You'll see he'll bark back."

And I leaned out from the balcony and barked down:

"U-u-u."

We couldn't control ourselves. And Emma was upset when she went inside and told our good mother that we laugh at the pedestrians and also bark at them.

"It was only a soldier," I tried to make an excuse for my behavior.

"It is not true, because he was a volunteer."

I tried to tell her that Emma was lying, but my two younger sisters were on her side. I will not sit with them on the balcony again, even if they ask me to!

Bad day.

We had cabbage for lunch. And I will never talk to Emma again. Only as much as necessary when we are with our parents, because my red ink was gone and I looked for it everywhere. And when Emma drank some water, she wiped her mouth with her handkerchief and I noticed a red dot on her handkerchief. I was dumbfounded.

"Did you steal my red ink?"

And I stepped to her desk and pulled out her drawer and everything fell out of it. And she was angry and I was angry too. And I grabbed her hair. Ethel hit my head with a ruler and Emma scratched my face with her nails.

My good mother ran into the room when she heard the great battle and she quickly disciplined us. My left cheek is still warmer. And I told her everything and Emma's left cheek is most likely warmer than mine. But my good father was more just. He only made Emma responsible. He said it was unheard of that a seventeen-year-old girl painted her lips and it was a disgrace. And my parents checked her face to see if it was painted but only her lips were.

And Emma cried like a trumpet and all three of the girls cried, like three trumpets, and they swore to repay me. But I am not afraid.

116

Exciting day.

As I was coming home from school in the afternoon I noticed Zulu in front of our house as he stood there and kept looking up. He was waiting for me, of course. He was even holding a cane!!!

It was lucky that I noticed him from a good distance. I wanted him to turn his back toward me so I could sneak in our entrance. I am afraid he will be looking for me in the morning again.

Bad day.

Today Yolanda asked me to do her homework in mathematics. And even my good mother ordered me to do it. I was truly upset, because they were just playing with puppets and I should be the only one who works.

Well, I did it, but I put some mistakes in it. Emma still looked at me without any emotion on her face and Ethel did not say a word to me either. She only said:

"Our relationship is dead."

"Peace to its remains!" I answered.

At least they won't bother me when I am in my room. Zulu did not show up in the morning, but when I looked out of the window after lunch I saw that he was waiting for me. I did not even go anywhere in the afternoon.

Mixed day.

Today we ate cherry for the first time this year.

I was barely able to get home in the afternoon. Zulu watched for me again with his cane. He must be a very unforgiving man.

When I studied in my room and looked over into the other room, I noticed that Emma sat by the window with her puppet and looked around fearfully. I thought she wanted to play with the puppet, because she is not allowed to do that anymore, but she still puts it into her lap in secret when we don't see it. I kept a close watch on her and when she looked at me I pretended I was reading my book. In a little while I noticed she was red and she was reading some kind of a letter. Soon I took off my shoes and tried to sneak up to her on tiptoes, but the floor crackled and she got scared and tried to hide the letter.

"Give it to me."

"No!"

We fought and she realized that her resistance was futile and I was about to capture her letter. She put the letter in her mouth and ate it. And she was very upset with me. She even cried. We said some unkind words to each other. And finally I said to her:

"I hate you, the same way I hate cabbages!"

117

And I saw that her eyes were fearful that evening, but why did she make me upset?

Mixed day.

Emma did not talk to me again all day and I am sure we would have been upset with each other forever, but something else happened. I was chasing a bumble bee with a carpet beater and the bumble bee landed on our porcelain lamp shade which had holly hock flowers painted on it. I hit the lampshade, and even though I did it gently, the lampshade cracked. And Emma saw what happened and her eyes shone with joy.

I begged her not to say anything to our parents and I promised her everything, but she said it was impossible for her to forgive me. But then she must have changed her mind. And when my good mother noticed the crack in the lamp shade during the evening, she became angry and asked:

"Who broke it?"

And Emma calmly answered:

"I broke it, dear mother, by accident."

Well, these girls... They are born masters of lying.

Exciting day.

Martha visited us and a girl we have not met before. She was a baroness' daughter and she had a camera with her. And Martha wore a new purple dress, because she turned twelve years old today. I would have liked to make fun of her, but I couldn't because of the girl who took some pictures. She is the baroness' daughter and she was very proud of her Kodak as well as her mother. She took various group pictures of us. And Emma asked her to take a picture of her alone and as she sat there with an innocent look on her face, I sneaked behind her and used my fingers to show the ears of a donkey on her head. And they really laughed and told her and there were no more plates in the camera.

She became so upset with me that she called me a brat and that made me upset with her. Nobody has the right to call me a brat in this world, except for my good father and good mother!

Ordinary day.

Zulu did not show himself. It is possible that he was looking for me on a street corner, but I was smart to walk in the middle of the road when I went to school and I frequently looked behind me. Perhaps he got tired of looking for me.

I saw in the afternoon that Emma sat by the window. There were two books in front of her and she was writing. I left the door open in case she wanted to talk. Well, she did come to me and said:

"Are you still upset?"

"I am," I answered.

And she then begged me and gave me a handful of almonds, so I would not be mad at her, and she asked me to look over her writing and check her spelling. I did.

Good day.

I painted a really nice tiger, as he stood in tall grass, and everyone liked it. My good mother gave me five koronas to get it framed so we could hang it in our dining room. I put my autograph on the picture and wrote on it that it was my first work of art and I titled it: *Tiger in the wild.* I put the date on it as well.

Bad day.

I had to go to get Emma because our maid was washing clothes. And as I was walking dreamily toward the school I almost stumbled into Zulu on Borz Street. He was only about three yards from me. I am sure he would have grabbed my collar but I jumped and ran away. And Emma came home by herself and I was scolded and did not get supper, except Emma gave me half of her roll in secret.

Bad day.

Emma had to take an exam today and Martha was also taking the same exam. I hardly recognized Martha in her new poppy colored clothes.

I didn't feel like playing with them because I will be the one sweating tomorrow, and if I get a bad question in Latin, I will fail.

And they whispered to each other in the dining room and laughed while they were looking at me and this made me angry.

When Martha stood in front of my painting, she spoke loudly, just so I could hear her.

"What kind of a sick cat is this? Does he perhaps live in a poor house? And why is he standing in toothpicks?"

And they all laughed.

And Emma answered her:

"It is not a cat. You can read under the picture what it is."

And they laughed again.

I wasn't allowed to close the door because the dining room needed some fresh air. And my anger was eating me inside. And I thought about what I could say to Martha, so the anger would eat her as well. I thought about messing up her hair, but she already new that trick. I decided to twist Emma's doll's leg and to straighten Ethel's curved comb. I planned to heat it on the stove and straighten it. I was going to make fun of Martha's clothes.

And I grabbed my book to go downstairs to the courtyard to study and I said to Martha:

"Your clothes should have been decorated with a seal."

"Why?"

"Because," I answered, "because its color is just like sealing wax."

And the girls laughed and Martha became pale in her anger.

Exciting day.

Our family walked together on Margaret Island in the afternoon. And Zulu sat there under a tree. I was terrified!

He got up as soon as he saw me and started to follow us... I went to the front of our group right away and pretended to be interested in the plants around us. But he just kept waiting for me to fall behind. He sat down at a nearby table in the restaurant. He was so mad at me that he followed us even on the way back. But I was smart enough to avoid him.

French day.

The girls got a French teacher and I have to study with them, but I just have to listen.

I thought it was very funny that in French *lo* means *water*, even though in Hungarian it means *horse*. From now on I will say to our maid:

"Please give me a glass of horse."

Big day!

I didn't fail in any of my classes. I was only scolded for barely passing some of them and I was told that the girls should be my examples. And I became discouraged and said when my good father left the table that the level of education in girl schools isn't worth much, which may explain why Emma can't spell.

Today I purchased six different colors of paint and a sea shell. And Emma got a new long dress this afternoon. She is proud of it, even though she looks ugly in it.

Peter and Paul's name day.

The volunteer was looking for me again. He stood in front of our house all afternoon.

"You can keep waiting for me!" I thought.

I did go out to the balcony with the girls in spite of him. And we had a good time. He is not a very witty man! And as Emma fiddled with her flowers one of her roses fell down by accident. Zulu picked it up and walked proudly with it. We just laughed at him, but we did put our hands in front of our mouth. Emma got upset with us anyway, but we didn't care about her.

"I will bring out a cigar butt," I said, "and I will through it down to him."

Emma ran inside and told our good mother what I was planning to do. She ruins all of our good fun since she got her new long dress.

Strange day.

We were sitting in French class when my good mother called Emma out of the room. Ethel sneaked out in a little while to see who was there. She was dumbfounded when she came back and whispered:

"Imagine. Zulu is here."

"The volunteer?"

"Him."

My blood circulation stopped. And as soon as our class ended I escaped to the attic. I sat there until the evening among drying clothes and things we stored there. I kept worrying. I was certain that my good father would beat me. And our maid came up for the clothes and said:

"What are you doing here young man? They are looking for you everywhere."

"Is the soldier still here?"

"He left a long time ago."

I was very tense, but wonder of wonders they only asked where I was. And my good father didn't even say a word. And Ethel pulled me aside and said she would tell me an incredibly big secret. And she said that the soldier is in love with Emma. I found this amazing. How can anyone be in love with Emma? No, that is impossible! He may have had bad intentions and tried to make them believe he is in love with Emma.

Good day.

I gathered up all my courage and went inside with some caution. Mr. Mishka was very glad to shake my hand and called me "my good friend, Erno." First I kept an eye on the door behind me, but then I saw that I was dealing with a calm and foolish man. His army uniform was the only thing scary about him. In reality he is a land owner, and supposedly got a law degree as well, but I am sure when he was in school his professors let him pass his classes out of pity.

Well, I had an excellent time. I saw how he kept looking at Emma!

"Emma is an angel!" he said.

I looked at Emma. She just sat there and looked so innocent that I had a hard time suppressing my laughter.

Happy day.

Emma looks in the mirror every five minutes and she is very upset with me. And even at lunch, when my father asked who baked the pie, I answered him:

"The angel."

And all three of us laughed and my good father scolded us.

Good day.

Mr. Mishka was in civilian clothes and brought a rose for Emma. He looks better in civilian clothes than in his army uniform. And he is a very good man. He said that my tiger is a true work of art and he will take me to a true artist, who is a friend of his, and he paints true pictures of farms, horses, oxen, hay stacks and sheep. But the artist is not home right now. He is vacationing in Szolnok with a friend of his called Hollosy.

A day of the arts.

I looked for a postcard which had a farm scene on it and I did find one which showed corn harvesting and a cart with oxen in the front. I showed it to Mr. Mishka and he really liked it too, but he suggested that I should paint only a small part from it. For example, one of the laborers or oxen, or just his head and then another small part on a different piece of paper. And I painted an enlarged picture of one of the oxen's head. The only thing that did not look good was the color of his horn. When Mr. Mishka comes back, I'll ask him about colors.

And my good mother really liked the picture and gave me two koronas to get it framed. And I wrote under it: *The head of an ox on a farm. Date. Name.*

Ordinary day.

Mr. Mishka truly liked my picture. And he told me to paint the tip of the ox's horn black, the bottom of it yellowish white and the middle of it white. And when I was the only one in the room with them for a minute in the hall, as I was writing down what he told me, I saw that he kissed Emma's hand.

Well, there must be something wrong in his head!

Bad day.

Martha had lunch with us and she wore her dandelion colored new dress. She was very proud of it and she envied Emma because of her long dress and her suitor. And when she saw the ox's head she laughed and whispered to the girls and they laughed as well, including Emma. And I asked them what was funny about my picture. And Yolanda told me that Martha asked whose picture it was. And they told her it was my picture. And they laughed so hard that they were wobbling. I was so mad at Martha that when she was leaving I wiped my inkbottle into her skirt.

Ordinary day.

From now on B.M. in my diary will mean Blind Mishka. Emma really has this man fooled! She does a good job playing a serious, smart, truth telling angel!

Good day.

I enrolled in my classes and purchased my books. We had grapes and peaches at lunch time. B.M. sent us grapes from his vineyard.

Exciting day.

B.M. and his father were at our house for lunch. And B.M. asked Emma to marry him. And my good parents will give him an answer in a few days. And I thought this was impossible, but my blood froze when I heard in the evening that they will give their consent.

Something bad will come out of this!

Bad day.

Emma called me immature and I was very upset. I told her that Mr. Mishka was an honest, nice gentleman and she is just fooling him. What if she marries him and then yawns into his face, like she does to us; and he will get to know her no matter what.

Mass.

During mass I thought about informing B.M. about Emma, because if he marries her he will send her home the next day, the same way my mother sends the bad bones back to our butcher. And I said to Ethel, "Come, I'll tell you something confidential, but swear not to tell anyone." She swore and I told her that something unlucky will come out of this! For a while Emma can act like she is someone else, but when he gets to know her and how bad she is, there will be some trouble. Ethel became worried and told our good mother what I said to her and my good mother called me a donkey.

Bad day.

I got an "F" in Latin the first day we had to recite our homework. And I told my teacher that seamstresses were making noise at my house, because they are making a wedding gown, but he didn't care.

I had the feeling ahead of time that we'd have cabbage for lunch.

Very bad day.

Today I sat in the hall for a while and heard that Emma called Mr. Mishka "Mishe" and once even "Mishice." I was astonished at this daring boldness and got into a fight with her, because I said: "How do you dare to call a man with a beard Mishe or Mishice?" And she called me dumb and I called her the same. And my good mother instead of scolding her called me dumb and told me not to interfere in their lives!

Ordinary day.

Emma begged me not to be upset. I knew what she was going to ask next. She wanted me to look over her letter and put punctuation marks in it and correct her grammar. She begged me on her knees and promised to give me punch cake and finally I gave in. And while I was putting punctuation marks in her letter she picked up her puppet and danced with it.

I wish Mishice would have seen her!

Very exciting day.

The day of the wedding. I wore new black clothes. There were eight of us. And I had to go with Martha. At first I was upset about it, but she pinned a flower on my jacket and tried to flatter me and off we went, hand in hand.

And I didn't quite comprehend the seriousness of what was happening until we reached the church, but I became very concerned when I heard Mr. Mishka swear: "I will never leave her..."

How can a grown man swear such a thing without thinking it over some more. After all, he doesn't even know Emma. What if he comes to the realization that his diamond princess is really just an ordinary girl!

The most beautiful part of the day was the dinner after the wedding, and Martha got the sugar rose from the wedding cake and she let me have it in secret. For this I have forgiven her sins against me.

And then Emma and B.M. said good bye, because they were traveling to Vienna and from there to Venice and Emma will not be coming back to our house from there. And she cried. And my good mother cried too and everyone did. Even I did! But then I thought it was a waste of water because he won't be able to put up with Emma for long.

Weeks passed. And every day I am waiting with terror that Emma will be sent home. Brother-in-law B.M. is a very good man and I would be sorry to lose him. But it appears that he still does not see Emma.

We got a letter from Emma. She wrote that they finished the grape harvest and she is very happy.

Well, even a kitten's eyes open up in eight days, but brother-in-law Mishka's eyes...

Good day.

I have not seen Emma for half a year. She gained so much weight that I hardly recognized her. When they arrived I was horrified that we would be witnessing dramatic scenes and there would be trouble in the house. And to my amazement nothing happened. Brother-in-law Mishka calls Emma his angel, his dove and he talks to her informally as if he were talking with a cobbler's apprentice.

This man became blind permanently.

Confession

I was reading the heroes section in the most recent newspaper. I was interested in the names honored in the big war, even without knowing them. I was glad when I saw Hungarian names too. My eyes stopped on the name, Sylvester Besztercey. Impossible! And on top of it, he was a gold medal hero! Impossible! Putting his name in the paper must have been some kind of a foolish joke. There were no two men with a name like his. I saw his regiment's number after his name and that he was a volunteer platoon leader.

Well, Sylvester…

It had not been a week since I had seen him, in his volunteer platoon leader uniform. It was true that he was in the army. But who had the courage to put his name among the heroes? A journalist? A typesetter? Well, it was a foolish joke!

All of his acquaintances knew he would not fire a gun. He had a rabbit-like face. He was blond and had round eyes. He was laid back when nothing bothered him. But if even a ten year old said something to him, he turned red and blinked with alarm. At times, he sat among us on Wednesday evenings, with his English pipe, and happily listened to every word, until midnight. But he never said anything. He rarely expressed his opinion, but when he did, he only said a short sentence. Even that he said very slowly, as if his tongue were made out of lead. Or he just nodded. But he never shook his head in disagreement. He wouldn't dare. But we liked him. Or perhaps we liked him because he was like that. We always like the person who listens to us, more than the person we have to listen to.

And he was not a worthless man, but a distinguished painter and an expert in drawing. He had already drawn every member of our group during dinner. He could draw anyone's face on paper with just a few lines. He illustrated the most beautiful calendars and also worked for some picture magazines. But he mostly worked for Zsolnay, where he painted flowers, grape leaves, birds, running horses, and things like these, on plates. Zsolnay paid him in gold.

He was a true artist. Even his legs stood like an easel. But still, I thought his imagination was rather limited. He only showed two or three kinds of pictures at exhibitions, the colors of fall, but always under blue skies, and water, but never without reeds. When it came to people, he always painted a young woman with red lips, brown eyes and a smiling face. She wore either white or blue clothes. At times she was dressed as an aristocrat, other times as a peasant. Sometime she was in the parlor, or in the snow-covered garden, or in the flower garden, but she was always the same woman, with red lips and playful eyes.

Well, he was a good painter and a good artist, only he did not see much from the millions of different things in this world. But he was an honest, nice gentleman. I admired him, even just for being a vegetarian. People who live on vegetables are all good people. They never end up in prison. His name was never involved in any duels, but neither was he in any newspapers either. What I don't understand is this: how did he become a platoon leader? And how did he get a medal for bravery?

I looked in different newspapers as well. His name appeared in them too. So it was not a publisher's joke. Well, I would visit him! A man who is celebrating is glad to have a visitor celebrate with him, even at midnight. And I had known him since he was a teenager. He brought his first drawing to my publisher ten years ago. But even then we did not talk much, or since then. I'd never been to his house either. I only knew that he lived on the Buda side of Budapest. He put his business card on my desk every time he came to my publisher.

"If perhaps you would have an assignment for me…"

I took care of the assignments through the mail. But I would visit him now. He was a good man, an honest man, and somehow he acted bravely. I would visit him. I was certain that he lived in an attic, among a lot of cans and tubes of paint. He probably had a bed in the corner, and his glasses and hairbrush were next to his tea pot. Artists usually live like that. I was very much surprised when I was directed to a beautiful villa with a garden.

A hunched peasant woman wearing a white apron ran to open the villa's door. She had a big spoon in her hand, and she humbly blinked, as if I were at least an emperor.

"Are you looking for Sylvester? He is home. Please go in through the glass door…"

I went through the glass door. I was even more amazed when a young, upper society woman greeted me in the house. She wore a peacock eye blue silk kimono and looked like the beautiful, red lipped woman in my friend's paintings!

"Are you looking for Sylvester? He is home. I am his wife."

I was astonished. This magnificent, intelligent looking, clean woman was my friend's wife?

"My husband is painting a model," she said with a smile. "If I could ask you to wait a little…"

She had three eggs in her hand. She was taking them into the kitchen, but first she led me into their parlor, which had light green wallpaper, a yellow velvet couch and some chairs. It was a nice little parlor, full of pictures.

"Please," she pointed to a chair, "I am very glad… My husband will be very glad too. But please forgive me. I have to give these eggs to my cook. She is getting impatient. She is not a maid from Pest. Maids from Pest are rather…"

And she sat down. She started chatting in her nice, flute-like voice, "maids from Pest cannot be trusted," and she told me that their previous maid stole her husband's razor for a foot soldier. And how they found - "horrendum!" the lady used this Latin word: "horrendum!"- how they found the foot solder drinking at their kitchen table at midnight and the words she exchanged with him. She did not

126

even want to mention little things like when the maid's stockings are the same as her employer's, and if the maid is so civilized that she takes care of her teeth with a toothbrush, it is advisable to make sure she does have such equipment. Finally, they had to get a maid from a village.

"But please excuse me," she smiled and picked up the three eggs again, "my cook is waiting. Are you here to see my husband about something urgent? I can call him out."

"I just came to congratulate him."

"For his medal of bravery? He is going to be very happy. Do you know why he received it?"

"I couldn't even guess."

"Oh, that is a terrible story. One morning, when my husband looked out from his camp, he noticed a Polish peasant, as he walked among the willow trees. He had a backpack on his back and a hoe on his shoulder. My husband became suspicious. He reported it. Two solders were sent after the peasant and he was brought back into the village. They took off his coat. He wore a dress shirt, which had a pocket inside and there were some papers in it. Right after this my husband was given the assignment of searching the forest with two other solders. The forest was a good distance from there. He had to see if there were any enemy positions and he was supposed to make a drawing of them. If no positions were found, they were supposed to walk through the forest to see if there were any Russians in it."

"There were some and unfortunately my husband was captured by them. The captain of the Russians interrogated him. Who was he? What was he? Which regiment did he belong to? Which village was he sent from?"

"Then the captain anxiously asked about a second-lieutenant, because one of his second-lieutenants was captured by our forces. He talked about the man dressed in peasant clothes."

"'What happened to him?'

"My husband would have told him that he was released, but he didn't answer. You know my husband, if he gets excited for some reason, or if he gets upset, he doesn't speak a word. Nobody can pull a word out of him, not even with a pair of pliers. The Russian captain became angry of course. He asked even louder. My husband closed his mouth tighter. 'Well,' said the captain:

"'I will hang you!'

"My husband did not respond to that either. His hands were tied at his back.

"'Are you going to talk or not?'

"They made him stand under a locust tree.

"'Are you going to talk or not?'

"They did not even send for a priest. Instead of a priest a cannon ball arrived from one of our cannons and blew away the locust tree, the hangman and even the captain. My husband was buried by dirt. By the time he was dug out and regained his consciousness, our soldiers were already there."

As she talked, she put the three eggs in a cigar ashtray on the table, so she could talk with her two hands as well. She was very animated with her hands. She opened them, closed them and then put them together.

"Please allow me one question," I asked her when she paused, "what you have told me is very interesting, and even though I am very much interested, I cannot think of anything else other than how the two of you ended up together?"

"With Sylvester?"

"Yes, with him. You were childhood friends, weren't you?"

"Oh no. He was already twenty eight years old when we first met. We met in Fured. I was nineteen years old... for the second year already... but everybody thought I was seventeen. Some men even made a bet about my age. Of course they asked my mother instead of me. They didn't ask her outright, just turned their conversation with her to my age. They bet on three bottles of champagne. One of them was a railway official. The other one called himself a composition writer for a town clerk, but he was really just an assistant. We didn't know them, just ran into them at a railway station."

"I have been wondering about one question since we have been talking. If you did not know each other since childhood, how did Sylvester court you and how did he confess his feeling for you?"

The lady shook her head with a smile.

"Oh please, those who belong together understand each other without words. Even mute people... Have you heard that mute men prefer to choose mute women for their partners..."

"Okay, but even if they understand each other, a man has to express somehow that he wants to marry the woman, or..."

"Well, he expressed it."

"But how? I have met with him at least a hundred times. We have often been together at lunch or even at dinner when we were younger, but I have never heard him say five words in a row."

The woman was surprised.

"Five words? That has not been my experience. We have regular conversations. After all, married couples always talk to each other. It is true that he stuttered when he was a child and that may be the reason he seems quiet. If someone he does not know talks to him, he always gets confused. But he doesn't stutter anymore. He can thank a teacher in his childhood village for that, because he really stuttered. The teacher told his parents that he could help their son get rid of his stutter for only one hundred forints. But he had to spend his summer vacation with him in Sumeg. The teacher's name was Kulcsar. When they returned from the vacation, my husband did not stutter any more. The teacher had his own invented

128

method of curing him. My husband says it was a simple method, but he does not like to think about it. He didn't even tell his parents. He only complained to Ms. Apollo, who used to be his nanny and is now our cook. Once I questioned him about it, because one of my girlfriend's sons stutters. He said he is better off stuttering, until he dies, than to have that teacher work with him.

"'But,' I burst out, 'if it only cost one hundred forints, and as you said, it was a simple system…'

"'It was simple all right,' my husband answered, 'I wish his hand would have fallen off…'

"And he didn't tell me.

"But my husband does not stutter any more, except if he gets excited over something. If he gets scared then he will stutter; he can't think of anything else and his tongue gets tied.

"Of course I did not know about this when I was single and it is amazing that we got together. Oh, every marriage has something amazing about how it got started. Two people have to arrive at the same place, like two trains arriving at a train station. To be honest with you, I didn't think when I first saw him… Oh, I have to take these eggs to the kitchen, because the cook… well I will just tell you quickly… The miracle happened to us at Fured. Isn't it amazing that miracles happen even at Fured? Fured has a lot of reeds. I didn't really like it when I first saw it. We are from Somogy and from that side Lake Balaton is a lot more beautiful. We only went across the lake the day after Saint King Steven's Day, because we heard there were a lot of guests. I didn't even know if I should have taken summer or fall clothes with me, because after King Steven's day the weather is often cooler. I only took two of my summer clothes, a white one and a satin dress with blue stripes. The satin dress looked very good on me. My straw hat's ribbon was the same blue color as the stripes on my clothes. I only took two parasols with me, one was white and the other was moss green, to go with my fall clothes. I also took six yards of gray material with me. I was going to make a cape out of it while I was there.

"We arrived late at the Elizabeth Hotel. We were lucky they were able to give us a little room.

"'Let's go to the restaurant, mother,' I was getting anxious around 8 o'clock. 'We are not going to get in if we are late.'

"The hotel's restaurant was already full. We had to go out to a nearby restaurant. There were seven of us, mother and my sister Klari - perhaps you know her as Melissza Somogyi, which is her stage name, but she was only a young twelve year old back then. And there was a pharmacy assistant with us from Pest. His last name was Forgacs, and he came with his parents. Oh, and Ms. Agnes was there too, my mother's girlfriend from Pest. She was vacationing nearby and she came over to be with us for the evening. Later, after I got married, I found out that we had gone there to meet the Forgacs family and they were there to meet us. Ms.

Agnes wrote to my mother that she had gotten to know a good family, the Forgacs family, and they had a twenty-four year old son, a very nice, educated young man, who would be good for me. He was studying to become a pharmacist. I found that letter in my mom's commode last year.

"Well, he was studying to become a pharmacist and had a bright future ahead of him. He planned to get a pharmacy permit in Budapest. Even though he wanted a large sum of money for this from my parents as my dowry, it was not payable until my death. He planned to get a loan, and they would have only had to pay the interest on it. This seemed to make a lot of sense. He had plenty of money to pay for his other expenses, because he was an only child. His parents had a two-story house on Attila Boulevard and also had a stone quarry in the county of Nograd. His father was a road surface contractor. Their family name used to be Forgaccio.

"I was twenty years old by then and my mother constantly worried that I would not find a husband. It is difficult for a girl in a village, because she is hidden from the world. Although when I was seventeen I was courted by a Lutheran minister. We met on New Years Eve at my godfather's house. He even visited us three times, twice for dinner and once for lunch. He ate a lot and talked little. My father liked him a lot, because he spoke good Latin. They kept talking to each other in Latin. Even the stuffed cabbages were offered to him in Latin by my Father.

"My father was a very educated man. I didn't even have to attend school after my elementary education. I only had to take a two month course on drawing from nuns in the town of Pecs. In reality, I did not even completely finish my elementary school. My father got into an argument with my teacher regarding a question on Hungarian grammar and he decided to pull me out of school because he disagreed with him. He taught me after that in our home. But I do know more than my friends who finished secondary school. I can write better than any of them. My grammar is better too. I only make mistakes with the letter "t". Sometimes I put more of them than I should and sometimes less. But a lot of people are the same way with that letter.

"What were we talking about?

"Oh yes, the Lutheran minister. Well, my father liked him very much. My mother only liked one thing about him. When the subject of the dowry came up, he just waved his hand."

"'When I get married,' he said, 'I am not going to look at my fiancé's dowry. I will only look at the person I will be spending the rest of my life with.'

"'He is a very honest man,' my mother thought after his visit, 'ten thousand koronas would be enough for him and a furnished apartment with a piano.'

"'I will also give them two cows,' said my father. 'You can choose any two, Ilka.'

"But the minister stopped coming to us. He told my godmother that I was a pretty girl, but that I talked too much. You can imagine how surprised I was. Even if I think of it now... I talk too much? As if I had two tongues, like the lion in the Csak

130

family crest. I would have liked to send him a message that nobody ever fell asleep while I was talking, but it is not unusual when a minister is speaking. But I did not jump into Lake Balaton. He had a stern look, as if he wanted to sue the person he was talking to, and his forehead was always wrinkled. I would have had a boring life with him.

"To be honest with you, I always dreamed that my husband would be a poet, and he would write beautiful poems, and he would write one or more about me. I like poems a lot. I always read the poems in the paper. I was hoping for a poet or a land owner, like my father. If I couldn't have a poet, that would have been fine with me too. Unfortunately poets don't visit villages any more.

"Well, I had no idea why Ms. Agnes invited us to Fured and why we met the Forgacs family right after we arrived. Meeting them was not uncomfortable for me. A girl is always happy if she has a young man floating nearby. But like I said, I had no idea.

"He must have known, because right from the first minute he was very attentive and tried to be very nice. He was the kind of man most women find attractive, because he wore different clothes every day and his pants were always ironed. He wore fine neckties and elegant shoes. His hair was greased. He had a gray top hat on his head in the morning, in the afternoon he wore a sailor hat and in the evening a soft black hat. I didn't know back then that this kind of elegance can be bought by anyone on Dorottya Street, even though Pest was not an unknown part of the world for me. My mother took me there occasionally for a ball and we also visited some theaters to further my education. Well, one evening we got plenty of it... What we saw was disgraceful... Mother was sweating... We left after the second act. That was an unfortunate day for us anyway. We ate at a restaurant called Hungaria. The chain of my mother's watch broke. She only noticed it as we were paying the bill, when she touched her neck and the watch was missing.

"'Oh no,' she said, 'my watch!'

"She looked down and saw that her chain was shining at the foot of her chair."

"'Well, great!'

"At that moment something crackled under her feet. She stepped on her watch."

"But where was I? Oh yes, I was talking about Forgacs. He had a handsome face and he wore five rings on his fingers. One of them was a thick signet ring. He had a black moustache and sometimes he even shaved twice during the same day. But he was a nice man in any case. At first his face appeared a little feminine, but later I saw he was rather masculine. I noticed especially in his eyes that he always had some kind of a hidden drawer nobody was able to look into. But it seemed like he always wanted to look into everyone else's drawers. He was looking with as much intensity as if he were trying to look through a keyhole.

"Well, we were going to dinner. All the tables were occupied when we arrived at the diner, even though it wasn't even eight o'clock yet. Still, we were able to find a table where only one lonely man sat. The table was next to a door inside. The smell of food was coming out of the kitchen and the waiters were going in and out of that door. But there was no other table and there was only one man sitting there. He had a little sailor pipe in his hand. He lit his pipe right then and started to blow the smoke. It was Sylvester. Of course I didn't know yet who he was. Forgacs approached him right away.

"'Is this table free?'

"Sylvester nodded and became red. He politely moved his chair from the head of the table to its side and put his pipe in his pocket. It was strange that he became so red. This young man must have been waiting for someone. I glanced at him. A man who is waiting for someone is always interesting for a girl. But he sure set his eyes on me when we sat down and even after that he stared at me a few times. It was even stranger that a young man who was waiting for someone observed me. But he tried to look without being noticed, as if I were some king of a pearl necklace and he were a thief. I wondered who he was. Could he be a poet? We did not talk with him of course.

"The next day there were some empty tables, but all of them had a small sign on them indicating that they were reserved. The owner apologized:"

"'Please, as soon as we have empty chairs we will hold them for you.'

"Well, we ended up going to the table where the painter was sitting. I did not know yet that he was a painter of course. He was by himself and sat at the head of the table again. He became red when he saw us and didn't even wait for us to talk to him, just moved his chair to the side. Forgacs didn't even ask him if the table was free. We just sat down in the same order as on the previous evening.

"At dinner time we arrived before him, but we didn't take his place. He did come. He had a big, flat book under his arm, as always. He went straight to his seat. He wore a blue neck tie with white dots, but his collar was open as before. He silently greeted us and became red. We didn't talk to him even then. It was as if we didn't even see him, even though we were all admiring him in secret, because he ate salad by itself. He put some oil and vinegar on it, but nothing else. He ate a bowl of salad and a boiled egg after that, nothing more. He had a kohlrabi dish for lunch the day before, but without any meat. Afterwards he asked the waiter:

"'What other vegetable dishes do you have?'

"The waiter thought about it.

"'I could bring you a string bean salad, which we usually serve with English mutton.'

"'Please bring me some,' nodded Sylvester.

"We laughed at him after he left, especially after he put a wide rimmed straw hat on his head.

"'He is a frugal man,' the old Forgacs joked. 'He only imagines eating meat with his salad. He doesn't have to pay for it.'

"'He only eats green things,' his son laughed. 'He should go to a pasture instead of coming here.'

"The next morning he arrived later than us again. We were not in a good mood, because my mother's new shoes were too tight and we could not even blame the shoe salesman from Pest. Ever since mother gained weight, she had always ordered size 7 ½ shoes with low heels. When we were going to Fured, she ordered yellow shoes in size 7. She had never worn yellow shoes before, but she wanted to be fashionable. She had a white lace dress, which we had seen in a magazine, but she didn't want to wear white shoes. She ordered yellow instead. She was able to put it on her feet, but half an hour later she was sorry. Well, I was sad too. I felt sorry for poor mother. I even told her to buy different shoes and that I would use her new shoes at home. I wear size 6 1/2.

"'What are you thinking?' she answered. 'We already spent a lot of money here. It will become larger over time.'

"And perhaps the bad soup we were served added to our unhappiness. It tasted like warm water and the dumplings in it were hard as rock. Then Sylvester came in his wide rimmed straw hat with his big book. He had his little sailor pipe in his mouth.

"'He is going to order dill without meat,' said Klari softly to cheer us up.

"We were smiling. Sylvester greeted us. He sat down and put his book behind him. He looked at the menu. The waiter came and Sylvester said to him seriously:

"'Dill sauce please.'

"At that moment we all tried to suppress our laughter. But a minute later Klari burst out laughing out loud and we all joined her. My mother even forgot the pain in her feet. She gasped for air as she said to Klari:

"'Are you crazy?'

"'But you are laughing too!' Klari chuckled. 'And my shoes are not even tight...'

"Sylvester just sat seriously among us. He looked at us and then continued reading the menu seriously. He glanced at me a few times. I was very embarrassed that we were laughing at him and tried to stop. I saw the rest of us were thinking the same thing. We tried to come down and started a serious conversation about motor boats and what a smart invention they were. But Klari did burst out in laughter from time to time. And then the waiter arrived and brought the dill without meat. Klari collapsed onto the table and laughed uncontrollably, and we all joined her. Even the old Forgacs chuckled, even though he was a very serious man.

"'How impolite,' mother scolded Klari. 'This gentleman will think we are laughing at him.'

"Sylvester turned a little red.

"'Please go ahead,' he whispered with a smile, 'please...'

"'But she is not laughing at you,' my mother apologized. 'She just gets a little crazy at times...'

133

"'Please go ahead... It is no problem,' Sylvester repeated kindly.

"'But no, no,' apologized Klari too, 'I am not laughing at you; I was just thinking about a little dog I saw earlier.'

"She lied of course. Still, we became embarrassed and tried to control ourselves. Sylvester ate the dill and glanced at me in secret. He ordered a potato dish after the dill, and he glanced at me again. There was meat on the potato dish, but he didn't touch it. He ordered fruit after that. The waiter brought him a plate with apples, pears, and grapes too. He paid his bill, nodded, and left. As soon as he left Forgacs smiled.

"'He forgot his book here.'

"Klari jumped to the book, picked it up and opened it. We saw right away that there were drawings in it, drawings of Lake Balaton. Some of them were colored, and all of them were beautiful. She kept turning the pages and all of a sudden shouted:

"'Ilka!'

"Well, it was really my picture, in water-color, and it was as lifelike as if I were looking at myself in the mirror. Even my straw hat with the blue velvet ribbon was on my head. What a miracle! How could he have painted it? When? Unbelievable! It is the picture hanging on our wall now. It is very good, don't you think? Forgacs was the only one who did not look at it and was not excited about the art.

"'What a cheap trick,' he said. 'He left his book here because he thought Klari would be curious. It is a business trick.'

"'It is like catching a bird,' smiled the old Forgacs.

"'He is going to make us pay for his dill,' laughed Klari.

"We all laughed.

"'We should play a joke on him by taking the picture out of his book,' said Forgacs.

"'No, we'll buy it,' I said, 'but he could have offered it to us without any tricks.'

"'We'll buy it,' my mother also said. 'A small picture like this one can't be too expensive.'

"'If you will allow me, dear Ilka,' said Forgacs politely, 'I would like to buy it for you as a souvenir.'

"I wasn't even able to answer him. Klari grabbed the book out of mother's hands and closed it. She quickly put it back on the chair. She saw through the window that the wide-rimmed straw hat was returning. He really did enter the restaurant. His face was red. He seemed suspicious as he looked at us. He put his book under his arm, the same way he always did.

"'Excuse me,' Forgacs said to him in an almost businesslike manner, 'we are interested in one of your pictures...'

"'If it is not too expensive,' my mother added.

"'Of course,' nodded Forgacs, 'after all it is only a small water color.'

"Sylvester looked at Forgacs as if he were looking at a trash bin in a hallway. Then he glanced at mother and then me too. But he did not look at me that way."

"'You probably know what we are talking about,' continued Forgacs, 'well, how much does that picture cost?'

"Sylvester looked like he had just been insulted.

"'It is not for sale for anything...'

"He nodded and left. We were silent, as if a gun had just been shot and no one knew where and why.

"'He must be crazy,' said the old Forgacs.

"'No, he is very smart,' answered his son. 'He knows we are going to be here tomorrow, and the day after tomorrow, and we want to buy that picture. He is a cunning man.'

"'Of course,' said my mother, 'that is why he painted it.'

"The painter did leave a feeling of disappointment in us. I have never had such a splendid picture of myself. I only had an old picture which was taken by a traveling photographer and was dried in the sun. You know them, bad glass, bad lighting, 'please smile,' a flash, and finally they draw in your pupils with ink. The people in the picture are ashamed they were born.

"Forgacs shrugged his shoulder.

"'Well, we may have to pay a little more for it, but we'll buy it,' he smiled as he tried to comfort me. 'But we have to be on our guard. If he comes here for dinner, we must not mention the picture to him. He will bring up the topic himself.'

"Sylvester did show up for dinner, and for lunch as well on the next day. But he did not say a thing. He just ate his vegetable dishes, pickles, cottage cheese noodles, and cooked roots, and drank water after his meals. He listened to our conversation with a smile on his face, and he glanced at me while he looked at the menu, from under his eyebrows, like a frog looks at the moon from the grass. But he did not say a word about the picture. We did not bring it up either. His silence made me even more anxious. I worried that eventually he would not show up at the table and all of a sudden he would disappear, as it usually happens at vacation spots. I even told my mother that we should start a conversation with him. After all, he was a gentleman. Of course I could not have started it, but mother could do it and then she could introduce me. Artists are respected everywhere. An artist is like a poet, a poet of colors. He must be a very interesting man.

"'What for?' answered mother.

"She thought if she introduced me, Forgacs would not be the only one around me any more.

"We walked over to Csopak to see Ms. Agnes around tea time. Forgacs came with us. By then his parents had already returned to Budapest. While we were on our way, we saw that Sylvester sat in front of a vineyard. He painted. We only saw him from a distance, but we recognized him by his huge straw hat. He had an easel with him which he painted on. Then I mentioned the picture to Forgacs.

"'It doesn't seem like my picture will come out of his book.'

"'Are you worried?' Forgacs asked politely. 'Well, we'll make it jump out of there this evening.'

"'Really?'

"'If I say so…'

"But what happened in the evening? As we entered the restaurant, the waiter joyfully informed us that a table opened up next to the one we used before. It was a better table in the corner. The painter was not yet there. He arrived a few minutes later. He saw from a distance that we were seated somewhere else. His face became red, but he still nodded toward us. He sat down with a gloomy face, again at the head of the table.

"'Salad please.'

"'Oh no,' I grumbled softly. 'Now he won't give us the picture; he'll think we abandoned him.'

"'Nonsense,' waved Forgacs with his hand. 'Only, it will be more expensive by five koronas.'

"And he addressed him nonchalantly:

"'Well, Mr. Painter, are we going to make a deal?'

"Sylvester looked up, but then he continued eating his salad calmly, as if the question were directed to someone else. Forgacs addressed him again:

"'Mr. Painter, please Mr. Painter…'

"Sylvester became red, even his ears were red. He looked at Forgacs.

"'I don't know who you are,' he answered coldly, 'and what gives you the right to keep addressing me.'

"He swallowed some salad and said nonchalantly:

"'I am not a salesman.'

"We were flabbergasted. Sylvester lost some of his color too. He blinked repeatedly and appeared deep in thought as he put the fish bones from his pike onto his fork.

"'He is offended,' I whispered. 'You see, he is offended. Oh no, I will never have that picture.'

"'Too bad.' Mother was sorry as well.

"Forgacs wiped off his mouth. He got up and went to the painter.

"'Forgive me, I didn't mean to offend you. I am Forgacs, a pharmacy apprentice from Budapest.'

"The painter stood up as well then. But he held his neck like a cock ready for a fight. But then he seemed to calm down and accepted Forgacs' hand for a handshake. He only said his name.

"'Sylvester.'

"Forgacs sat down next to him.

"'If you allow me... I only brought up the picture because I thought it was for sale. Please don't be upset. After all, that is how painters make money...'

"'It is not for sale,' Sylvester shook his head.

"'Isn't that why you painted it? Isn't that why pictures are painted?'

"'No.'

"'Then why?'

"'For myself.'

"'For yourself? Why would you do it for yourself?'

"Sylvester shrugged his shoulder.

"'That is my business.'

"'But if I would pay for it.'

"'That is not possible.'

"'Why isn't it possible?'

"'It doesn't have a price.'

"We listened apprehensively. Even Forgacs did not know what to say next. He twisted his moustache and appeared confused. His eyes were blinking.

"'But still, well...'

"Sylvester looked at me; then he continued eating, as if Forgacs did not even sit there. He was putting three or four leaves of lettuce on his fork at a time. I didn't know back then how healthy salads were.

"'I know,' Forgacs started again, 'I know you are an artist. I even know your name from a picture magazine. And artists are stubborn. But I would like to have that picture.'

"Sylvester shook his head.

"'I won't give it to you.'

"'Not even for one hundred koronas?'

"'Not even for a thousand.'

"'But,' stuttered Forgacs, 'but...'

"'Not even for a thousand,' repeated the painter.

"'But why would that picture be more precious to you than to me?'

"Sylvester was silent. He picked up a menu and glanced at me from behind it. I usually did not look at him, just felt that he was observing me, but at that moment I looked at him with a sad expression on my face. And when our eyes met, I don't know how, but I felt I was going to become his wife. I can't really express the feeling I had in words, but somehow I felt a connection with him. It was presentiment. Later, after we were married, I even told him, and he told me he had that feeling the first time he had seen me. He fell in love with me the first day, or if I use his words: he was in love with me from the needle of my hat to the heels of my shoes. He observed me so much in the first hour that he was able to draw me from memory, and the next day he put the colors of my face on it.

"But of course his presentiment was just like a dream. He thought he would now see me again. That was the reason he painted the picture.

"'I am not going to force you,' Forgacs retreated. 'I can tell you are not in the mood to sell any pictures. But still, it is a picture of a lady who does not belong to you...'

"'Well, does she belong to you?'

"That question was like a hit on his chest. Forgacs nearly moved back from it.

"'To me? Well... I am one of her admirers.'

"'Me too,' answered the painter loudly. Then he pulled out the Evening News from his pocket and started to read it.

"Forgacs got up. He seemed disappointed as he returned to us.

"'Strange man,' he said softly, 'but still, we will have that picture.'

"'I doubt it,' I sighed. 'I heard every word.'

"Gypsies started to play music in one corner of the room. We couldn't talk to each other any more.

"Forgacs encouraged me once more when we were parting for the night.

"'We'll get that picture. I will go back and tell him I am one of his distant relatives. I will even have a drink with him, but the picture will not leave Fured.'

"I wasn't able to sleep well that night. I was really sad that I was not getting the picture. But still, somehow I liked that he wouldn't have sold it, even for a thousand koronas. Why was that picture so important to him? By that time I really liked Sylvester. I thought it was strange that one minute he was red like a little girl, but in the next minute he was so manly.

"The next day Forgacs was happy to tell us his news.

"'I was successful! I got it!'

"'Impossible!'

"'I got it! I don't have it in my hands yet, but still I got it. I know the way to it. He is a very stubborn man. We drank until midnight. Imagine, we drank raspberry juice. He doesn't drink anything else, so I had to drink the same thing. I will never drink raspberry juice again. I got sick of it.'

"'But what happened with the picture?'

"'We'll have it. Rest assured Ilka, we'll get it!'

"'Did he say he will sell it? Did he tell you for sure?'

"'No, he didn't say that. I didn't even ask. Just leave it to me. I have to be tricky. I am from the capital. I know how to go about this. I didn't even bring up the picture, but that is why we'll have it. I know about these things. He is going to paint at Csopak today. We are going to sit next to him from lunch until tea time and we will keep praising all of his brush strokes. He is a very good artist, but wild as a bison.'

"'But what if it doesn't work?'

"'I know for sure it will work.'

138

"'I don't.'

"'It is certain. If in the end he won't give us that picture, I'll have him make a copy of it. He can make one that will look exactly the same.'

"'I don't believe he will copy it. He was offended that we sat at a different table and even laughed at him before that. We didn't even talk to him.'

"'Perhaps, but I will remedy that. I will visit him in the morning, and we will invite him to sit at our table. We will be very kind to him, and that will tame him.'

"Mother was a little reluctant, but I thought it was a good idea.

"I would have been glad to have any painter at our table, because I had never talked with any of them. There was a nun who painted with us for a couple of weeks, when I was a student. Her name was Klarissa. She painted pots, plates and flowers too. I would have always liked to ask a painter how flowers are painted. The ones I painted looked like they were made of painted sheet iron. The colors didn't come together. I would have liked to paint some portraits too, but first I would have to learn how to do it.

"Forgacs really did bring the painter with him at lunch time. He was holding his arm as if he were afraid that he would break loose and run away. Sylvester did not seem to want to get away. He seemed to be happy to be able to join us.

"'I would have invited you earlier,' mother apologized reluctantly, 'but I was afraid you would not want to join us.'

"'Thank you,' Sylvester said politely, 'I am used to being alone.'

"'And here we have a better opportunity to talk about the picture too,' mother got right down to the subject, 'you are probably upset that we looked at your book. My daughter Klari likes to put her nose into everything! Since we have already seen the picture, it is understandable... Would you consider selling it?'

"Sylvester was silent, as if he weren't even part of the conversation.

"I spoke to him as well.

"'It is an amazingly beautiful work. You are a great artist.'

"Sylvester's eyes were already bright, but they were shining when I told him that.

"'If you will allow me,' he whispered, 'I would be much obliged if you would accept it... As a souvenir...'

"And he already reached for his book.

"'If it is not expensive,' mother said anxiously.

"Sylvester removed my picture from his book.

"'Here you go,' he handed it to me joyfully.

"'But,' mother worried, 'we haven't even bought it yet.'

"'It doesn't have a price,' Sylvester smiled, 'it is a souvenir from Fured. But wait, I won't give it to you like this. I will get if framed first.'

"'No, we won't let you do that,' I answered happily. 'That will be our expense.'

"Sylvester shook his head.

"'That is no expense. I am the only one who knows what color and how wide the frame should be. I will take it to have it framed right after lunch.'

"And he put the picture back into his book.

"'Please make a painting of me too,' Klari begged him.

"But mother stopped her.

"'Do you think he is here to paint every spring chicken?'

"'Sometime I will,' the painter encouraged her. 'Her face has very nice colors too. I will do it if she calls me Mr. Sylvester, or just Mr. Sili.'

"'Mr. Sylva,' Klari laughed, 'but you aren't upset?'

"Well, all of a sudden he won mother's good will, because he gave us the picture. She asked him all kinds of nice questions. Where had he studied art? And:

"'Can you make a living doing this?'

"Sylvester gave short, one or two word answers. He didn't learn his art from anyone, but his drawings were praised even when he was a young school boy, and he drew more and more. He was asked to illustrate a book while he was still a student.

"'Are you able to live on what you are paid?' mother wondered.

"'Yes I am,' nodded Sylvester, 'I even have some money left which I put into my savings account.'

"'In your savings account?'

"'Yes, five or six thousand koronas a year, but last year I was able to put away ten thousand. It is true that my living expenses are modest.'

"Forgacs reached behind the painter's back and signaled that he was lying. Klari laughed so loud the whole restaurant looked at us.

"'We saw yesterday,' I said to divert his attention, 'we saw that you painted at Csopak.'

"'I painted a couple of grapevines,' answered Sylvester joyfully. 'I can see Lake Balaton right behind those grapevines. The leaves are already turning yellow.'

"'And the yellow color,' I said enthusiastically, 'goes well with the blue.'

"Sylvester's eyes shone as he looked at me.

"'You are right.' he said, 'that is the reason I am painting them.'

"'We would like to take a look,' I tried to seize the opportunity, 'unless we would be an interruption. I would very much like to see how you paint.'

"'You are welcome to observe,' he answered happily, 'but I am already putting the finishing touches on the picture. What time would you like to come?'

"'After tea time, or should we come earlier?'

"'After tea time will be good. I will start painting a little later than I planned.'

"Our conversation was primarily just small talk, but by the way he looked at me and talked to me I felt as if something connected us. Kind of like two siblings who met each other in adult life, after they had been separated when they were babies, due to some circumstance. My father read a story like that. We wept when we heard it. It happened in America. Twin babies were separated during a flood. The water took one of them away while he was in his cradle.

"But where did I begin? Oh yes, we were going to look at how he painted.

"Mother didn't come with us because of her shoes. Klari and Forgacs were the only ones who joined me. We arrived there around five o'clock. The weather was sunny and still very summer like. I remember I wore my white batiste clothes and carried a white parasol. Sylvester was already painting. He had his English pipe in his mouth and wore a hat which covered his eyes. The picture he was painting depicted two grapevines. Both of them had lovely yellow leaves and bloomy green grapes. But the grapes still looked like they were made out of some kind of green material.

"'Please continue painting, Sylvester, as if we were not even here.'

"We stood behind him and I observed with great interest how he put light colored dots on the grapes and how they turned transparent and soft, one by one, after one or two turpentine smelling brushstroke. All of a sudden, a big, beautiful carriage turned onto the road, and was slowly approaching us. Two priests who wore black cassocks walked about twenty feet before the carriage. One of them was very old and quite thin. They got closer to us. We didn't pay much attention to them until they were about ten feet from us. Klari whispered:

"'The Cardinal!'

"She was right. I recognized him from his picture. But in real life everyone looks different. I couldn't see on his picture how black his eyes were. It was hard to see anything other than his eyes on his thin face. Sylvester barely looked up. He calmly continued working on his picture. He cleaned the ash out of his pipe before he put it away in his pocket. The two priests reached us and stopped. Forgacs greeted them silently. I bowed toward them too. Sylvester stood up from his chair, took off his hat and bowed. It was a very graceful move. I liked it. The cardinal stepped closer. He looked at the painting.

"'Outstanding,' he nodded, 'outstanding. You are obviously a true artist. What is your name, if I may ask?'

"I saw that Sylvester became red and he stared like Hamlet at his father's ghost.

"'What is your name?' the cardinal repeated.

"Sylvester tried to make a 'B' sound, to start his last name, but he remained silent.

"'What is the artist's name?' asked the other priest even louder, 'His Eminence would like to know.'

"He may have thought that he was deaf.

"Sylvester stared silently. His jaws were tightly kept together as if he were getting ready to say his name, but he remained silent.

"I was dumfounded as I watched him.

"He was silent.

"'Isn't he Hungarian?' asked the cardinal.

141

"At the same time the other priest asked the artist:

"'*Sind sie vielleicht ein deutscher, mein Herr? Etes-vous francais, monsieur?*'

"The painter kept silent.

"'Are you an English gentleman, Sir?'

"We were surprised that Sylvester would not answer.

"Finally he moved and reached into his pocket. He pulled out his valet and took out one of his business cards from it. He gave it to the cardinal. At the same time, as if a cork held his name, he almost shouted:

"'Bbbesztercey.'

"He was breathing like a carp which had just been pulled out of water. The cardinal smiled and nodded.

"'It is a very beautiful picture,' he said kindly.

"He gave his secretary the business card and continued his walk. Sylvester put his brush into the paint again and continued airing the turpentine smell. We were also silent. His behavior was so incomprehensible that we were stunned. Why hadn't he said his name? Why had his tongue frozen all of a sudden? He wasn't red by then, but had turned rather pale. His hand moved the brush as calmly as if nothing had happened. There was not even one grape that needed correction. He finished them all and then wiped his brush with a rag.

"'I am ready,' he said calmly. 'Will you wait for me until I put the picture away? I usually put it into the cottage here.'

"He folded his easel and his chair as well, and took them inside.

"Then he joined us. We walked together.

"I would have liked to ask him:

"'Why didn't you tell your name right away to the cardinal?'

"We did not have a close relationship yet. I suspected some kind of a big secret, as if I stood in front of an old iron gate. What could be behind this? Of course I know now. But back then I felt there was some kind of a fictional mystery behind it.

"Klari interrupted my daydreaming as she danced the Faust waltz in front of us on the street. She sang and danced. We laughed at her.

"'Well, this is how I will paint her,' said Sylvester, 'the way she is dancing, but in a red, poppy colored skirt.'

"'But when?' Klari asked impatiently.

"'I will let you know later.'

"'Later, later… You are just making a fool out of me, Mr. Sylva.'

"But she really did like the idea of the red skirt. Then we talked about the cardinal and how removed he was from the world. Nobody would be allowed to go into his house.

"'I would like to see so much,' I said. 'What kind of a house does he live in?'

"'You will see,' answered Forgacs. 'Tomorrow or the day after, you will see it.'

"'Later, later,' Klari made fun of him.

"'Well, tomorrow for sure!' Forgacs was determined.

"But a whole week passed by before he announced:

"'The cardinal is going to Csopak to visit a sick friend this afternoon at four. They attended school together a long time ago.'

"Well, it really did happen. He bribed one of the servants and he let us in.

"Sylvester came with us. From the time we were introduced to each other, he became one of my inseparable knights, just like Forgacs. He didn't go away to paint any more. He took out his book and pencils only when we sat down, and drew for a little while. He liked that I watched with interest his every line.

"Well, the cardinal's rooms were not interesting. They weren't pompous. They were like the rooms of most elderly priests, decorated with crosses and pictures of saints on every wall; only there was a canary chirping in one of the rooms. But his garden was wonderful. There were roses blooming, which I had never seen before. There was a white rose which had red stripes on its petals and its base was also red.

"'Marvelous!'

"'His Eminence's favorite flower,' said the servant. 'He walks here every morning to see how much it has opened.'

"There were only two flowers on the plant. One of them was in full bloom; the other one was burst. I looked at the burst bud with craving eyes. Its petals were barely white yet, and I could also see a white dot on it. Some kind of a bug tasted it. I was observing it.

"'Well, I will dream with this,' I said. 'Oh, I have never seen anything as wonderful! Have you ever seen anything like this?'

"Both of my suitors were shaking their heads.

"'It is almost incomprehensible,' Sylvester wondered. 'All kinds of flowers can be found on St. Margaret's Island, but such striped roses...'

"'Cross breeding,' waved Forgacs. 'The white rose graft was old, and the red was weak when it was grafted. Perhaps the graft was weak which was grafted into the plant. They grow these in the king of England's garden. It can only be seen there in the world other than here.'

"He turned to the servant.

"'The lady likes the rose, and perhaps you like gold.'

"He took out his purse.

"The servant was frightened when he refused him.

"'Absolutely not! Like I said, this is His Eminence's favorite flower.'

"'But,' Sylvester tried to encourage him, 'one of these will be wilted by tomorrow and the other one will open up.'

"'You could say,' Forgacs tried to convince him, 'that it was wilted by the afternoon and you cut it off.'

"'Absolutely not!' the servant replied, 'His Eminence must not even find out that someone has seen it. Nobody is allowed to set foot in here.'

"He almost pushed us out of the garden.

"The night that followed was very restless for me. I really did dream about the roses. If only I had a rose like that, I would pin one on my blouse every day, and all the women who saw it would turn yellow from envy. Well, I would like to get a graft from it, regardless of the cost!

"I was also getting worried that I would have to choose between the pharmacist and the artist. They were getting increasingly impatient toward each other.

"When Forgacs was my only suitor, we had to wait for him several times. We used to walk up and down the chestnut trees until he appeared from the café or the pharmacy. After Sylvester started to pay attention to me they were both sitting at the hotel's entrance until I arrived, because neither of them wanted the other one to have the opportunity to be with me alone. In the morning, at noon, at tea time, they were always waiting when we were up in our room. When I was with them, one of them was keeping an eye on me from the right, the other one from the left. When I dropped something, they almost fought over it. They were jealous of each other, like little puppies over a bone. They appeared to be good friends on the surface, but under the surface they were gnashing their teeth toward each other.

"Forgacs however was quicker, wittier. For example, that morning he brought me scented water in a little bottle. He sat next to me at lunch, and we smelled the little bottle, and then he stole it back from my purse. After we returned to our room, he knocked on the door.

"'You forgot this...'

"Mother already lay down in the inner room. She soaked her feet and lay down. By then we were able to get two rooms overlooking the park, after some of the guests left the Elisabeth Hotel.

"So, mother lay down. Klari and I sewed. I sewed all my clothes ever since I was a little girl. I sewed a grey cape for myself when we were there. I thought the evenings were already getting cooler. Ash grey color always looked really good on me, as long as the collar was made of navy blue or black velvet. Forgacs very much enjoyed seeing me while I sewed. Of course I wanted to be polite and offered him a seat.

"'Well, where did you leave your friend?' I asked softly, because I did not want to disturb mother.

"'The fool is standing downstairs,' he winked happily, 'I told him I would just give you the little bottle.'

"It was somewhat unpleasant for me that he called Sylvester a fool. This may have been an indication that I felt what the future held for me. But I really liked that he was able to cut in line to be able to see me. I almost laughed when he turned to Klari and told her he was sorry that he left a sugar coated almond at the pharmacy.

"'I wanted to give you a beautiful, pink, sugar coated almond, dear Klari, but I talked so much that I forgot it on the pharmacy table. It bothers me a great deal!'

"Klari looked at him as if a thorn had just gone into her feet.

"'Thank you for forgetting; at least I won't upset my stomach.'

"'But you can upset it, don't be sorry, you can upset it, if you don't mind going down to get it. Here is my card. It will be given to you when they see it. But wait, I will write a word on it just to make sure the sugar coated almond will be yours.'

"Klari of course jumped at this opportunity. I could have said that we could get it around dinner time, but felt he wanted to confess.

"Nobody had confessed to me until then. But I was always trembling from excitement when one of my girlfriends in school told me that the man who was trying to pursue her confessed and she told me the small details of how he did it. This was extremely interesting for me as it would be for any girl.

"Well, finally the long awaited minute had arrived for me as well: Forgacs was going to confess!

"Forgacs was deep in thought as he wrote on his card, but his eyelashes were almost dancing. He looked at his card as if he were looking through an eye of a needle instead of a keyhole.

"I saw from the corner of my eye that he wrote in Latin. He must have written for his colleague to give a few sugar coated almonds to Klari, but that he should make her wait for a long time.

"Klari took off. We were left alone.

"'Well, finally,' he exhaled loudly, as if he had just arrived on top of a mountain, 'finally I can have a talk with you… in private… I have been waiting for an opportunity like this for the past two weeks, but I wasn't able to get to you from that hay eating painter. I wasn't able to get rid of him even for a minute. And you have also encouraged him…'

"'Me?'

"'Yes you, dear Ilka, because you are so kind to him. Well, don't look at me so seriously, I know you are grateful to him for the picture he gave you. That picture… if I would have known…'

"'I am not any kinder to him than I am to you.'

"I was so exited that my coil of thread fell out of my hand and rolled all the way to the stove.

"'But what I would like,' he blurted out, as he hurried to pick up my thread, 'I would like you not to be kind to him at all.'

"He sat back in his seat. He twisted the thread onto the coil.

"'This tick will not leave me alone even for a minute. He waits for me at the entrance of the Elisabeth Hotel in the morning. He doesn't leave me until the evening, when I step into my room. His room is next to mine now. He did everything possible to get a place next to me. If I wanted to be ridiculous, I would be jealous of him.'

"And he laughed. He looked at me with loving eyes.

"I think I was a little red from the anticipation. I was diligently stitching and barely looked up from my sewing.

"'He is a great artist,' I said, just to say something.

"'Artists are smart people,' he answered and shook his head, 'but this one... He sits next to me for hours and I don't hear a word from him. He is probably chewing the cud at those times.'

"And he laughed. He touched his tie and continued in a softer tone.

"'But I would like to talk to you about something else, dear Ilka, if you allow me...'

"I am sure I would have said that I allow him, but his words of, *'chewing the cud'*, were unpleasant for me, because my father does not talk much either. But perhaps I didn't feel that way because of my father, but because of Sylvester... I didn't even realize how fond of Sylvester I had become.

"'You are mistaken Forgacs,' I said with a smile, 'in that you think quiet people are fools. My father is so smart even our minister respects him. Even though our minister studied abroad and won several awards at the University of Jena. You should see his library. One of his rooms is full of books and none of them are fiction. He only has one book on poems, *"The Run of Szalan"*, but he doesn't read that. So you see, he is a very knowledgeable man, and when he comes to our house to have dinner with us every Sunday, he asks my father questions about Latin and Greek expressions. And you know our minister is a quiet person too. Sometimes they don't even say anything to each other for half an hour; they are just thinking as they smoke their pipes. Both of them are academic and are very smart. Even the minister's poor wife was very knowledgeable. She passed away during the winter. She was only fifty years old, but she needed to be operated on. She was taken to Budapest in a private railroad coach into a sanitarium. But then...'

"We heard the knock of a chair in the inner room.

"'I can't sleep,' mother began, while she was still inside, 'did you say you want a button made out of bone on your cape?'

"She came into the room we were in with sleepy eyes, just as she was dressed: barefoot, in petticoat, wearing a night dress. I was extremely embarrassed. She just stood there wondering what Forgacs was doing there winding the thread.

"'How did you get here?'

"Mother was very strict when it came to morals and respectability.

"'How did you get here?'

"Well, the confession was nipped in the bud. But it was evident that he wanted to confess. I thought; mother stepped on the gold watch again, but this time it was mine.

"Forgacs tried to come up with some excuses. He said he just wanted to give me the little bottle, because he didn't want me to think it was lost. Then he talked about Klari and the pharmacy. He turned the conversation from the pharmacy to his own pharmacy, which did not exist yet, but some doorknobs were being shined for his permit already.

"'Just a minute,' said mother, 'I'll put on my slippers.'

"And she quickly returned in stockings, slippers, wearing a blouse and black skirt.

"The conversation that would have followed would have gone something like this:

"'I only need a woman and some money to get the pharmacy started.'

"Mother would have put her own card on it.

"'Well, why don't you get married?'

"However Forgacs would have been ready with his own card:

"'It is difficult for a pharmacist; he needs a large foundation.'

"Mother would have been ready to say:

"'Everything is possible over time, but love is the most important foundation.'

"Forgacs would have been ready to say:

"'That is exactly what I wanted to talk to Ilka about.'

"And I could have become a fiancé in that hour, if I wanted to. If only... If only...

"But we didn't even get a chance to put out our cards. Klari stormed in through the door. She had a bag of candy in her hand. She was extremely happy.

"'He is going to paint me! Mr. Sylva will paint me! He is going to do it today! In a minute! He is standing outside the door, and he will paint me, if you allow him. He is in the hallway and he would very much like to paint me right away. Can I invite him inside?'

"She didn't even wait for our answer, just jumped to the door and opened it.

"'Please come in Mr. Sylva! Please! Welcome.'

"Even her knees trembled from the excitement. The painter came in bashfully with red cheeks. His eyes flashed on me and Forgacs from the door. My two admirers were inseparable, but at the same time truly resented each other.

"That night I brooded over which one of them I should choose.

"Forgacs' vacation would be over in two weeks. If he went home without getting engaged to me, and saw that the painter stayed near me, I was sure my name would not be Mrs. Forgacs. But should it become Mrs. Besztercey?

"I had to choose that week, oh no, I had to choose!

"Forgacs was a smart, attractive, elegant boy. He had nice black hair. He was also wealthy and must have been a diligent man. He would have a beautiful house: carved furniture, hardwood floors, oil paintings and nice carpets. I would have a separate dressing room with a large stand alone mirror next to the window.

"Sylvester was blond and less aggressive. He was four years older than Forgacs. He was stronger and healthier. His eyes were full of goodness and honesty. And it was not true that he was dumb; he only got confused at times, and when it happened, it was hard for him to speak. This was an unpleasant experience. But when he was calm, he was just as resourceful as Forgacs. And who knew what kind of an artist he would become over time? Perhaps he'd become one great painter. After all, even the cardinal admired his work.

"Sylvester would try to accommodate his wife. Forgacs wouldn't. Forgacs would most likely become the kind of husband who only knows his own will in his house and constantly has to be asked:

"'How would you like it dear?'

"Sylvester would ask me that question. I would get used to his faults. For example, he didn't eat meat, not even fried chicken. Was that a problem? I would eat the chicken, he would eat the salad. We could easily eat like that, even in restaurants.

"Forgacs would perhaps make me a cashier in his pharmacy. It was true that pharmacies are beautiful and smell pleasant, but should I spend my life in one of them?

"Sylvester was more fun. We would wander to different places and we would paint in forests, fields, villages, near lakes, under the beautiful sky. Oh, a field full of flowers is more beautiful than a waxed hardwood floor. I would learn his art as well. I would never learn how to run a pharmacy, but I would learn to paint.

"But Forgacs was very wealthy. He was expecting a large inheritance... The purse opens without a sigh. I could go to theaters or to concerts in the evenings. And I could have Klari live with me. It would be easier to find a husband for her that way.

"I wasn't able to choose. Both of them appealed to me equally. Forgacs for his city lifestyle, and Sylvester for his country lifestyle. Forgacs for being witty and Sylvester for being open and honest.

"I talked with mother about them, but she never gave me any advice regarding which one of them I should choose. There was already an unfortunate marriage in our family. The parents hammered it together. The unfortunate couple never blamed the parents, but the parents kept bitterly saying:

"'It would have been better if we would have let them choose their own mates.'

"Mother told me several times:

"'I will advise you in everything, but I want you to choose your own mate. I am not going to approve or disapprove anyone. Your heart will tell you who your true mate is. Listen to your heart.'

"And it goes without saying that I am grateful my mother and father thought that way.

"Still, mother did make some remarks, which led me to believe that she would prefer to have Forgacs as her son-in-law. She would have gotten rid of Sylvester sooner or later. But Sylvester was smart and promised to paint her too. He said he'd use oil paint and the painting would be a gift to her. Mother made sure right away that there would not be any incidental expenses for her. She looked at him with friendlier eyes from then on. That day she even said he was a nice man. It is true that she only said it to Klari.

"She was still waiting too. Oh, a mother's heart senses a lot of things. Even if she did not feel Sylvester was a clear choice, she didn't feel Forgacs was either. She just had Forgacs' house in Budapest revolving in her thoughts.

"I thought I would wait until the end of the week. If I chose Forgacs, I could tell him on the last day too, and then Sylvester would most likely return to the capital with him. If I didn't choose Forgacs, Sylvester would stay here longer and I would get him to confess. I would get him to confess this week. After all, he was just waiting for the opportunity.

"I felt like a pharmacist who is trying to weigh something. If I put a little weight on one side, it would tilt the scale. Perhaps tomorrow I would find that something.

"I was tired when I woke up the next morning. I could hear the music from downstairs already. I looked out the window. My two admirers were already walking under the dewy trees in front of the hotel. I could tell it was cold outside, because Forgacs' collar was turned up.

"During the previous evening we had talked about going to Siofok to have lunch there. We planned to return in the afternoon.

"I had already finished my cape.

"They brought me flowers every morning. Both of my suitors waited for me with flowers every morning. I always made one bouquet out of the two and gave the leftovers to Klari.

"On that day as I looked down, I saw that both of them had flowers with them. Sylvester had them in a wrapping paper and Forgacs carried a white paper box.

"Sylvester was dressed for the trip.

"'Good morning! Good morning.'

"They handed me the flowers. Sylvester brought five carnations, Forgacs... imagine what Forgacs handed me from the opened box. Oh, it was the wonderful rose! The cardinal's rose! I noticed right away that it was the rose bud. It opened at night, and Forgacs brought it for me. Well, I thought I was going to kiss him in public, where we were on the sidewalk, in front of a hundred people! And if he would have asked me to marry him in that moment, I would have shaken his hand. I can't really express in words how happy I was as I pinned the rose on my blouse. I did not put it together with the carnations and left its green leaves on the stem. Later I pinned the five carnations on my hat. I wore my straw hat with the blue ribbon. The flowers looked very good on it.

"Every woman noticed my flowers and their teeth were rattling with envy.

"I was happy. I held my moss green parasol. It matched my cape well, and the flowers even better!

"We talked while we took a little walk. The clouds were scattering and that made us happy. We started to feel the warm sunshine. But the leaves on the chestnut trees were already turning red. It was a sign of the approaching fall.

"We kept talking during our walk.

"The eyes of women were following me everywhere. Perhaps I may even say that the eyes of men did too.

"Mother had to sit down on a bench around ten o'clock. I told her not to put on her size 7 shoes.

"Well, we sat and chatted as we waited for our departure time. The hotel's director Mr. Moys stopped in front of us to call our attention to a well known actor and actress who walked nearby. We only knew them from the theater. Three years later Klari got to know them while she was learning to become an actress herself. But back then she just looked at them with great admiration.

"A child sold postcards nearby. We bought a few of them. We wrote to my father, as we did every day. Forgacs wrote to his mother, as he did every day. Sylvester wrote to a woman named Ms. Appolonia Balogh, not every day, but often. He wrote to her that day too, but he only put the address on the card. I thought she was a high society woman from the address, and I even asked him:

"'Please tell me, who is Ms. Balogh to you? You know we women are curious.'

"He smiled.

"'She was my nanny. She can't read.'

"I really liked that he sent her cards.

"His nanny is with us even now, but now she is our cook. She is the little hunched back woman who opened the door for you. Oh no, these eggs are still here. I will tell you only in a few words how the confession happened.

"Well, we sat there and chatted while we wrote on the postcards.

"All of a sudden I looked at my watch.

"'Oh no, it is eleven!'

"We took off in a hurry and were almost running to the ship landing dock. The ship usually departed at eleven. It was full and we could already hear its horn.

"'We are going to be late!'

"Klari ran ahead of us like a quail, if there was a pink quail in this world. She wore a new, pink blouse which had a white sailor collar. It was very pretty. There were red porcelain bottoms on it. Well, she flew in front of us. I followed her with Forgacs. Mother was left behind. Sylvester stayed behind to keep her company.

"'Oh no!' I was terrified on the bridge. 'My parasol! I left my parasol on the bench!'

"I had never lost my parasol in my entire life. I lost a bag, my watch, a pocket book, things I bought, theater binoculars, railway tickets, everything, but that was the only time I lost my parasol. I had leaned it against the back of the bench when we looked at the postcards. When we jumped up, I held my cape to prevent it from waving, and I completely forgot about the parasol.

"'Forgacs, my parasol!'

"Forgacs turned around and ran back like an ostrich.

"'What is it! What is it!' mother gasped for air.

"'My parasol… Someone will take my parasol! My magnificent, expensive, beautiful parasol! Oh!'

"'Never mind,' smiled Sylvester, and he pulled out my parasol from under his coat. He also pulled out my bag or purse as they call it in Budapest.

"'Why didn't you tell Forgacs? Shout after him!'

"Forgacs however was far among the trees. We only saw his checkered pants appear at times, like the spokes of a wheel in the distance.

"'If only the ship would not leave until he got back.'

"We anxiously waited for Forgacs to appear again. He wouldn't even be able to find the bench we sat on.

"The ship was whistling, ringing. But it was still standing.

"'What is taking him so long?'

"I looked at my watch and it was two minutes after eleven. I was glad we were departing late.

"'Oh no, they are pulling in the boarding bridge.'

"'Please talk to the captain, Sylvester. Ask him to wait just a minute, just a tiny minute. He is coming already! He is running over there.' Sylvester jumped obediently to talk to the captain, but he was busy at the time. He was mad at one of his sailors. His face was red as a cooked lobster and his fist was twitching as if he were holding hot metal. He pulled out his watch and shouted down through a copper pipe:

"'Let's go!'

"The ship splashed as it pulled away.

"Oh, I was so mad at Sylvester! We were still turning around when Forgacs ran out of the woods like a sprinter. The spectators laughed, and the laughter grew louder, because Forgacs didn't see that the ship was moving. He just kept running with his head down, even after he got to the dock. Well, the people roared with laughter when his spokes slowed down and stopped. He looked desperate as he wiped his face with his handkerchief.

"Klari laughed.

"'Come on,' she shouted, 'run on the water!'

"Mother and I were the only ones upset.

"'Unbelievable,' grumbled mother, 'why didn't you tell Forgacs that you had the parasol?'

"Sylvester shrugged his shoulder.

"'How would I have known why the pharmacist was running back?'

"The ship picked up speed. It plowed a long furrow in the water. Fured was fading from our sight.

"I still stood at the back of the ship, in the sunshine, and Sylvester was next to me. There were some other people there too who waived handkerchiefs. Everyone was on the deck, except for mother and Klari. They went down to the hall. Mother was tired from the running and she rested all the way to Siofok.

"Well, the two of us just stood silently at the back of the ship. We did not say a word for over fifteen minutes. Finally Sylvester spoke:

"'He'll come after us in a motor boat. Are you really sorry?'

"And he looked at me. Oh, I will never forget how he looked at me.

"'Well,' I answered, 'of course I am sorry. He missed the ship because of me... He is a good boy.'

"And I smelled the rose.

"I felt that he smiled and I lightened up on the situation.

"'It would have made me unhappy if anyone missed the ship because of me. And Forgacs was especially nice today. He brought me the cardinal's rose. It is unbelievable that it is from the cardinal's garden... Who wouldn't think it was a treasure? I will press it after it wilts and will put it in a frame. I will put a little sign on it: *The cardinal's rose*. It is too bad it will lose its color.'

"We rested our elbows on the ship's railing and I looked at him with friendlier eyes by then because I did not want my words to weigh down his heart.

"'If that rose is so precious to you,' he answered politely, 'I will paint it for you.'

"'Would you do it?'

"'Today, at lunch. But it would not be too late tomorrow either. I can do a finer job with oil paint.'

"I reached to shake his hand to express my gratitude. He grabbed my hand with even greater gratitude. And perhaps that move was the reason, or the pin was too short, I don't really know, but in that second my rose turned a summersault and fell into the water.

"'Oh no!' I screamed.

"Sylvester just stared at me.

"In the next second he threw down his coat, his book, his hat and jumped onto the rail, but more quickly than I am telling you this. By the time I was able to speak he jumped! Down into the water! The water splashed up four feet high.

"I screamed so loud that the echo of Tihany became silent out of fear. But other people shouted:

"'Help! Help! Lifeboat!'

"Well, all of a sudden everyone crowded that side of the ship. The women cried for help, the men just stared. The sailors untied the lifeboat and put a lifejacket in it. The ship stopped. Sylvester swam like a seal and periodically lifted his head out

152

of the water. All of a sudden he turned around and swam calmly back toward us. He held the rose in his mouth.

"Well, I won't even talk about how the captain swore and how the water dripped off of Sylvester. He calmly paid a twenty korona fine with a wet bill. The captain didn't even take it, instead he signaled to his sailors:

"'This money is yours. I won't tolerate jokes like this! I will leave him in the water if he jumps again! Unbelievable!'

"I scolded him too of course; oh, every part of my body was still trembling; but inside I was really pleased with him. After all, every woman saw how he brought the rose, which was mine, out of the water. They saw how he brought it in his mouth and how he handed it to me with an elegant move.

"Well, all the women and even the girls seemed envious of me. They moved to the other side of the ship, but still kept looking back. I didn't even look at them of course. I just stood calmly, with pride, at my place, as if the whole thing wasn't even unusual for me, as if my admirers jumped off of ships and towers regularly.

"Sylvester joyfully dried himself in the sunshine. One of the sailors put a jute mat on the floor for him to stand on because he was dripping. He just stood on it and kept dripping. He pulled out a pipe, blew the water out of it and lighted it up. He calmly continued dripping. I didn't even look at him. I just leaned my elbow on the railing toward our destination.

"I kept wondering which one of them loved me more. The one who gets a rose out of the garden of impossibility?   Or the one who rescues it for me from the lake of death?

"If I chose Forgacs to be my husband, he'd get me everything I wished for. If I chose Sylvester, he would be ready even to die for me. '

"But how did Forgacs get that rose? Did he buy it from the gardener?'

"Impossible.'

"The gardener must have known how precious that rose was to the cardinal. He was the one who truly knew! He knew every flower and how much they meant to the cardinal. If the gardener couldn't sleep, it was because he was worried that the cardinal would not be pleased. The rose was at a highly visible place. The gardener must have been proud of it. He may have even expected a reward for it from the cardinal. Perhaps he had even gotten it already.

"The gardener couldn't have sold the rose.

"If it was a different rose, but the same kind, I could still think that it was from there. But the rose was truly the same rose, which was still just opening up yesterday. The little hole which was on the green leaf covering the bud was still there. It had curled to the bottom, but the little hole could be seen on it. The rose was the cardinal's rose, the same one we saw.

"Did he steal it?

"Well, he must have stolen it. When we left, he had stayed a step behind, broken off the bud and put it in his pocket. He had kept it in a glass of water overnight and it had opened up by the morning.

"I looked at the stem of the flower. It was cut with a knife. It was possible that instead of breaking it off he cut it with a small knife. But he could have broken it off too and later made the stem more appealing.

"He stole it! The same way he had wanted to steal my picture out of Sylvester's book. The same way he had taken the scented water bottle out of my bag. He stole it! But what did the cardinal say when he did not find his precious rose?

"All of a sudden the sunny Lake Balaton turned cloudy to me. This thought had crossed my mind even the morning when Forgacs gave me the rose. But my joy had such a big flame that I did not pay attention to it. I thought it was Forgacs' business how he got it. The main thing was that the rose was mine.

"By the time I was on the ship, I thought about the cardinal's servant. He let curious people in the house secretly for maybe two or three coronas. He even let us into the garden. Oh, what happened to that poor man if the cardinal found out that his flower was gone? Was he upset with him? Did he chase him away? Did he lose his employment? He might have even had a family...

"This thought almost shook me. That unfortunate man had a family! My eyes welled up with tears, but I wiped them off right away. I didn't want Sylvester to see them and think I was crying after Forgacs.

"Poor Sylvester was like a wet mouse at the back of the ship. Water dripped off of him even when we arrived at the shore. All of his steps left a watery footprint, even on the asphalt road of the Grand Hotel. The travelers laughed at him and admired him as well.

"The women still looked at me with yellow eyes as they got off the ship and looked at Sylvester with admiration. They looked at my left hand and were even more envious when they did not see an engagement ring on it.

"Sylvester did not even look at them. He just kept walking and dripping. Klari laughed at him.

"'Mr. Sylva, do you have any candy in your pocket?'

"Even mother smiled at him with satisfaction.

"'Buy at least a new shirt at the store,' I said to him cordially. 'We'll wait for you until you get back.'

"'Never inconvenience yourselves because of me,' Sylvester said politely. 'Just go ahead and have lunch. I will join you as soon as I can. Or did you want to wait for Forgacs?'

"I looked back at Lake Balaton when he said that, but did not see any motor boats.

"'No,' I answered, 'we'll just wait for you.'

"It took an entire hour for him to get back, but he looked great. His clothes were completely dry. They were ironed, and he wore a brand new shirt. Only his hair and shoes remained wet.

"Mother lay down right after lunch, although she was very unhappy that she had to pay for a full day even for just an hour rest at the hotel. But the running really took her strength away.

"'At least your shoes widened,' Klari tried to comfort her.

"She lay down. We walked down to a park. Klari was with us. I was thinking: 'how could I get Klari to leave us alone? If she left us alone, Sylvester would confess!'

"I noticed a suitable white bench under a large tree. There were four or five girls playing with a ball not far from there. They had two governesses with them. I thought Klari would be interested in playing ball with them. She'd get up from the bench and would be about ten steps from us.

"The sun shone very brightly there and that was a little unpleasant. No problem, I held my parasol.

"I sat down on the bench as soon as we reached it. I sat on its end. Klari sat in the middle and Sylvester at the other end. He opened the book he was drawing in and his folding chair. He took out his colored chalks.

"'Your face is very interesting,' he said, 'in the green shade of the parasol.'

"'Are you saying that my face is green? Oh, please don't scare me, Sylvester!'

"'No, the sun is shining through the green silk... It is something wonderful.'

"And he asked if he could paint me.

"'You can keep talking,' he said. 'A painter is not a photographer. Please keep your face toward me. It looks wonderful!'

"He sat in front of me on his small folding chair. Klari seemed interested, but I saw in her eyes that she was sleepy.

"Well, she would be resting between the two of us. She did not even look at the children who were playing with the ball. Mother must have told her not to leave us alone.

"'Klari, have you heard what the girl with the black hair said about you?'

"'About me?'

"'About you, as they passed by us. They sat at a table behind us.'

"Klari's eyes seemed refreshed all of a sudden.

"'What did she say?'

"'She said your pink blouse with the white collar looks great on you. The other girl also complimented you, the one catching the ball right now.'

"Klari showed more interest in the girls and turned toward them.

"I continued to babble.

"'After soup, the bigger girl said she'd like to get to know you because you have nice eyes. I am surprised you didn't hear it.'

"Klari seemed energized. She opened her parasol. She looked toward the girls but remained on the bench.

"'It would be nice if you would go over to them. They would talk to you right away.'

"Klari jumped up and started to walk toward the girls. But she didn't even take five steps before she turned back.

"'But, how are you going to stay here?'

"She covered her mouth and laughed.

"'Well, just go,' I encouraged her. 'After all, you'll be close. Those girls are very nice. They even have governesses.'

"The ball rolled toward us. Klari picked it up and she smiled.

"'Watch out!' shouted Klari, 'I will throw it high. I bet she is going to drop it!'

"'No way!' the girl from Budapest shouted joyfully.

"The next minute Klari was in their company. We were left alone.

"Our backs were toward Lake Balaton as we sat on the bench. One of the reasons I chose to sit there was that I did not want Sylvester to think I was looking for Forgacs. Besides, we had to turn our backs to the sun because it shone into our eyes.

"'Am I green enough?'

"'You are wonderful enough,' Sylvester paid me a compliment.

"But I did not even think about Forgacs then, and he did not come after us. He made up some excuse in the evening. The motor boat company had all of their boats reserved for a usual trip to Tihany. It was not worth it for him to come over by the time it was four o'clock.

"Well, only the two of us sat there. Well, now; I thought, now...

"'But what should I answer him? I had not even chosen between the two of them yet. I would tell him that... Somehow I would delay the matter, the same way I did with Forgacs.'

"And since Klari was already playing ball, I became silent.

"He really did look at me with affectionate eyes. The colored chalk moved slower in his hand. I gave him an encouraging look. If he could have read in my eyes he would have read:

"'Speak; this is the moment for your confession.'

"He proved to be illiterate in reading eyes. He was silent as a fish.

"An aggressive fly landed on his left cheek. He drove it away. The fly just turned around once and returned right away. He drove it away about ten times with a calm wave of his hand. I would have liked to tell him to hit the fly in the head, but he had unprecedented patience. I had to wait until that annoying fly got tired of his place. Finally Sylvester put his finger in the turpentine, wiped it in his handkerchief and rubbed his face where the fly usually landed. The fly did not return any more.

"'Well'; I thought, ' well, now, now...'

"He did speak:

"'Your lips,' he said sweetly, 'they are especially wonderful.'

"He said these words with a lot of feeling and not as quickly as I am talking now.

"Of course I was most interested in how he was going to begin. I really liked that he started this way. But the minutes went by. Sylvester was silent and admired me and his paper, but just kept on drawing. Finally in my vanity I had to ask him:

"'What makes you say my mouth is special? I have never noticed anything special about it.'

"Well, speaking at that moment was a mistake, because he sat down next to me to explain what common lips were like and how my lips were different from them. But he sat next to me by then and spoke slower and with more pauses. I had to put him back on the right track.

"'Well, don't common lips look like mine?'

"'No.'

"'Smaller?'

"'No.'

"'Bigger?'

"'Bigger.'

"'Like on statues?'

"'Greek statues don't have them...'

"'Beautiful lips? Greek statues don't have beautiful lips?'

"'Textbook like.'

"'Textbook like? I don't understand. Aren't my lips textbook like? Why aren't they textbook like?'

"'They are finer.'

"'But finer how? Well, tell me an example.'

"'A petal of a rose.'

"And he stared at me with devotion. He was barely breathing.

"'Continue drawing,' I encouraged him so he could get some air.

"He drew and kept looking into my eyes affectionately. He even sighed three times.

"I made a mistake again by starting to talk about my family pictures and who resembled who. My features look like my grandmother's on my father's side of the family.

"I started to tell the story about how my grandfather got married. He was attacked once by some men when he sold his land and one of the robbers was his own gardener.

"I came to a halt right there. If I told him the whole story, he would not get to speak; I thought.

"He just looked at me and waited.

"'Please continue talking,' he said, 'continue. I really like to listen to you...'

"I liked that he asked me to speak. And I told him about our gardener too and how we hired him out of pity, because he was sick. He had some kind of an illness... from straining... Father arranged for him to be operated on and thought he would be faithful to us until he died. But he was wicked...

"I was upset with myself as we were going back. Why did I have to tell him all sorts of stories? Sylvester would have confessed and now I would be able to choose between the two of them. I would talk to mother in the evening and I would choose by the morning.

"I thought about Sylvester a lot by then. I realized he was a very nice man. He didn't have as many ties as Forgacs, but I was no longer a little girl whose thermometer would go up and down based on ties.

"Wealth does not say much about a young man either. Money is also a liquid, it flows out of some people's hand, regardless how much is put into it. Cards, horse races...

"I was sure Sylvester did not play cards. And who knew; a dirty little paintbrush might be a bigger asset than an expensive, elegant pharmacy. If he already had ten or fifteen thousand koronas, he might be paid even better in the future.

"On the way back I asked Sylvester on the ship:

"'If you were a child again, would you choose to become a painter?'

"'Yes,' he answered with surprise, 'Yes.'

"'Well, wouldn't you rather become... for example a pharmacist?'

"'Me? A pharmacist?' he seemed shocked.

"'Why not?'

"'I would rather mix paint than ointment.'

"'But it is a beautiful occupation and pharmacists are very well respected in small towns. They even get to go hunt with princes and counts.'

"He shrugged his shoulder.

"'Perhaps. I would not hunt even if I were a pharmacist.'

"'But still, for some reason you don't like pharmacists.'

"'Why should I like them?'

"'They all get rich.'

"'People who don't sleep well are not rich.'

"'How do you know they don't sleep well?'

"'People who sleep on bags of money don't sleep well.'

"'People who have to pay a bill and don't have the money don't sleep well.'

"He shook his head.

"'Smart people don't take on debt. They don't live beyond their means and they sleep well.'

"'What you are saying is that people who sleep well are rich.'

"'People who don't carry their treasure in a purse are rich.'

"'People who keep it in a safe.'

"'In their heart.'

"'That is a nice thought, but…'

"'I am talking about people who are not only driven by the pursuit of money.'

"'Instead…'

"'It is different for different people. For me it is my art.'

"I didn't really understand back then what he was talking about. But I liked what he said. Oh, my husband is a very smart man, except he doesn't brag about it. But like I said, I did not really understand him back then.

"I was truly a poor person that night. I couldn't fall asleep. I was most concerned about the cardinal's servant. What a bad person I was. I ruined a family because of a rose which would wilt in just a day. And I saw in my imagination a poor household. A narrow faced woman who wore a ragged skirt and slippers; oh, she had five pale little children around her and they faintly cried:

"'We are hungry…'

"And I saw the poor servant as he gazed in front of himself with tired eyes. Sighs, cries, discouraging hopelessness, empty bread basket, empty pot, ragged lives. Only because in my foolish greed I wished for a flower.

"Seeing five pale little children tormented me so much that I kept turning in my bed, with tears in my eyes, until dawn. Why did I imagine five children instead of four or six? I still don't know. I didn't ask the servant about his family. I had no idea if he even had a family or not. I just kept struggling with the image of those five children until morning.

"I would go to see the cardinal; I thought, I will kneel down before him and will beg him to forgive the servant.

"'I am the one to blame! The young man who brought me the flower did it for me. Perhaps the servant who let us into the garden did not commit such a big crime. For a man with a family earning one or two extra koronas this way is forgivable.'

"When I looked in the mirror in the morning, my face was so drawn I looked like I had slept in a crypt. Perhaps this was one of the reasons I verbally attacked Forgacs so furiously in the morning:

"'What have you done? You have ruined a family. You took away their bread. Perhaps they even became homeless. Didn't that poor man tell us that rose was the cardinal's favorite flower? You stole it! You stole it and did not think about throwing a family into the dust of the road with your action.'

"Forgacs was astounded.

"'Who told you I stole it? Who was trying to slander me?'

"'Well, if you didn't steal it, you bought it. It is the same thing. You made that poor man commit a crime! You made him become unfaithful toward his employer! Even worse! There are two criminals instead of one!'

"'But,' Forgacs said nervously, 'who told you I bought the rose. Who was that…'

"'Well, you have either bought it or stolen it. You can't fool me so easily. And I will save that man! I am a brave girl and am not afraid to talk to even twelve cardinals.'

"At nine o'clock I went to the cardinal's home and rang the bell.

"'I would like to speak with the cardinal. Please tell him that the girl from Somogy is here and would like to talk to him about something important.'

"The servant, who was not the same servant that was with us, stared at me with a long face. He shook his head.

"'His Eminence does not see ladies and sees only very few men!'

"'I am not a lady. I am a human. I want to save the life of a fellow human. Do you understand? The life of human! Tell me, is your coworker, the other poor man still here?'

"'I don't know who you are asking about.'

"'The one who showed us the cardinal's rooms the day before yesterday. He was a tall, serious, older man, and had a humble expression.'

"He thought about it as he looked at me.

"'Did he show you?'

"'That is not the question. The question is: did the cardinal fire him? Or did he not? You must know!'

"He shook his head.

"'Nobody was fired here. That is not something that happens around here.'

"'Well, even better. Then I arrived in time. Announce me! It would be futile to talk me out of what I determined! I will keep ringing the bell until your cardinal comes here.'

"The servant got scared.

"'Just a minute,' he whispered, 'just a minute. I will announce you to His Eminence. Please wait a little... Who should I say is here to see him?'

"And he started going inside. But he didn't even go as far as that door is from here when a bishop quickly came out. He was the cardinal's secretary. He had a stern face and was very much surprised.

"'What is happening here? What is all this noise about? We can hear it inside the rooms.'

"He came to me when he noticed me.

"'Please excuse me bishop,' I said, 'but I came here regarding a very important matter. It is about a family's misfortune. The day before yesterday we were in the cardinal's garden and admired his rose. A young man who was with us at the time brought me that rose yesterday. He either stole it or bought it. I thought about that poor servant last night that he may lose his employment.'

"I don't know what else I chattered. The only thing I remember is that I was very brave. I told him that I came to beg for the forgiveness of that man. I am the one to blame, because I desired that rose when I looked at it. His Eminence would

160

forgive his servant if a girl asked him, but not because he was asked, but because of his kind heart. He would not let the servant's innocent children hunger.

"The bishop listened seriously with amazement. He pointed to a chair for me to sit on if I wanted to, but I did not sit down. He remained standing too until I was done talking. Finally he turned to the servant.

"'Who was on duty the day before yesterday?'

"'Miklos, my lord, Miklos was here in the afternoon.'

"'Have him come here.'

"The servant quickly went upstairs and entered a hallway. The bishop was deep in thought as he looked at me.

"'Were you here with the painter, Miss?'

"'Yes, there were the four of us.'

"'That painter is a very gifted artist. I have seen many of his pictures. How are you related to him?'

"'I am his fiancé,' I answered nervously.

"I still don't know why I lied. I don't usually lie. Perhaps I wanted to impress him so my effort would be more successful.

"'Congratulations,' he nodded with a bored expression on his face, 'congratulation. He is a great artist.'

"We heard the servant's footsteps in the hallway. He quickly appeared in the next minute. He was bare headed, wore an apron and held a broom in his hand. He became red when he saw me.

"'What rose is this lady talking about?' asked the bishop calmly, 'and you allow visitors in here, Miklos?'

"'Please forgive him,' I begged with my hands put together and with tears in my eyes, 'for his children...'

"The bishop looked at the man with surprise.

"'And you have children too, Miklos?'

"The servant became even redder.

"'Of course not. How could I?'

"And he was dumbfounded as he looked at me.

"'I don't have a wife or any children. I never did.'

"'What about the rose?' the bishop interrogated him.

"'The rose? Well, my lord, a young man from Budapest gave me ten koronas and asked me to put a rose in the garden and tell this lady that it was His Eminence's favorite rose. He gave me ten koronas so I put the pot into my room. When His Eminence left, I planted it in the garden as I had discussed it with the young man. Later that evening he took it with him.'

"'But you let visitors in here, Miklos?'

"The servant was embarrassed.

"'Well, my lord, well... I wasn't told it was not allowed. But if it is not allowed, it is not allowed, I will not let anyone in here in the future.'

"I don't even know how I left that place. I felt ashamed and upset at the same time. Oh, what a foolish thing I had done for that servant! How crazy that liar made me over the cardinal's rose!

"The first thing I did was to throw the rose out of the window. But when I looked at my face in the mirror I scared myself. I looked as if I had just gotten up after three weeks of sickness. That was the only time in my life I wished I had pink powder. How could I go among people like this?

"I did not send out for powder even then. I am proud to say that I never put flour on my face. You can look at my dresser. You won't find any powder, cream, or even paint on it. I only have a small perfume bottle by my wash basin, but that is not make-up.

"You should have seen the cold reception I gave to Forgacs when we went down to have lunch. A thermometer would not have been able to register the degree of coldness I showed toward him when I looked at him.

"Of course he started to make excuses right away, but just increased my anger.

"Well, he just kept lying! That he did not steal the rose and he did not buy it either, but he asked the cardinal in person to give it to him. He told the cardinal that perhaps his future depended on that rose, and he was so kind that he cut down the flower himself.

"'Here you go, my young friend. If such a small thing makes you happy, how could I deny it?'

"I was more and more annoyed. I looked at him.

"'But when were you at the cardinal's? We were together until eleven last night and I saw you sitting on the bench with the rose at seven in the morning. I saw you when I looked out my window.'

"'I talked to him at dawn,' he answered without batting an eye, 'I found out from the servant that he holds a mass at five.'

"'In the garden?'

"'Of course not in the garden. He just goes through the garden on his way to the chapel by his home. He was already standing at the hallway when I saw him. I sent in my card. I wrote a few words on it ahead of time:'

   I need to speak to you regarding a matter of life or death...

"'Nothing else. Although I did write under my name:'

   It is not at all about money.

"'I thought people might try to approach the cardinal for money with all kinds of tricks.'

"He was lying so well, I had to laugh.

"Sylvester sat next to us with a sour expression on his face, as if he had eaten every pickled cucumber around Lake Balaton. I saw on his face that he would have

162

preferred to sit in the lake with Forgacs, instead of sitting at the same table. He probably would have pushed his head under water.

"'The cardinal was very gracious when he received me,' repeated Forgacs, 'even though he was already dressed for mass. He wore a cardinal's hat on his head and had a silver shepherd's staff in his hand. He came out into the garden like that. 'Please hold my staff for a second,' he said. And I held the big, heavy silver staff while he cut the rose.'

"Mother was really pleased with Forgacs. What a nice young man!

"I burst out laughing and during my laughter my attitude softened toward him. I even liked that he kept such a calm face as he made up all that nonsense. He would have deserved an honorary doctorate degree for his skill in lying.

"It appealed to me. After all, I thought, he loves me with extraordinary passion, if he gets me a rose which does not exist anywhere in the world. And on top of it he thinks of a way to make me feel the rose is even more precious. How resourceful and what an effort! The lad is deceitful, but he loves me a lot.

"Poor Sylvester just kind of lagged behind us after we left the restaurant, like a king whose crown was knocked down. Nobody looked at him. Still, when mother sat down to rest, he joined me as usual. I had Forgacs on one side and him on the other. And we walked for a little while under the trees.

"I still just talked with Forgacs.

"'But how was it, what did the cardinal say?'

"And Forgacs didn't understand why I laughed so much at his story, even though it was a serious and moving tale.

"Well, Forgacs had reached again the height of possibilities, like the top of a watermill wheel, before it stops, but finally what was at the top ends up at the bottom.

"We walked under the chestnut trees. We didn't even take ten steps when I saw the cardinal's secretary. He was quickly coming toward us. I saw that he looked toward us from a distance.

"At that moment I remembered what I had lied to him. I had told him I was Sylvester's fiancé. What would happen if he joined us and said something, perhaps about the picture of Csopak that he would like to buy, and he might even congratulate Sylvester. All of a sudden I got scared and grabbed Sylvester's arm.

"'Let's go down to the water, Sylvester. I am feeling parched and it is nicer over there.'

"We turned around. I was still holding Sylvester's arm, because I wanted the bishop to see that I did not lie. I was really scared. But the bishop was not the only one who saw that I hung on Sylvester's arm; Forgacs noticed it as well. I didn't think about that.

"I noticed his color had changed when I looked at him. He became silent and stern. He looked at me as if he were looking through a keyhole. We didn't even get down to the water when he said:

"'I have something to take care of.'

"He raised his hat and left us. He left me. I have not seen him since.

"I have only seen his name twice. Once in the paper, when he got his pharmacy permit. I don't know who he married. The second time I saw his name was in Klari's keepsake album.

"Klari asked one of her composer friends to take her album and get a few words in it from famous people. After about three weeks, the composer returned the book with a few scribbles from famous and not so famous people. There were even some nice drawings in it. There was a beautiful watercolor from Muhlbeck. There were also some music notes here and there and lots of autographs from famous people.

"I don't know how Forgacs got among them. He even wrote a mean, stinging line in it.

"A not well known playwright wrote a short poem in it called: *Drama*

"The poem was something about drama being a thought without a body and how an actor gives a body to the writer's thought. Forgacs wrote under this the following:

> So the writer is a thought without a body and an actor is a thoughtless body.

"Klari erased it.

"But where was I? Oh yes, he said good bye on the shore of Lake Balaton and left us.

"I stayed just the way I was and still held Sylvester's arm. And a strange feeling got over me. Kind of as if I was in a dream. As if I would have been together with Sylvester for a long time, in some kind of a close relationship and we would not be separated ever again. He pressed my arm softly and I felt a sweet tingle around my heart.

"I came to my senses only when Forgacs said good bye.

"'Oh, I am sorry, Sylvester,' I said bashfully as I withdrew my arm from his, 'I am so absent minded today. I just wanted to turn you around so we would walk downhill and I forgot to withdraw my arm. How impolite! You must really disapprove of me now.'

"'Of course not,' he whispered, 'Of course not…'

"His face was red and his eyes were almost teary.

"I worried that mother may have seen us and I would have to listen to a lesson on morals. But I was relieved when I saw that the bench she sat on was empty. They had gone up to the room to go to bed.

"We silently walked toward the hotel. I thought about Forgacs' face, how cold he looked and sounded when he departed. What was he going to be like when he'd be angry after he became a husband? Disagreements happen even among brothers with or without reason and they look at each other with angry eyes. It is an ugly sight. Anger can turn the most beautiful face ugly.

"Forgacs' good bye was somehow scary and cold. He was like a stubborn horse whose bridle was pulled forcefully. What would he be like when he was screaming in anger? And then there were his lies... If he was so good at lying, he would deceive his wife too. He could deceive her every hour. He could deceive her throughout her whole life.

"That was when I thought about the rose too. Wasn't that rose itself a lie? I remembered that my father had a small book on magic. I don't remember its title. I read it a lot when I was a small girl. But then one of our relatives, a little boy called Elek, borrowed it for a day. Of course it never turned up again. In that book I read that if someone puts certain chemicals into the pot of a rose, the red rose turns yellow or white, and the yellow rose turns red.

"Now I understand why the cardinal's rose was so unique. This kind of thing is child's play for a pharmacist.

"We reached our hotel.

"'I could paint the rose now,' said Sylvester joyfully, 'if you'd allow me, that in your room... I just have to run home for my paint.'

"I looked at him. And my feelings clearly and directly confessed:

"This was my mate!

"And he also looked at me in a way that his eyes almost bulged out.

"But of course this was only interaction between our eyes. First we had to get through the formalities. The door which had a sign on it: Order.

"'The rose?' I repeated almost mechanically.

"'The rose,' he answered with joy, 'or you. Same thing.'

"'Same thing? How are we the same thing?'

"'Well... you are a rose too. Whichever rose you want.'

"It was evident that what he said was from his heart. His tongue was not used to saying empty words of affection.

"'A little later,' I answered. 'Let's walk some more Sylvester, let's go into the pine forest. I like the smell of pines very much.'

"And then it happened. He confessed."

And the young lady smiled. The eggs were still there, even if not in her hand. She put them into an ashtray on the table while she talked. Her cook must have been waiting for them for a long time.

"Excuse me," I said, "but that is exactly what I am interested in. How did he confess? I have known him for quite some time, but I have never heard a ten word sentence from him. I can't imagine…"

The young lady smiled.

"He did confess, nicely, beautifully."

"But how? Tell me, how did he confess? I can't imagine that he could make a confession."

"He was able to do it. Oh, it was a beautiful hour… I remember every detail, as if it happened today. After all, the hour is celebrated in every woman's life when a man confesses love to her. Although it is foolish, isn't it? What is it good for? Every lover has confessed long before they express their feeling in words. But if that is the custom, if that is how it has to be, if that is the order."

"Well, it happened after we turned our walk into the pine forest. The reason I told him to go there was that I was afraid Klari would see us from the window and would report to mother that we were there alone. Mother was still on Forgacs' side. She would have sent Klari down to be the insulator."

"'Let's go into the shade of the pines.'

"We walked into the forest, but not completely, only to a bench by the edge of it.

"Sylvester felt that the celebrated hour had arrived, and if he wasted it who knew if it would ever return again. His face was red and his eyes shone and were moist from being moved. I sat down on one side of the bench and pointed to the other side with the tip of my parasol, for him to sit there. I was resolved not to start any stories about my family, and not to say anything else either.

"Well, I just sat down and remained silent. I waited. Oh, I was moved too by this occasion. I was silent. I only just said:

"'I love the smell of pines.'

"And he answered:

"'Me too.'

"Then I was silent.

"He held his book of drawings with both of his hands. He was silent. I gave him an encouraging look. He looked back and remained silent.

"A nanny pushed a stroller toward us. She fanned the baby. It is true that it was a rather warm day in September. The flies attacked just like on a hot day.

"I thought he just waited for the nanny to pass by.

"The nanny got closer and closer. She looked at us.

"She got in front of us and squinted toward us. She kept going.

"She looked back even then. Finally she disappeared under the pines at the curve.

"Sylvester was silent. He looked at me lovingly and kept silent.

"'Poor nanny,' I spoke, 'the baby is not even hers but she has to push her.'

"'She is pushing her,' whispered Sylvester, as if he were talking in his sleep.

"I almost started to tell him how much my heart sinks every time I see a nanny. There was also a girl in our village. Her name was Ilona. She was a poor peasant girl and had beautiful blue eyes. Her mother sent her into the city to become a servant. She said:

"'Get a little money, Ilona, otherwise you won't be able to get married.'

"Ilona did go, but she returned in less than a year. She didn't get money… the poor girl returned… with her big problem. Ten days after her little girl was born she was hired in the neighboring village as a nanny by a shopkeeper. She kept escaping at night to come home to nurse her own daughter too. She had to walk three hours to get home and back…

"Like I said, I had this story on the tip of my tongue, of course not in so many words. Now I can take my time because I am a wife. I only wanted to tell him in a few words, but I kept it to myself, even though I almost burst.

"In the meantime I thought that Sylvester might not even have any intention of getting married. What if he was just playing with me? In that case I could go back to our village and stay up at nights worrying over not being able to find a husband. Now I can talk with all honesty. Otherwise I was always honest. I would not have gotten married against my heart and my parents would not have forced me to. But the thought of staying single until I died was dreadful to me.

"I looked at Sylvester. He looked like a burning bush.

"No, this man was not just playing with me. He looked at me like a child of a beggar at the candy in a store. A woman's decision is of vital importance to a man who loves her. His whole existence depends on her.

"Perhaps he wasn't able to speak because of the importance of this minute; no not the importance, instead the heavy weight of it was weighing down his heart.

"But he was going to speak! Even the stone speaks up when it is truly in love!

"I waited. I was moved too, in all honesty, but I would have been able to speak, if I had wanted to.

"I silently waited. I only glanced toward my side to look at him once in a while.

"A ladybug landed on his hand and walked up and down on the back of it. He didn't get rid of it, just kept looking at me. Even his ears were red in his excitement.

"I silently pushed the dust with the tip of my parasol.

"I got tired too by the weight of the happy anticipation and I was a little irritated with him; oh why didn't he speak already? When even the trees looked at us and the blades of grass straightened up to listen as well. Even the bees stopped for a minute and buzzed with encouragement.

"And he was silent…

"I would have liked to stamp my feet.

"'Say something already! Get down on your knees! Not in front of me, but in front of the happiness that is awaiting you.'

"And he was silent…

"Finally I looked at this face.

"His face was completely red.

"His lips trembled.

"'What do you want to say?' I asked softly. 'Just say it.'

"Sylvester just looked at me.

"I encouraged him again:

"'Or don't you want to say anything?'

"'But I do,' he answered with as much difficulty as if the biggest rock of St. Gellert Hill weighed on his chest.

"'Well, just say it,' I whispered with encouragement , 'you can tell me anything Sylvester. I know you are not a liar like... Let's not talk about that. Just speak freely, honestly about what you feel.'

"And I looked at his face to encourage him. His lips trembled like the leaves on the trees during summer. His chest moved as if the words got stuck in his throat.

"'Well,' I began to put the words in his mouth.

"'Well...'

"'You want to say that you love me, don't you?'

"And then finally the confession burst out of him, like the cork out of a champagne bottle.

"'YES!'"